Bloody Water

Clay Warrior Stories
Book #3

J. Clifton Slater

Bloody Water is a work of fiction. While some characters are historical figures, the majority are fictional. Any resemblance to persons living or dead is purely coincidental.

This story takes place in 265 B.C. when Rome was a Republic and before the Imperial Roman Empire conquered the world. While I have attempted to stay true to the era, I am not a historian. If you are a true aficionado of the times, I apologize in advance for my errors.

I'd like to thank my editor Hollis Jones for her work in correcting my rambling sentences and overly flowery prose. Also, I am grateful to Denise Scherschel for her help in structuring the editorial flow of the book. Her amazing illustrated book <u>Zippy McZoomerman Gears Up</u> is a must read for children with disabilities.

Now… Forget your car, your television, your computer and smart phone - it's time to journey back to when making clay bricks and steel were the height of technology.

J. Clifton Slater

Website: www.JCliftonSlater.com

E-Mail: <u>GalacticCouncilRealm@gmail.com</u>

Bloody Water

Act 1

Qart Hadasht means New City in Phoenician. Today it's known as Carthage. In 265 BC, Qart Hadasht was a vast trading and military empire. The empire stretched across the northern coast of Africa with settlements around the Mediterranean and beyond. As with all empires, Qart Hadasht sought expansion and influence wherever possible.

Sicilia, or Sicily, at its closest point, was a bowshot across the Straits of Messina from Roman Republic soil. With the empire's encroachment, the Roman Senate was forced to debate the threat on their southern coastline. In addition to Qart Hadasht seeking more of Sicilia, the Republic was challenged by mercenaries occupying the city of Messina, and the restless king of the City State of Syracuse.

In the ancient world, the tension between foreign states created anxiety for their neighbors. Athens, Macedonia, Egypt, Sparta, Qart Hadasht, and the rogues of Illyria struggled for power, dominance, wealth, and survival. International politics is not new. It's as old as mankind and just as convoluted.

Chapter 1 – Warship Rowing

Over the past few days, transferees drifted in and reported to headquarters Southern Legion. The port town of Rhegium offered few diversions. And, the docks were dangerous because the Sons of Mars sometime attacked the piers in their travels up and down the strait. For these reasons, few men delayed in registering for their assignments which included a bed and food rations.

Due to the unrest in the area and the unique nature of the southern territory, the Legion put each new Legionary through additional training. Six men to a training unit and the First Optio saw to it that the units were assembled as each man reported in. This prevented a delay in bringing the Legionaries up to Southern Legion standards.

***

The newest team of men waited in the dark for their teacher. Lance Corporal Alerio Sisera stood with the others in the cool mist of predawn.

"Good morning, Legionaries," a deep, raspy voice greeted them. He spoked from just beyond the lantern light that encircled the trainees. "My name is Sergeant Martius. Some in the Southern Legion call me Chief of Boats. Some have less savory terms to describe me. For you, right now, I am your rowing instructor."

A few Legionaries groaned.

"I take it from your enthusiastic responses that some of you have boating experience," Martius continued from the shadows. He was still an invisible, disembodied specter from the dark while the training unit stood between four bright lanterns. "But I'm not asking about fishing boats, merchant ships, nor rowing your lass around on a pond; I'm asking for attack rowing experience. Those of you trained in warship rowing raise your right hand."

None of the Legionaries responded.

"Strip off your armor, gladius belts, and helmets. Place your gear on the ground behind you," the rowing instructor ordered. "On the beach is a sixteen-oar river patrol boat. Shove it into the water, get in, and row to the south."

Lance Corporal Sisera pulled off his helmet, unstrapped his gladius belt, the protective skirt, the shoulder pieces, and the back and front chest sections. After carefully stacking the equipment, he crept out of the light towards the dark beach.

The six-man training unit stumbled around until one Legionary shouted, "Boat. Over here."

They converged on the voice and grabbed the gunwale. Except all six were standing on the same side of the boat. It took a while, but finally, they had three men to a side. Once evenly distributed, they heaved and shoved the vessel off the beach.

The water was cold. By the time the boat was fully floated, the Legionaries were waist deep and shivering. Quickly, they climbed into the vessel.

"Paddles? Where are the paddles?" one man in the training unit asked.

"I can't find any," another replied.

The six Legionaries felt around but none could locate an oar. Meanwhile, the river patrol boat had caught the current in the Messina Strait and started to drift north.

"Where are you taking my patrol boat?" Martius growled from the beach. "Bring my boat back. Right now, people."

Alerio realized the only way to return the boat to the Optio was to swim it back.

"In the water," he ordered. "Unless you want to beach it and carry the boat back to the Sergeant."

Alerio was the first. Reluctantly, the other five slid over the sides and joined him in the cold water. After spinning the boat around, the first thing they noticed was the current pushing against the hull. As they kicked, the boat simply held its position.

Martius' voice carried over the sounds of thrashing legs and churning water, "The vessel you are propelling is a river patrol boat. It is forty feet long and eight feet wide with oarlocks for sixteen rowers. It's a single-bank meaning she'll have eight oarsmen on each side."

The rowing instructor's raspy tone cut through the aquatic noises. Due to a person's natural tendency to move toward a source of authority in times of stress, they angled the boat in the direction of the beach. As the bottom of the strait inclined upward, the swimmers on the beach side found footing on the rocks and sand. Soon they had the river patrol boat moving slowly southward.

Chapter 2 – Oars, not Paddles

Between pulling from the beach side and the kicking on the other, the patrol boat was returned to the initial site of its launch.

"Attack rowers know their equipment, their boat, and their position. In the Legion we store our oars, not paddles, on shore," explained Martius. A lantern flashed into life and below it appeared a rack of oars sticking up above the glow. "Grab an oar, form a line, and hold the oar over your head."

Once the six Legionaries were lined up, the rowing instructor walked behind them. He slowly moved from one to the next grabbing the center of each man's oar before pulling it back to test the man's strength.

"First and third men, take the forward rowing stations," he ordered. "Second and sixth, the aft rowing stations. Fourth and fifth man take the center rowing section."

Alerio was fourth in the line. He followed directions and carried his oar back to the patrol boat. As the training unit converged on the vessel, the first rays of sunlight began to peek over the mountains from the east.

"This is your machina locus, your engine. Always place your strongest rowers mid-ship," Sergeant Martius advised as he pointed to the pair at the center rowing area. Still a shadow, the instructor rapped on a u-shaped cutout in the boat's railing and a feature on the oar. "This is your oarlock. You'll find a leather sleeve on the oar. Place the sleeve in the oarlock with the collar inside the gunwale. The collar prevents your oar from going for a swim without you."

Alerio listened as the instructor pointed and named boat parts. He also watched as the soft morning light revealed the frame of Sergeant Martius. Where previously he had been a gravelly voiced ghost cloaked in the shadows of the night, in daylight, he was revealed to be a scarred beast.

Chapter 3 – Barbarian Ax

The instructions continued on the beached river patrol boat. The six Legionaries followed directions and commands until their arms were exhausted from holding and rotating the oars. After each drill, they held the oar blades suspended off the sand and gravel of the beach.

"Port and starboard fall in," commanded the Sergeant for the hundredth time. "Stroke, stroke, power ten in two."

The left side rowers and those on the right side jumped into the patrol boat and pulled twice slowly. Then they began ten fast repetitions as directed.

"Port side, check it down," he ordered.

The left side held their blades steady while the starboard side continued rowing. In theory, they turned the boat to the right.

"Let-her-run," Martius stated and the blades were lifted. "Ship oars and fall out."

The blades swung high overhead before the training unit rested them beside the hull and stepped out of the boat.

"Meal time," the instructor said as he limped away from the vessel. Over his shoulder, he announced. "Afterwards, we'll launch and see if you've learned anything."

Alerio rested his oar on the sand beside the boat and marched up the beach with the others. Bread, meat, cheese, and wineskins filled with watered wine lay on a table just off the beach. While the rest of the training unit gathered together, Alerio carried his breakfast to where the instructor sat.

"Sergeant Martius. Do you mind if I join you?" he asked.

Like the other men in the training unit, Alerio was naked except for his wool undershorts. Martius surveyed the fresh scar on the young Legionary's side, the ragged lines on his arms, the parallel scars on his shoulder, and the odd crescent shaped wound on his head.

"Yes, if you can explain those," Martius said while pointing to the multiple blade marks.

"Lance Corporal Alerio Sisera, formally of the Raiders in the Eastern Legion," Alerio reported as he sat. He explained while motioning to each scar. "Four rebels, a rebel Captain, a sword competition gone wrong, and a disagreement with a gang in the Capital. And, you?"

He was pointing to Martius' mangled right leg. Short scars crisscrossed the Optio's arms, chest, and his thigh. While prominent, the scars on his body paled in comparison to the mangled right leg. A wide scar ran down the front of the Optio's shin. It ended part way across the top of his foot.

"Barbarian ax on the western frontier," Martius stated without emotion. Then he inhaled deeply, closed his eyes, and began to recall. "I was just a Private. The Right-Side pivot for my squad, but still, only a simple infantryman. We formed our double lines when the tribes came out of the woods. Two Centuries of infantrymen, about one hundred and ninety shields, against six hundred barbarians."

"Those are ugly odds," suggested Alerio.

"We had them held but the General pulled our cavalry," Martius explained. "Seems the barbarian horsemen had targeted the headquarters' Century and they needed the cavalry more than us."

The Sergeant reached down and punched his thigh twice as if to accent a point.

"There was still over a hundred of us able to fight, so we formed a fighting square. With the wounded and our mules in the center, we broke wave after wave of barbarian attacks," he stated with pride. "The lads were in it and the ranks held. Held until another troop of mounted tribesmen joined the fray."

"They charged our northwest corner while the horde smashed at our ranks," he explained. "The Centurion pulled my squad off the back line and sent us to reinforce the corner. I remember the Legionaries doubling up behind the men at the corner. I remember them falling back as three tribesmen sacrificed their ponies on Legion gladii. I remember a burning pain in my thigh. I don't remember the ax that split my leg."

"I woke up in a field hospital. The medics had set the bone and stitched the flesh, but the foot was fused, and had little feeling," explained the Optio. "I took a medical discharge and limped back to my village. After a winter of pity and handouts from my neighbors, I packed my belongings and left."

"To most of the Legions, the Southern Legion has a bad reputation. We're not infantry, except for the patrols in the high hills along the rivers," Martius explained. "Mostly, we're on boats or in small garrisons along the coast. Legionaries don't respect fighting from boats or walking guard posts with seagulls. So, they look down on us. Well, I needed a place that was desperate for experience. I arrived and was turned down by the Senior Centurion. But, I persisted. For a year, I rowed on any merchant vessel that would have a crippled oarsman. I studied the art of the oar. Then I read about warship-attacks, and discussed the tactics with every old Captain I could find. You'd be amazed how many served in the Greek, Illyrian, Syracuse, or even the Qart Hadasht navies."

"Almost a year to the day, I limped into the Centurion's office and presented him with a plan to improve his rowers and the maintenance of his patrol boats," declared Martius. "He made me a reserve Corporal and watched me for six months. At the end of my probation, he called me into his office. I thought he was going to relieve me. Instead, he offered me the Chief of Boats position with the rank of

9

Optio. And now, every Legionary joining the Southern Legion has to go through me to qualify."

Chapter 4 – Blisters

"Hold-water," Martius shouted from the aft of the boat.

The training unit leaned over their oars and gasped lungs full of air. They had rowed south along the shore of the Messina Strait. Then made a wide turn placing the river patrol boat in the center channel stream and rowed south. Both directions were against the current. Now they rested with the oars in the water.

"Dip this in the saltwater and wrap it around your blisters," the Sergeant instructed.

A bundle of wool cloth pieces was passed along the lines of rowers. Each took a piece and soon five of the Legionaries had dipped the cloth over the side and wrapped it around their raw left hand. All the rowers except one.

"Sisera. The cloth is for your blisters," Martius advised. "Not for your head."

"No blisters, Optio. But, the damp cloth is refreshing," Alerio replied. The cloth drooped over his ears and dripped saltwater onto his shoulders. He had to peek out from under it to see the instructor.

"All Legionaries have tough skin on their right hand from gladius practice," offered Martius. "Rowing always draws blood from the left until it toughens up. What makes you special?"

"Gladius instructor, Sergeant. I practice with both hands," explained Alerio.

"Port and Starboard, ready oars," Martius said ignoring the hearsay of a Legionary admitting to using his left hand to wield a gladius. "Stroke, stroke, stroke."

The river patrol boat moved slowly towards the beach. With six rowers, instead of the normal crew of sixteen, the vessel was woefully underpowered. Despite the shortage of oars in the water and the exhaustion of the six, the boat held steady as it cut across the current that tried to push the hull northward.

"Back-it-down," Martius ordered when the bow of the boat was two yards from the shore.

The oarsmen reversed their strokes and the boat slowed until it nudged gently against the beach.

"Fall out," Martius directed.

The six Legionaries climbed over the sides of the gunwale and splashed into the water.

"Beach her," Martius instructed.

The Chief of Boats sat in the rear while the oarsmen heaved and shoved the boat out of the water. Once it was high enough on the sand, Martius rolled over the side and pushed on the rail so he could stand.

"Stack your oars in the rack and grab something to eat," he said while pointing up the beach to a table laden with bread, meat, and fruit.

Seemed the Southern Legion was generous with the rations, Alerio thought. Then he realized that he was really hungry. While running, jumping, blade practice and even wrestling worked up an appetite, rowing left him starved. He placed the oar in the rack and joined the ravenous training unit at the meal table.

Lectures on boat handling filled the afternoon. A few of the Legionaries snoozed and others barely paid attention. Alerio listened to every word.

Late in the afternoon, a boat appeared far down the shoreline. At first, the vessel was a dot on the water. As it drew closer the training unit noted it angled left then right as if the oarsmen were out of sync. It eventually came close enough to be recognizable as a full-sized patrol boat.

When the bow drifted to starboard, the current caught the fore section and began turning the boat away from the shore. Sergeant Martius, who had been watching the boat struggle as he talked, pointed down the beach.

"Something's wrong," he declared. Indicating one member of the training unit, Martius ordered. "You, go fetch a medic. The rest of you double time down there and secure that boat."

Alerio jumped to his feet and raced toward the stricken vessel.

Chapter 5 – Attack Aftershock

Alerio splashed into the surf just behind another Legionary. By the time they started swimming, the current had grabbed the hull of the distressed patrol boat and propelled it further from the beach. The bow caught the edge of the central channel's flow. Between the opposing currents of the strait and the water at the shoreline, the vessel began to spin.

Even though Alerio was right behind the first swimmer, he ended up on the opposite side of the rotating boat.

The Legionaries pulled on the rails and both came out of the water at the same time. As their arms hoisted their chests above gunwale height, they looked down into the patrol boat.

A Legionary with one arm leaned unconscious on the rearward-facing oar. The nub of the other arm was tied off at his bicep. Three bodies lay on the central beam unmoving. The last occupants were ten men slumped over their oars. All ten were dripping fat, red drops into the bloody water collecting in the bottom of the boat.

As the other three trainees climbed in, Alerio said to the smallest, "Take the rear oar. Guide us into mid channel. We'll use the northern current to help us."

With only four oarsmen, it was impossible to move the patrol boat against the southern current running along the shore. Once over the edge of the opposing currents, they rowed with the flow.

Martius watched from the beach. Behind the Sergeant, ranks of men stood at the ready.

Alerio didn't call for a reverse stroke as the boat neared the shore. He let it run hard onto the sand. Legionaries on the beach hoisted the vessel out of the water.

"Medics, stand by! We'll bring the wounded to you," shouted Martius once he saw the slaughterhouse of the interior. To the Legionaries, he ordered. "Lift them out and carry the wounded to the medics."

Once all fourteen injured were in the treatment area, Alerio walked down to the boat. Martius was leaning in and pulling gladii, javelins, and arrows from the red tinted water.

"The appropriate order is back-it-down," the Optio scolded.

"With only four oarsmen, we were barely able to keep forward movement," explained Alerio. "I was afraid if we slowed, the boat would stall away from the beach."

"What you need to be afraid of are hidden rocks ripping out the bottom of my boat," Martius sneered as he pulled another gladius from the water and tossed it to the sand. "If you land a boat that fast on an uncharted beach, you'll be marching back to Rhegium. Where I might add, I'll be waiting to ask you about my boat."

"I understand, Optio," replied Alerio. "What happened to the boat's crew?"

"That's a good question Lance Corporal Sisera," Martius remarked as he pulled an arrow from the wood of the gunwale. "Let's go find out."

The fourteen Legionaries from the patrol boat were laid out in a circle with their feet towards the center. medics tended to the living. The dead required no treatment.

"These are all that's left of our three-squad garrison at Occhio," a Centurion informed Martius and Sisera as they approached the triage area. "A merchant ship came up the inlet and its Captain started yelling for the Legionaries. Ten men and their Optio began rowing across the river. Before they could reach the merchant, an Illyrian bireme came upstream."

"What was so valuable a pirate ship would dare attack a settlement with a Legion garrison?" asked Martius.

"No one knows. The Illyrian ship cut between the patrol boat and our garrison dock," continued the officer. "With our forces split, the Legionaries couldn't link up. The Illyrians rained arrows and spears down on the patrol boat while sending fighters down a ramp to the Legion's dock."

"The Legionaries on the garrison side fought a retreat down the river," reported the Centurion. "Once the patrol boat managed to get out from under the shadow of the Illyrian ship, they rowed to meet them. One squad leader and three men formed a shield wall on the riverbank. They held off the Illyrians while the injured jumped for the boat. The fourteen who rowed back are the only survivors."

The officer stared at the circle of wounded and dead Legionaries. Shaking his head to clear the image, he focused on Optio Martius.

"Or should I say, these are the ones who made it back," he ventured, narrowing his eyes. "I want those Pirates up on crosses; every last one of them. But, they'll be gone by morning. We can't counterattack, and we have no way of knowing why they chanced tangling with a Legion garrison at an unimportant farming village."

It was late in the day. Half the sun had dipped below the mountaintop on the island across the Messina Strait.

"I don't understand, Sir," Alerio inquired. "Why can't we go after them now?"

"Because the Southern Legion is scattered up and down the coast," the Centurion explained. "It'll take half the night to gather our forces. We'll have to wait for sunrise to move our ships and men down the coast for a coordinated attack."

"And the Pirates will row out at first light?" guessed Alerio.

"That's right. Without a direction, we wouldn't know where they're headed," confirmed the Centurion. "They'll be at sea before we arrive."

"Let me take a crew and drop off a spotter," offered Martius. "It's only five miles to the beach at the Occhio inlet. The farming village and docks are a little over a mile inland. Once our spotter is landed, we'll breach at Point Ravagnese and watch for his signal."

16

"Do you have someone in mind for the job?" asked the Centurion.

"Excuse me, sir," broke in Alerio. "I'd like to volunteer. I've had experience sneaking up on rebels. I can't imagine pirates will provide more of a challenge."

"Optio. Your opinion?" inquired the officer.

"If Lance Corporal Sisera wants the job, it's fine with me," Martius remarked. "But, we need to get started before it's fully dark."

"All right, Sisera. You're our spotter," the Centurion ordered. "Collect your gear and go with the Sergeant."

"Yes, sir. Sergeant Martius can you have someone load my armor in the boat?" Alerio asked. "If I'm going to sneak around, I'll need to grab something from my quarters first."

Act 2

Chapter 6 - Moonless Rowing

Martius clutched and unclutched the rearward facing oar handle while he bobbed in the patrol boat. His fifteen oarsmen on the port side were holding water. The fifteen rowers on the starboard side stood in knee-deep water. Between them, the boat remained near the shore even as the Chief of Boats grew more tense with each passing moment.

The Sergeant watched as the young Lance Corporal jogged onto the beach. Leather straps fell over his shoulders and the Legionary was fastening them together as he ran. When he neared the boat, Martius noticed two gladii hilts jutting up on either side of Sisera's neck.

"Starboard side, push off and fall in," Martius ordered while Alerio climbed over the side. The fifteen rowers on the left shoved the patrol boat and scurried over the gunwale. Once their oars were in hand, the Sergeant announced, "Rowers, standby. Stroke, stroke, stroke."

Martius shoved the rear oar so the patrol boat angled away from the shoreline as it surged ahead. Unlike the undermanned river patrol boat, the training unit had rowed earlier, the larger coastline patrol boat with thirty oars cut sharply through the salty water of the strait.

"Here's a fire kit," Martius said handing Alerio a small wooden box sealed in wax. "If the Illyrians row straight out of the inlet light one signal fire to indicate they're heading for Sicilia across the strait. Light two if they turn south and set sail; that means they're heading for open water and home. If they turn south and continue rowing, light three. That would be the best scenario for us because they're staying near our shoreline. We can then hunt them down and crucify the cūlus pirates."

"What if they stay at the dock?" Alerio asked.

"Then they are stupid and they will die," Martius assured Lance Corporal Sisera.

***

The patrol boat cruised south as the sunlight faded. Even when darkness fell and the shoreline vanished, the oarsmen continued their steady strokes.

"Are you navigating by the stars?" inquired Alerio. "I've heard mariners can do that."

"No Lance Corporal. I'm using the fires from the fishing village at Point Ravagnese as a guide," Martius replied. "Their cook fires will show me the point. We'll turn once the flames are behind us."

In the distance, several candle sized flames danced in the dark. As the patrol boat traveled, the lights moved from ahead to off the starboard side. When the fishermen's fires were over their left shoulders, Martius eased the oar so the boat curved in the direction of the dark shoreline.

"Back-it-down," called the Sergeant ordered the oarsmen. "Let-her-run."

The oarsmen reversed stroked once before lifting their blades from the water. With the patrol boat slowed from the backstroke and the oars hovering above the water, the boat gently nudged into the dark beach.

"The inlet is off to your right. Follow the beach," Martius directed. "As you face inland, the garrison, fields, and grain storage buildings are on the right bank. The village is on the left bank and uphill from the water."

"Why is the village not near the fields?" Alerio asked. The farmer's son couldn't understand the unusual layout.

"Flooding. In the spring and after heavy rains in the mountains, the fiumare at the end of the inlet floods over its banks," Martius replied. "The fields flood and sometimes the garrison building floods. We have to rebuild the stockade every year. Now go."

Alerio slid over the side and into the chest deep water. Holding his armor and helmet over his head, he waded towards the beach. Behind him, he heard Martius call to the oarsmen.

"Back-her-down. Back. Back," the Optio ordered. The patrol boat moved away from the beach and vanished in the dark.

Chapter 7 – Survivor

Alerio heard the waves lapping at the shoreline. Where the land curved around forming the bank of the inlet, he dropped his armor and helmet on the rocky beach. By following the curving bank, he arrived at an area with thick reeds and a crop of trees. There he collected an armload of dry branches.

Back on the beach, he piled dirt into three piles before patting the top of each flat. From behind his back, Alerio pulled a long, curved dagger with a yellow stripe on a black hilt. It was more than a fine weapon. It identified him as an Ally of the Golden Valley, and a friend to the assassins of the Dulce Pugno, the valley's protectors. After shaving off kindling with the dagger, he tented branches and the thin wood strips on the three raised flat surfaces. Finally, he dug out a depression in the beach and laid the last of the branches in the bottom.

Once the three unlit signal fires were set, he unstrapped the dual gladius rig and slipped on his armor and helmet. He resettled the gladius harness over his armor and tied it down before setting off towards the village of Occhio.

A mile in daylight over roughly plowed fields was a simple march. In the dark, it was a tortuous path and bruising on the ankles and knees. Alerio smiled at the mounds and valleys of the planted rows, the smell of freshly turned soil, and the aroma of green growing plants. It reminded him of home.

The fields on the flat land soon transitioned to cultivated hillsides. As Alerio climbed, he left the small grain field behind and arrived at a row of beans. His early work on a farm prevented him from simply bashing through the vine plants. Out of respect for the farmers, he walked to the end of the row before proceeding up the hill.

"You can't go," a voice whispered from a few rows to the front.

Drawing his hip gladius, Alerio crept forward.

Another voice choked back a reply, "I've got to free them."

A third voice caused Alerio to relax.

"Lance Corporal, you are injured," a man stated. "If you stumble into the pirates in your present condition, you will be killed."

"Someone has to…" and the weak voice trailed off.

"How is he?" another voice inquired. "Is he dead?"

"No. But his breathing is ragged and shallow," came the reply.

Alerio looked up to see a slice of the moon over the mountain. He squatted down to wait. Shortly, there would be some illumination. He figured it was better to meet the voices in shadowy moonlight rather than stumbling into a group of strangers in total darkness.

"What are we going to do?" pleaded another man.

"There's not much a handful of farmers can do against those Illyrians," someone answered. "If we rush down there, we'll be killed."

The half-moon drifted slowly above the mountain spilling weak light over the rows of bean.

"Stand down citizens," Alerio said as he moved forward to join the group. "I'm a Legionary. Lance Corporal Sisera. What's going on here?"

The question was asked for two reasons. One it occupied the speakers so they would think instead of attacking a form appearing from the dark. The other reason, Alerio was curious.

"Is the Legion here?" a man asked hopefully.

"Not until morning," Alerio responded.

"It'll be too late," another one whined. "They'll row out at first light. It'll be too late."

"First things first," Alerio commented. "Where is the Lance Corporal?"

"He's here. We fished him out of the water after the Illyrians knocked him off the bank," a kneeling man reported. "He must have been alert enough to take off his armor. When he floated to the surface, we paddled out and brought him to shore. I'm afraid he's cut up bad. I've bandaged him but he's not doing well."

Alerio dropped to his knees and ran a hand over the Legionary. Rough cloth covered his arms and lower legs but the worrisome bandage was the wet cloth wrapped around his stomach. The light wasn't necessary to recognize the sticky dampness on the wrap. It was blood.

"Thank you for taking care of him," Alerio offered. "Now. Why will the morning be too late? Too late for what?"

"They've rounded up our old, our women, and our children," stated another man. "They said if we attack, they'd cut their throats."

"They'll take them as slaves when they row out," added another farmer. "It's the fault of the merchant ship that brought them."

"What was so important about the merchant that the Illyrians chanced attacking a Legion garrison?" questioned Alerio.

"We've discussed that but we have no idea," another farmer admitted. "Other than piracy."

"The man they took off the merchant ship was tall, thin and swarthy," described the farmer kneeling beside the wounded Legionary. "He was dressed in a gold embroidered robe."

"Him and the four slaves carrying the big coin chest," another farmer stated. "And a man in strange pants toting stacks of parchment and scrolls."

"The coin chest is enough to warrant an attack," Alerio suggested. "Tell me about your families?"

"The Illyrians rounded up everyone in the village. Then they marched them across the fiumare," a farmer reported. "We were in the fields and couldn't get back in time. Their leader said if we attacked, they'd kill them all. Now, our families are under guard in the grain storage building."

"How many?" inquired Alerio.

"Twenty-five," came the answer.

"Twenty-five guards?" asked a shocked Alerio.

"No, no, women, children, and our elders," the farmer corrected. "There are six Illyrians guarding them. Can you help us?"

Alerio was conflicted. On one hand, he had an assignment to report the direction of the Illyrian ship. On the other hand, he was confronted with the need to save a farming community. However, if killed in the process, he wouldn't complete his initial assignment.

From the bean terrace, he could see moonlight on the inlet. Gentle ripples flowed down toward the strait. Across the water, the fields were black with no surface to reflect light.

"Where is the grain storage building?" he asked.

"You can't see it from here. The hills with our village block the view," the kneeling man informed him. "Can you? Will you help us?"

"I need you to carry the Lance Corporal to the crop of trees at the beach and hide there," answered Alerio. "When the Illyrian ship leaves, you'll need to light signal fires to alert the Legion. If you do that, I'll free your families. Or die trying."

"Oh, Laetitia blesses us this night," a farmer gushed.

"Don't celebrate yet," warned Alerio. "Let me rescue them before you start invoking a Goddess."

"Still, you've given us hope," the kneeling man said. "We'll carry the Lance Corporal to the beach and come back to help you."

"No. I'll need two men to guide me to your families," instructed Alerio. "If I have too many citizens running around in the dark…well. let's just say someone could get hurt if it becomes a melee."

"Cimon. Marcissus. Go with the Legionary," the kneeling man ordered. "Row him across and show him the grain storage building. Then, follow his directions."

Two men stepped closer to Alerio. One was tall and thin while the other was short and stocky.

"I am Cimon," the thin farmer introduced himself before pulling the stocky man close in. "He's Marcissus. When do we get started?"

"As soon as the rest are on the way to the beach," Alerio told him.

It took little time for two farmers to pull up a pair of anchoring poles from the bean rows. Soon they had strips of goatskin stretched between the poles and the injured Legionary placed on the stretcher. As the group of twenty-three farmers moved down the terrace, Alerio turned to Cimon and Marcissus.

"Two questions. How do we cross the inlet?" he asked. "And, what material did you use to construct the grain storage building?"

"We have a flat bottom boat," Marcissus replied. "We use it to transfer men and supplies across the inlet. We can row you all the way to where the inlet meets the fiumare."

"No. We'll cross here and approach from the fields behind the building," Alerio explained. "What about the storage building?"

"It's brick," Cimon stated with pride. "Brick with a mud layer. Our productivity is good because we don't lose the harvest to vermin or rot when it rains."

"At my father's farm, the village's storage buildings have bricks for the first three feet and the rest is wood," said Alerio.

"You're a farmer?" asked Marcissus.

"My father is the farmer. I'm a simple Legionary," Alerio replied. "And we have a mission. Show me to the boat."

Chapter 8 - Grain Storage and Hostages

Lantern and torchlight lined the pier but Alerio couldn't make out details from the flat bottom boat. What he could see was the black hull of a long ship that blocked the light as Cimon and Marcissus paddled them across the inlet. By the time they reached the right bank, the lights of the village on the hills came into view.

"Most of the pirates are in the village," Cimon commented.

"Let's hope they stay there," Alerio replied.

They tied the boat to a post and the three men climbed up the embankment. As they entered the grain fields, Alerio had to nudge Marcissus when the farmer turned left.

"The Legion stockade is just up there," Marcissus whispered.

"Go further into the field. We need to approach the grain building from the rear," Alerio advised.

They walked deeper into the field before angling around. When Alerio saw campfires in the distance, he grabbed the farmers and had them squat down.

"Who has experience with a sword?" he whispered.

"I'm good with an ax, but with a sword, no," replied Marcissus.

"No sword, but I can plow a field all day," confessed Cimon. "I'm strong."

"Marcissus. Take this and stay behind me," Alerio instructed while handing Marcissus his hip gladius. "Once I clear the guards, you get the elders, the women, and the children out of the building. Cimon. You lead them away from the storage building. Marcissus will bring up the rear. If any Illyrians chase you, chop them down like an old pine tree."

"Like a pine tree?" asked Marcissus.

"You know, big chunks and lots of gooey sap," replied Alerio. The farmers chuckled and relaxed.

Alerio learned swordsmanship during harvest times on his father's farm. During his formative years, a Centurion and an Optio from the Northern Legion came annually to work the harvest. While there, they taught former Sergeant Sisera's son military tactics and gladius work. One of the lessons involved surviving hard and difficult tasks; when faced with the impossible, sing and keep a good sense of humor.

Alerio needed the farmers loose and thinking, rather than freezing up at the first sign of trouble.

"Humor and singing," Alerio mumbled to himself before asking. "Do either of you know a song?"

He was disappointed when both replied no.

"Marcissus, remember to stay behind me. Cimon, stay at the edge of the grain field so you can lead the families deeper into the fields," Alerio repeated the assignments before stepping forward. "Breathe deep, stay loose, and follow me."

Moments later, Alerio stood stooped over so his eyes were just at the top of the grain stalks. In front of him a domed structure occupied a cleared area near the inlet. From his vantage point, the dark storage building partially blocked light from campfires to the left and right. He could see pairs of men sitting at the fires. If the farmers were correct, two more men were somewhere in front of the grain storage building.

From across the inlet and high up on the hill, singing carried from the village. In response to the faraway voices, the Illyrians guarding the hostages sat up and joined in the ditty. At the first note, Alerio reached over his shoulders and unsheathed both gladii.

Look around me, the view never changes
For I am a rower in the Greek navy
My vista is steady, if not picturesque
It's of benches, wood sides, oak oars and dreck
With a peek at the blue sea, out the oar hole, at its best
No matter the landfall
To my eyes and nose, there's no rest
For I work on a bench, surrounded by pests

Look around me, the view never changes
For I am a rower in the Greek navy
His back hairs thicken, on every cruise
From behind curses, garlic breath, endlessly spews
Hold your fluids from below, spit flies, gas roars, from on high
It's better than farming
Or hauling big loads, proudly says I
This life in the navy, without dirt or sky

Look around me, the view never changes
For I am a rower in the Greek navy
My view on the bench, is a rower's lament
Unseen green coast, the blue sea, horizon sunset
Row faster, slower, cruise, power those oars, and we bank
No matter the cruise
To my sight and smell, there's just planks
For I work on a bench, surrounded by stank

Look around me, the view never changes
For I am a rower in the Greek navy
My scene's consistent, even in battle
Ship oars, increase strokes, and attack angles
I row to the drums, I pray, row all the day, as if addled
No matter the foe
To my eyes and nostrils, there's no battle
For I work on a bench, surrounded by cattle

Alerio smiled at the song. The Illyrians and Greeks had been at each other's throats for decades. It wasn't hard to understand the song as a barb at Greek oarsmen. Especially those assigned to the center tier in the Greek's large fleet of quinqueremes.

The smile faded as Alerio stepped out of the grain field and began to sing.

Chapter 9 - Fight on the Right Bank

Alerio hooked around and approached from behind the left campfire. The two Illyrians at the fire were unaware a fight was about to start.

"Look around me, the view never changes," Alerio sang. *"For I am a rower, in the Greek navy."*

Swinging inward with the two gladii, his strikes slammed the pirates on their temples. The two fell together and ended up resting on each other.

One pirate near the storage building door wondered why his companions decided to whisper in the middle of a song. His curiosity ended when a single figure leaped over the flame. It landed and raced at him.

"My vista is steady, if not picturesque," Alerio crooned as he jumped at the third pirate. *"It's of benches, wood sides, oak oars and dreck."*

The other pirate at the door was in full voice with his face lifted as if to compete in volume with the crewmen in the village. He jerked when his partner punched his shoulder in warning, but it came too late. Alerio ran his gladius through the first pirate's right side. Stepping beyond the crumpling man, he conked his partner on the crown of the head. The singing pirate fell silent and toppled to the ground.

"Marcissus. Free your people," Alerio ordered with a turn of his face. Looking ahead at the final two pirates, he picked up the song. *"No matter the landfall. To my eyes and nose, there's no rest."*

The last two pirates drew long curved knives and shuffled forward in a coordinated attack. Holding their sicas high, they aimed for the Legionary's unarmored neck. Alerio ran at them, and the Illyrians leaned forward expecting to meet their foe face-to-face.

Two feet from the points of the knives, Alerio dropped to his knees and slid under the sicas. One of his gladius' tips faced downward and he drove it into the top of a pirate's foot. Sharp, narrow steel penetrated the foot and the bone split. With his balance gone and agony flashing up from the foot, the pirate collapsed and grabbed at the wound.

The second gladius pointed upward. Alerio pushed it into the pirate's throat, through the soft palate, and up to the base of the man's skull where it nicked the bone. Although by the time the nick occurred, the Illyrian was too busy trying to suck air past the gurgling hole in his throat to care. He was the only pirate to die in the initial confrontation.

"For I work on a bench, surrounded by pests," sang Alerio as he stood between the two pirates.

In a straightforward duel or swordfight, killing your foe was easy once you fought through their defenses. When attacking a group, it proved faster to simply disable the enemy. Except for the last pirate, the other five sustained survivable wounds.

Alerio spun to check on the four Illyrian pirates on the ground. Two stirred but didn't seem as if they were ready to stand and fight.

Shrieks, wailing, and moaning came from the direction of the grain storage building. Glancing over, Alerio saw a woman emerge through the doorway with two small, limp forms draped over her arms. Behind her, another woman stepped into the torchlight with a dead child cradled in her arms.

"Marcissus. What's the problem?" Alerio asked. He was unable to comprehend the meaning of the tiny bodies carried by the women.

The farmer turned from where he was helping the women and older children out of the storage building.

"The Illyrians killed our young, and our old men, and our old women," he uttered with tears streaming down his face. "Then. Then, they tossed the bodies in with the living."

Alerio grasped why the pirates had eliminated slaves that were too young or old to be productive and wouldn't sell for top coin. Weeding out the weak made sense economically. But, tossing the dead in with their families was cruel. Cruelty and economics, he understood intellectually. Emotionally, he imagined his own mother and his two sisters among the dead farmers. He lost his temper.

Chapter 10 - Massacre at Occhio

Two of the pirates were regaining consciousness. They rolled over and placed their hands on the ground to push up. In their confused state, they didn't understand when hands gripped their collars. The idea, that everything wasn't as it should be, came to them when they were bodily dragged across the ground, and dropped between two torches.

"I will have the name of your Captain," Alerio screamed. His voice carried across the inlet, up the hill, and reached the village.

To no avail, the singing of the pirates drowned out his voice. He crushed one of the pirate's ears between his fingers and forced the man to his feet. With the other hand, he reached back and drew the Ally of the Golden Valley dagger.

"I will have the name of your Captain," he repeated while slicing the pirate's throat.

His voice didn't carry, but the sight of one of their own gushing blood caught the attention of a few. When the Legionary slung the dying man away and pulled another to his feet, they ran to alert their Captain. By then, the singing was hushed and the crewmen gathered on the hillside.

"I. Will. Have. The. Name. Of. Your. Captain," shouted Alerio as he drew the curved blade across the other pirate's throat.

That dying pirate was tossed aside and the Legionary marched to the doorway. He returned dragging two more pirates.

"The name," he ordered as he placed the point of the knife in a pirate's ear.

Not waiting for a reply, he drove the blade through the ear and into the man's brain. Pushing away the dead Illyrian, he reached down and pulled the other to his feet.

"The name of your leader?" he yelled. "Where is he?"

A large man shoved through the ranks of pirates and strutted to the very edge of the hill. Two men with torches flanked him so he was well lit although far away.

"I am the leader. Legionary," the big man shouted.

Alerio held up the knife as if to signal for the man to wait. Then, he stuck the blade through the side of the injured pirate's neck and yanked until the blade burst out the front of the man's throat.

"I asked for your name. Not a conversation," Alerio yelled back.

Without waiting for a reply, Lance Corporal Sisera marched to the last living pirate on the right bank. The wounded man was crying and sobbing as he crawled away from the fate that befell his shipmates. Alerio grabbed the foot with the split bone and dragged the man back towards the torches. There were claw marks in the hard ground where the man attempted to stop the movement with his fingertips.

"Your name," demanded Alerio of the pirate leader. He pulled the wounded pirate to his feet.

"Navarch Martinus Cetea of the Illyrian Navy," came the reply. After a pause, he added. "Your name Legionary? I will have your name."

"Alerio Sisera. Lance Corporal of the Southern Legion," Alerio spit back. "You murdered the old and the innocent. I will see you on a cross."

"We are Illyrians. The sea provides. And what she doesn't, we take. Those who died brought no profit so we made them sport," Cetea thundered back. "I will gut you. Before you die, you'll watch as we make sport of every farmer in the village."

A hand tapped Alerio on the arm. Looking over his shoulder, he saw Marcissus stepping out of blade distance.

"There are pirates sneaking down to the fiumare," the farmer advised him.

"Go. Get your people as far from here as possible," Alerio said. "By morning the pirates will be gone. Or they will fall to the Legion. For now, go and hide in the fields."

Marcissus inched away as if afraid to turn his back on the blood-soaked Legionary. As with most people when confronted by the reality of vengeance, he relished the idea of revenge but was disgusted by the brutality of the act. And was leery of a man who could extract the full measure of retribution.

"Navarch Martinus Cetea. You will die by my hand," promised Alerio turning back to face the inlet.

Cetea shifted his stance. From a proud and arrogant stiff back, the pirate leader relaxed. He held his hands out wide as if to show he was unarmed.

"We should talk," suggested Cetea. "Any man who could overwhelm six Illyrians would be valuable to me. Valuable to the Illyrian Navy. What say you?"

Despite the offer, Alerio knew a war party of Illyrians was creeping down to the shallow head of the inlet. Once across the low summer stream, they'd attack quickly.

"I already have a job. But here's a parting gift for you," Alerio said as he jammed the knife between the pirate's ribs and twisted the blade. "You killed old people and babies. You aren't a navy, you are pirates."

With those final words, he let the body fall, faded back out of the light, and ran into the grain field. Moments later arrows fell from the sky. As if planted in ragged rows, the shafts filled the space between the two torches.

Chapter 11 - Signal Fires

Twice an Illyrian pirate screamed out and disappeared in the grain field before a horn sounded. The remainder of the war party sent to deal with the Legionary retreated to the safety of the village and their fellow crewmembers. Although they wouldn't admit it, they were happy when the recall sounded.

Alerio followed them to the edge of the field. He watched their shadowy figures climb into the riverbed, splash through the stream, and scramble up the far bank. Once sure they wouldn't return to hunt him or chase the escaped farmers, he turned downstream.

Skirting the wall of the Legion stockade before venturing to the bank of the inlet, Alerio located the path down to the boat. A misstep as he climbed down sent him sliding into the water. While standing in it knee deep, he took time to rinse off his hands before stepping into the flat-bottomed boat. Rather than paddling across to the far bank, he aimed the boat towards the strait.

A short while later, the water became rougher as the inlet met the Messina strait. At the mouth of the inlet, he beached the boat.

"Most of the women and children are safe," Alerio stated as he entered the ring of farmers. Then he delivered the bad news. "Unfortunately, the Illyrians killed the oldest and youngest of your families."

Gasps and curses came from many of the farmers at the announcement. Ignoring the anguish of the grieving men, Alerio asked about the wounded Legion Decanus.

"He's the same. Which is good considering his injuries," a farmer replied.

Alerio found an unoccupied tree and sat down. He closed his eyes as he leaned against the trunk. Someone placed the waxed firebox in his lap.

"Wake me at first light. Or if the pirates row out," he said.

"But what happened at the grain building?" another farmer inquired. "Who's dead and who's alive?"

"You'll have to ask Cimon and Marcissus in the morning," Alerio replied. "I was busy having a conversation with Navarch Martinus Cetea."

"You were talking to the pirate leader?" another farmer asked.

"Just a brief chat. I think we came to an understanding," Alerio stated.

"An understanding? What understanding?" questioned the farmer.

"That one of us will die when we meet again," Alerio said as he dozed off.

It was still dark when a hand nudged Alerio.

"The Illyrians are boarding their ship," announced a farmer.

Drifting down from far up the inlet, male voices shouted unintelligible orders. Individually an oar wouldn't make enough noise to reach Alerio and the farmers. But one hundred and twenty oars clicking into place was a cacophony that traveled.

Alerio pulled his knife and sliced away the wax. In the box were dry shavings of wood, a flint, and a small iron bar.

As the kindling flared to life, a farmer commented, "Won't the pirates see the fire."

"If they do, it'll be on the beach," Alerio informed him, but he also warned. "They may shoot arrows into the trees as they row out. Everyone, move away from the beach."

Alerio stood up carefully with the burning kindling and walked to the depression in the shoreline. After laying the fire in the small pit, he blew on the branches until the flames flared assuring him the fire would burn until he returned.

A drum beating a slow rhythm announced the Illyrian vessel before it appeared in the predawn light. Alerio jogged back to the trees. Finding a thick one, he scooted in behind the trunk and watched the inlet.

The ship was about eighty feet long and ten feet across the middle. Two banks of thirty oars dipped into the water in time with the drum. Alerio figured with sixty oarsmen on each side plus commanders and sailors, the Illyrian pirates numbered at least one hundred and seventy-one when they arrived. Now they rowed out with eight less. He wished it could have been fewer.

Behind the Illyrian bireme, a merchant ship rowed slowly down the inlet. Only six oars propelled it. Even with the slow pace of the larger vessel, the underpowered transport was falling behind.

Alerio leaned farther around the tree trunk trying to get a better look at the ship and the pirate leader. As the two banks of oars rose and fell, the sideboards of the ship slid by. There was no sign of the ship's captain. It was disappointing to be this close and not have a javelin handy even if he couldn't identify Cetea.

From Alerio's left rear, someone shouted. A moment later, a young farmer broke from the trees and ran onto the beach. He held a tree branch and waved it over his head like a club.

"Come back here and fight, you piece of merda," the young farmer screamed as he sprinted toward the inlet's mouth. "I'll perfututum you up for what you did to my sons."

The aft of the boat had just entered the mouth of the inlet and suddenly, the broad shoulders and short brown hair of a man appeared.

"Skew him," he ordered while pointing at the charging farmer.

Alerio recognized the voice and now could put a face to the pirate, Navarch Martinus Cetea.

Five archers stood up mid-ship, notched arrows and released. The farmer was knee deep in when two arrows plunked into the water on either side of him. Then, three arrows sank into his chest. He managed one more step before disappearing beneath the waves.

Occhio inlet had been gouged out of the soft soil along the coast for thousands of years. In that time, the water flowed from the mountains in torrents dragging soil and carving out the riverbed. The river water ate through the soil creating a deep inlet before dissipating into the Strait of Messina. The farmer's last step put him over the edge of the inlet's steep channel.

"Stand down," Cetea ordered.

The Illyrian ship cruised from the mouth of the inlet and rocked as it rowed into the swift current of the strait. Behind it, the merchant vessel wobbled as it floated into the same current.

"I didn't mean to," pleaded Cimon. "I only wanted to tell him about his mother and sons. How was I to know he'd charge the pirate ship?"

It seemed Cimon had followed the Illyrian ship and reported the horror of the night before to the farmers. One of them had reacted rashly to the news. The group of farmers wandered out of the woods to watch the pirates sail away in the soft dawn light.

"Charybdis has claimed him," another farmer said. "A horrible way to die; being gulped down by a sea monster."

Alerio stared at the waves seeking signs of the mad farmer. When nothing broke the surface or bobbed in the waves, he figured a Goddess of the deep had consumed the farmer. Looking up, he watched as the Illyrian ship tracked to the south and set its sail.

The Lance Corporal ran to the beach, blew on the fire pit, and lifted out two flaming sticks. After two of the signals mounds were ablaze, he sat down on the rocky beach to wait.

Chapter 12 – Beach Landing

Optio Martius' boat was leading four other patrol boats. The flotilla rounded Point Ravagnese and rowed feverishly in the direction of the inlet. Alerio relaxed. After judging the speeds of the approaching Legion boats, and the under sail retreating Illyrian ships, he decided no sea battle would be fought today.

Sooner than he expected, the five patrol boats beached and over a hundred Legionaries leaped to shore. Alerio stood, brushed off his posterior, and saluted as a Centurion shoved through the line of charging Legionaries.

The infantry officer looked at the dried blood on the armor, helmet, arms, and face of the young Legionary. When the Lance Corporal left Rhégion to be the spotter, he seemed fresh faced and eager. Now, coated in blood, he had bags under his eyes.

"Report," ordered the Centurion.

"Lance Corporal Alerio Sisera, Sir. The farmers have an injured Decanus in the tree line," he explained while pointing up the beach. Then, he pointed out to sea, "The Illyrian ship and the merchant ship have sailed."

"Medic to the crop of trees," directed the Centurion before he shifted back to Alerio. "What happened to you?"

"The pirates killed the oldest farmers and the babies. They spared the women and children to sell as slaves," Alerio reported. "I couldn't let the Illyrians take them and destroy the farming community. There are dead pirates at the grain storage building and in the grain fields."

"You sound like a farm boy," suggested the Centurion.

"Yes, sir," admitted Alerio.

"As am I. So, thank you," the officer said before turning to a Legionary NCO. "Optio Cletus. Take a squad to the village and be sure the Illyrians didn't leave any surprises for the community. Especially, in the well."

"Yes, Centurion. Decanus Eligius. Take Sixth Squad to the village," the Sergeant ordered. "I'll be joining you. Corporal Domitian. Put two squads around the village, send

44

another to the grain storage area, and keep two on the beach."

While the Sergeant was organizing the distribution of the squads, their Centurion crossed the beach to another officer. They spoke a few words and by the time the Centurion returned, two of the patrol boats were launching. From the woods, a medic accompanied four men carrying a stretcher. The injured Legionary was loaded on the fourth patrol boat under the watchful eye of the crippled Sergeant.

"Optio Martius. I'm keeping Sisera with me for the day," the Centurion said as he turned from Sergeant Cletus. "You can have him back tomorrow."

"Yes, Sir," Martius replied before turning to his boat crew. "We have an injured Legionary, five miles of rough seas, and we are tired. If it was you laying on that stretcher, what would you want your oarsmen to do?"

"Row like my oversized cōleī were on fire," a rower responded.

"That's what I'd want as well. Fall in," Martius ordered.

They pushed the boat off the beach and the twenty oarsmen, the medic, and the Optio climbed into the boat.

"Stroke, stroke," Martius shouted as the patrol boat headed out for the trip around Point Ravagnese.

Act 3

Chapter 13 - Well, Well Duty

Lance Corporal Eligius motioned for Alerio to join him as the Sixth Squad marched up the beach.

"The name's Ovid Eligius. You look a mess," the squad's Decanus stated as they reached the tree line.

"Alerio Sisera," he replied. "And you should see the other guys."

"The Illyrians have been active in the past few months," Eligius offered as they entered the small grain field. Looking ahead, the squad leader shouted at his two leading Legionaries. "No more than a two-shield distance apart. If someone gets between you, it'll be a bad day."

The Legionaries angled inward and touched the edges of their shields together. They hadn't broken stride, but now there was less space between them. Following behind, the eight other members of the squad adjusted so if attacked they could rapidly form a shield wall.

"As I was saying, the Illyrians have become more active and bolder," Eligius stated. "They've never attacked this far up the strait. Something has them riled up. Have you been in the village?"

"No, Decanus. Last night I did all my work across the inlet at the grain storage building," Alerio said. "Is there something unique about the village?"

"Call me Ovid or Eligius. Save the rank for ceremonies," Eligius directed. "Not that I know of, it's just I've never been to this village. Until three weeks ago, I was the Right-Pivot for First Squad, Third Century."

"Congratulation on your promotion," Alerio commented. "Whose squad did you take over?"

"No one's squad. The Senate decided to finally add Centuries to the Southern Legion," Eligius informed Alerio. "We've been thirty under strength Centuries for as long as anyone can remember. Now they suddenly allocate coin for additional squads bringing the Centuries up to what a Legion should have."

"Why now?" asked Alerio. "Is there an increase in rebel activity?"

"Not that I've seen and I was with the Bovesia Garrison until last year," Eligius replied. "There's a big river, not the fiumare like here, a good-sized trading town and farming communities. If there were rebel activity, it would be at Bovesia. No, I don't think its rebels. But something has the Senate nervous and I don't think it's only the Illyrian raiders."

The squad stepped out of the grain field and started the climb up to the first terrace. Alerio finally saw the rows of beans and the stakes for the bean plants in daylight.

"There's a trail on the right side," suggested Alerio.

"Lead element, angle right," ordered Eligius. "Follow the trail."

Two terraces later, the land flattened and low buildings came into view. They were constructed of mud, ill formed bricks, and rough wooden planks.

"Not much to look at," observed Eligius.

"I agree," Alerio said. He pointed across the inlet to the grain fields stretching out far beyond the right bank of the waterway. "That's their treasure."

A group of women and older children were brushing through the grain stalks. Leading them was a squat farmer swinging a gladius.

"Is he a problem?" asked Eligius.

"That's Marcissus. He helped me free the hostages last night," Alerio commented.

"Is that where you picked up the stains on your armor?" teased Eligius. "How many pirates did it take to accumulate that much grunge?"

"Six at first," stated Alerio.

"At first? How many in total?" Eligius questions. Before Alerio could reply, the Decanus bellowed. "Sixth Squad, form on line and halt."

"Eight by the time they recalled the war party," Alerio related.

One of the Privates turned around, and with his opened mouthed, stared at Alerio.

"If a horde of barbarians came charging at you from behind those buildings," Eligius warned the preoccupied infantryman. "The man on your right and left would die because you weren't ready to set the line."

"I'm sorry Decanus," the Legionary offered.

"Don't apologize to me," Eligius scolded. "Apologize to the man on your right and left because that's who died because your shield wasn't there. Do it!"

The Private turned to his right and mumbled a few words. Next, he faced the man on his left and apologized. Afterwards, he stood stiffly in line looking straight ahead.

"Squad, stand by," Eligius ordered.

"Ready," replied the squad as they stomped their right feet into the dry dirt of the village.

"This is a house to house search," Eligius commanded. "Pair off by twos, and keep an eye on your partner. Call out if you see anything dangerous, interesting, funny, or perverted. Especially perverted so we can all enjoy it. Draw. Forward march."

As the eight Legionaries split apart and began going through the houses, a noise behind Alerio drew his attention. Coming up the trail was Optio Cletus and the Centurion.

"Alerio, a word," requested the Sergeant. "The farmers said you had a conversation with the pirate Captain. Is this where you talked to him?"

"No Optio. He was standing at the edge of that hill," Alerio said while indicating the top of a steep slope off to the side of the village.

"And, where were you?" asked the Centurion.

"I was over there, sir," replied Alerio holding out a finger and aiming it at a brick and mud dome. "Where the bodies are."

Even at the distance from the trail to the grain storage building, they could clearly see six corpses. Five of the dead were sprawled on the ground between two closely space torches. It wasn't the dead pirates that caused the Centurion to wince. It was the raw wounds on four of their necks, one with dried blood on his ear, and another with a chest and foot wound.

"You left two throats intact," observed the Optio.

"I already had the pirate leader's name by then," Alerio replied. "and my hand was so wet, it was easier to stab."

The Centurion cocked his head and studied the fresh-faced Lance Corporal. There was something not-quite-right between the look and manners of the young Decanus and his actions. Despite the incongruity, the Centurion asked, "What is the Illyrian Captain's name?"

"Navarch Martinus Cetea," answered Alerio. "Tall man, well built with short brown hair."

"Navarch? You said Navarch?" stammered the Centurion.

"Yes, sir. Navarch Martinus Cetea, that's what he said," Alerio confirmed.

The Centurion turned his head and looked into the distance. From the hill, the waters of the Straits of Messina reflected the morning light and further in the distance, rose a hazy view of the mountains on the island.

"Sisera. Navarch isn't a name. It's a title," explained Centurion Narcissus. "In Greek, Navarch means leader of many ships. Who you spoke with wasn't simply a pirate Captain. He was an Illyrian Admiral."

"Sir, if Martinus Cetea is an Admiral, where are his other ships?" inquired the Sergeant.

"That, Optio Cletus, is the question of the day. Where were his other ships?" repeated the Centurion. "For the ships, I haven't a clue. Or why he left?"

"Left, sir?" asked Sergeant Cletus. "They took the merchant ship and, according to the farmers, a chest of coins. Seems like a pretty good day's work."

"Navarch Cetea chanced attacking a garrisoned inlet to capture a rich foreign merchant. Why?" inquired the Centurion. "How much coin is it worth for war between the Republic and the Illyrian Kingdom. We're missing something."

A shout rose from the village followed by a call from Lance Corporal Eligius.

"Centurion. Optio. You'll want to see this," the squad leader yelled.

Alerio trailed behind as the officer and the NCO marched toward the largest hut in the village. On the way, they passed a water well. Standing beside the well was the

Legionary, who had been distracted and out of line. He stood with a rope tied around his waist.

"It's easy. We drop you in the well and you feel around for anything foul," another Private explained. He held the other end of the rope. "After you check, we pull you up."

The well was a dark hole in the center of the village with a single course of stone ringing it. Adding to the man's terror, the well only opened the width of the Private's shoulders.

"Who would poison a well?" asked the Private. "Can't we just pull up a bucket, look at the water and sample it? That should tell us if it's clean."

"Carcasses rot over time," another Legionary explained. "Right now, it may be drinkable. In a week, you'll pull up a bucket of fur and maggots. In you go."

Two Legionaries held him upside down. Five others fed rope out hand-over-hand until the Private's hobnailed boots disappeared below street level.

Alerio cringed at the infantryman's claustrophobic duty and rushed to catch up with the officer and the NCO.

Chapter 14 - It's Greek to Me

"Having the grandest house in a rural farming community was like having two deaf and blind oxen," thought Alerio. "It sounded good until you saw the results."

Lance Corporal Eligius stood on the porch of the shabby structure with a wide grin on his face.

"This better not be another display of debauchery like the last time," warned Sergeant Cletus as he approached.

"You've got to admit those portraits were extraordinary," Eligius replied. "Nothing salacious in here, Optio, unless you're a scholar."

Ducking through the goatskin door covering, Alerio followed the officer and the NCOs. Scattered around the dirt floor and over the rickety table and chairs were unrolled scrolls and pieces of parchment.

"What's this?" demanded Cletus. "It's parchment. So, what?"

Eligius strutted to a scattered stack and snatched up a piece of a scroll. While walking back, he held it out so the Sergeant and the Centurion could see the writing.

Alerio looked but couldn't make out the language. Thanks to his mother, he wrote Latin. Plus, he spoke a spattering of other languages. Mostly learned from friends of his father as he grew up. But this script made no sense to him.

"I don't know what it says," admitted Eligius. "But I know symbols. On the bottom is the imprint of Ra, the Egyptian Sun God. However, the writing is Greek. I think."

"Egyptian officials writing to the Greeks. A merchant ship with a large coin chest," the Centurion summarized. "Being chased into a Republic port by an Illyrian Kingdom ship. All right, Sergeant, I want every scrap of parchment stacked and carefully bundled up, water tight, for transport back to Fort Rhegium. Let's see if Planning and Strategies can make sense of this."

A short time later, the goatskin door had been repurposed as water tight wrapping for the sheets. During packing, the Centurion noticed the parchment in the corner was pasted to the dirt floor with blood. Even though these pages were barely legible, they were packed separately and tossed in the big package.

"Sisera. Take charge of the documents," ordered the infantry officer. He handed over the bundle. "We'll assign two squads to row you to Rhegium. Report to Planning and Strategies, give them the package, and tell them what you know."

"Yes, sir. What happened here?" asked Sisera.

"It seems Navarch Martinus Cetea isn't a reader. Or he got preoccupied and just forgot those," the officer replied while poking the bundle with a finger. "In any case, he's left us clues and we're going to figure it out. Now get to the beach."

"Yes, sir," Alerio said as he stepped through the door frame.

Outside, Alerio noticed the Legionary who'd been lowered into the well was back on solid ground. Bent over and dripping wet, the man vomited volumes of liquid.

"I take it the well-dive didn't go well," ventured Alerio to Lance Corporal Eligius.

"It served a purpose," Eligius replied. "Poor lad got dunked by his squad mates. They thought it was hilarious when he began to scream. It wasn't until he was up that they found out when they dunked him, he came face-to-face with a dead man."

"Are you going to get him out?" asked Alerio.

"We're pulling the corpse up now," Eligius answered.

Sixth Squad had lashed a three-pole structure together over the hole so they could bring the body out fully before swinging it to the ground. A pair of sandals appeared and when a pair of brightly striped pants came into view, Alerio raced back to the hut.

"Sir. The man from the merchant ship carrying the parchment and scrolls was just pulled from the well," he explained. "The farmers described him as having strange pants."

"It seems Cetea wasn't just a non-reader; he didn't like scribes either," the officer stated. "Sergeant. I need the body on the boat with Sisera and the bundle."

"Yes, sir. I'll pull the squads from the grain storage area and the defensive perimeter," Cletus explained.

"Sisera. Wait for the squads. Once they have the body, go with them to the beach," the Centurion ordered. "Unless you discover something else."

"Yes, sir," Alerio responded. He left the hut for the second time balancing the wrapped scrolls and pieces of parchment in his arms.

Act 4

Chapter 15 – Rhegium Garrison Southern Legion

No one bothered to wake Alerio. He dozed, curled up in the bow of the patrol boat. But the sudden talking between oarsmen alerted him they were nearing their destination.

"Liberty in Rhegium tonight," a rower said voicing his anticipation of a night on the town.

"I'm with you," another stated. "If nothing else they have good vino."

Alerio sat up and glanced over his shoulder. The solid blocks of the Rhegium tower were easily seen in the distance. With a raised view of the opposite shore, it provided the best place to scrutinize the edge of Messina. While the city's walls blocked a view of the harbor on the far shore, the height allowed Legionaries to monitor ships entering and departing the port.

The port of Rhegium occupied the shoreline north of the tower. On this side of the strait, the city of Rhegium stretched from the flat land at the harbor to where the mountains began to climb. A few of the buildings on the elevated ground actually had a view of Messina. But, they were far enough back the view was obscured.

On this side of the tower, the garrison's wall ran from the base of the tower to a tree line. Along the walls rested patrol boats; some under construction and others beached for repairs of broken boards, or for re-caulking. Over the wall, the clay shingled roofs of Legion buildings could be seen.

The patrol boat drifted the last two yards and nudged against the beach.

Alerio jumped onto solid ground and walked up the beach to get out of the crew's way. After they pulled the boat clear of the water, four Legionaries slid the stretcher and the unknown corpse off the boat.

"Where to Lance Corporal?" a stretcher-bearer asked.

"Planning and Strategies," replied Alerio. "Wherever that is?"

Sergeant Martius limped to the grass at the top of the beach.

"In the command building," he directed while pointing at the main gate. "Cross the quad. The entrance is around back."

"Thank you, Optio," Alerio acknowledged as he began to angle up the shoreline.

"Sisera. You might want to wash off and clean your gear before meeting with the command staff," suggested Martius.

"I'd also like to have a hot meal and a large mug of vino," Alerio replied. "But Centurion Narcissus said this bundle, that body, and my report were rush items."

"Carry on, Decanus Sisera," Martius ordered as he limped down to inspect the patrol boat.

Chapter 16 - Southern Legion Planning and Strategies

Alerio guided the bearers through the gate, across the parade ground, and along the side of the command building. In the rear, he found a shaded courtyard with a small flower garden. An elderly man in a duty tunic was on his knees turning soil at the base of a flowing vine. Alerio paused and started to ask directions. But, after spotting an entrance, he didn't. Instead, he made for the doorway.

"Set it down and wait here," he ordered the Legionaries with the stretcher. As he stepped over the threshold, he announced. "Lance Corporal Sisera. Reporting per orders of Centurion Narcissus."

From a desk in a corner, an Optio looked over a stack of parchment.

"You are filthy, Decanus," the staff NCO observed. "Don't you think you should have cleaned up before reporting to command?"

"I've just come from the Occhio Inlet with these," he replied while holding out the bundle. "Plus, a foreign body and my report. The Centurion said it was urgent."

"Stand by," the Optio instructed. He stood and marched through a door behind his desk.

Alerio glanced around the room. There were two other desks piled with parchment shoved against a wall. The positioning was necessary as a large table occupied the center of the room. A sheet of animal skin covered its surface, hiding lumpy objects that rested on the tabletop. Around the room, shelves lined every wall except where a desk and chair rested or the three doorways prevented storage.

The Sergeant returned and behind him marched First Optio Gerontius and a Senior Centurion.

"Sir. Yesterday the garrison at Occhio was attacked by the Illyrian Navy," Alerio began but stopped when the Centurion held up a hand.

"Velius. Would you like to join us?" the officer shouted in the direction of the backdoor. When there was no reply, the senior officer called out again. "Tribune Velius. Your presence is requested."

It was almost humorous to have the Senior Centurion, the First Optio, and a staff NCO of the Southern Legion's command staff standing around waiting. Alerio almost lost it but the narrowed eyes of the other three reminded him of his lowly position. He bit down on his tongue.

The old man from the garden eventually shuffled through the door.

"Tribune Velius," began the Centurion, but the old man laid a finger over his own lips to silence the senior officer.

"Pardon me Senior Centurion Patroclus," Tribune Velius said as he shuffled to a desk. Once there, he swept the surface clear. "The body is of an Egyptian. Based on the ink stains on his right hand and left fingers, he was a clerk or an accountant. However, from the band creases around his head, I'd say a royal scribe. The creases would be from the headdress he wore at the court of the King of Egypt."

"What was a royal scribe doing on a merchant ship in Occhio?" questioned the senior officer.

"Senior Centurion Patroclus, if we knew the answer to that, it wouldn't be a mystery. Would it?" stated Velius. Turning to Alerio, he asked. "Is that bundle for me, Lance Corporal?"

"Yes, Tribune. It's parchment and scrolls the royal scribe carried," reported Alerio.

"Please, place them on the desk," Velius ordered while indicating the empty desk. Turning to the staff NCO, he asked. "Staff Sergeant Octavian, if you would begin sorting the documents? Now, Lance Corporal if you would relate the details as you know them."

Alerio was partway through his story when First Sergeant Gerontius interrupted.

"Navarch? An Illyrian Admiral commanded the attack?" he asked while grinding his teeth. "He killed and wounded my Legionaries. For what? A chest of coins. I want to kill him slowly. With my bare hands."

"First Optio. If you would have the stretcher-bearers carry the Egyptian to medical," suggested Velius. "Have the medics pack the body in salt. I have a feeling, we'll be returning him to his King."

Growling as he made for the door, Alerio realized the First Sergeant was personally upset at the loss of the

Legionaries. Like a father who had lost sons, he was grieving, angry, and frustrated at not being able to extract revenge.

"Decanus Sisera, please continue," Velius urged.

While Alerio went through the sequence of events, the First Sergeant returned and pulled up a chair where he sat quietly fuming. Senior Centurion Patroclus collected a chair and sat off to the side. The only people standing were Tribune Velius and Alerio.

During the report, the sun went down and Staff Sergeant Octavian sorted all the documents into piles. Except for a few questions by Velius, Alerio told them the entire story uninterrupted.

"Very well, Lance Corporal Sisera. I'd like you back here at first light," Velius instructed at the end. Then turning to Gerontius asked. "If that's all right with you, First Sergeant?"

"Sisera. Report to me at the front desk in the morning," instructed Gerontius. "Clean your gear but leave it in your quarters. Report in a duty uniform. Dismissed."

Alerio saluted by slamming his right fist into his chest. Flakes of dried blood broke loose and fell. In shock, he looked down at the chips floating to the floor.

Tribune Velius studied the flakes as they created an irregular pattern on the tiles. A slight smile crossed his face before he looked up and locked eyes with the young Legionary.

"Don't worry about it, Lance Corporal," the Tribune said. "Go and clean up. I'll see you in the morning."

Alerio marched to the rear door and stepped out into the night.

Chapter 17 – Beware the Dark Arts

Unable to sleep, Alerio strapped on his hobnailed boots and slid a loose tunic over his head. As he stepped from the transit barracks, he took in a deep breath. Although sunrise was still half the night away, he felt restless and needed a run. At the rear gate of the garrison, he nodded at the duty Legionary and headed for town.

After a few blocks, he turned right on a dark road and started up into the hills. When he reached the edge of the settlement, he stopped and looked back. Over the town, across the moon lit waters, and slightly to the north weak lights from the city of Messina glowed softly. The only thing he could gather from the view; Messina seemed to be about the size of Rhegium.

Alerio retraced his route downhill and ended up at the docks. Running along the piers, he noted the number of valuable merchant ships lashed to the pilings. They were anchored, just two-arrow flights distance from where the pirates known as the Sons of Mars lived in Messina. At the end of the dock, he jogged in a half circle and headed towards the garrison.

Lighting a lantern at the gladius training pit, he secured two wooden training gladii from the supply shed. Once loosened up, he began to attack the training post. In short order, he was running simultaneous right and left sword drills.

"Up early, Sisera?" a voice asked loud enough to be heard over the hammering of the gladii.

With a final slap at the post, Alerio turned and blinked away the sweat from his eyes.

"Good morning, First Sergeant Gerontius," he said once he identified the speaker. "Seemed like a good idea to get a workout in before reporting to you."

"I'm heading to the baths," said the senior Optio. "Put away your toys and join me. There are a number of things we need to discuss."

Alerio shelved the heavy wooden gladii, blew out the lantern, and ran to catch up with the Southern Legion's First Sergeant.

They soaped in one bath, rinsed off in another, and did a final cleansing in a third. Then they sat on benches with curved brass scrapers, slushing off the water while massaging their muscles.

"Do you know what Tribune Velius does for the Legion?" Patroclus asked as he scoured at his moist skin.

"Planning and Strategies I assume," replied Alerio. "Although I'm not sure what that is to start with."

"Before a Legion takes the field, it gets a number of things. New recruits to create squads so the Centuries are brought to full strength. A Senior Tribune from an important

64

political family and a General chosen from the Consuls. Along with the General comes a gaggle of young Tribunes," explained Patroclus. He stopped speaking as he reached back and scraped behind his shoulder blades. Once finished with the awkward position, he asked. "What do all those additions to the Legion have in common?"

"I'm not sure First Optio," admitted Alerio. "What do they have in common?"

"None of them have military training, or the first idea of how to deploy a Legion," Gerontius stated. "It's why we have a full time Colonel, a Senior Centurion, a First Sergeant, and on the Century level, Centurions, Optios, Tesserarii and Decani. We are the military professionals who know maneuvers and how to fight a Legion."

"So, for planning and strategies we need people experienced with battlefield tactics," offered Alerio. "The Tribune and the Staff Optio are here to advise the command staff on the best way to approach an enemy."

"But Lance Corporal, the Southern Legion hasn't been ordered to take the field. We're on garrison duty," Gerontius proposed while slipping a duty tunic over his head. "There is something that comes before calling up a full Legion to fight. First, you've got to study and learn as much as you can about an enemy."

"Intelligence. Tribune Velius and Staff Sergeant Octavian are gathering intelligence," guessed Alerio.

"There's another word for them," Patroclus suggested as he walked to the exit. "Spies, masters of the dark arts. I'll see you in my office at dawn."

Chapter 18 - The Big Picture

"First Sergeant Gerontius. Lance Corporal Sisera reporting as ordered," Alerio said as he entered the command building.

The sun had yet to appear over the mountains but the brightening sky qualified as predawn. Gerontius looked up from his desk. He eyed the olive tunic with the Decanus band of woven bronze thread around the right sleeve. Then, he shifted to the Legion gladius instructor tab on the young Legionary's chest and the Eastern Legion Raider sash with a rising sun over cresting waves painted on the silk.

"Better than yesterday," scowled the First Sergeant in appreciation of the duty tunic. Any sign of the relaxed conversation in the baths had evaporated. "You are meeting with Tribune Velius this morning. When he's finished with you, report back to me for your orders."

"Orders?" asked Alerio.

"Did I mumble?" inquired Gerontius. He jerked his thumb indicating a door behind his desk. "Don't keep the Tribune waiting."

Alerio circled the First Optio's desk and pushed open a door. There he found a long hallway with doors to offices on one side and several small windows on the other. At the end of the hall, he opened a door and stepped into the large rear room. In front of him was the Staff Optio's unoccupied desk.

"Lance Corporal Sisera. Kind of you to join me," Tribune Velius said as if Alerio had a choice in the matter. "Let me assure you, I was very pleased with your report yesterday. As well as your heroic act in saving the women and children of the farming community. I suppose you have questions."

"Good morning, Tribune Velius," Alerio replied. "I have no questions, sir. Just reporting as ordered."

"Perhaps you have no questions because you lack knowledge," pondered Velius. He shuffled to an end of the large table. "Please, help me with this."

The old Tribune gathered up a corner of the goatskin sheet with one wrinkled hand. He pointed to where he wanted Alerio. Together, they carefully lifted and folded the sheet until the lumpy items on the table top were revealed.

Puzzled at first by a shiny, wide ribbon of blue separating two brown lumps, Alerio studied the tabletop. Eventually, something looked familiar and he walked to the other end of the table.

"This looks like the inlet at Occhio and Point Ravagnese," Alerio offered while pointing at a carved-out piece of brown next to the blue band.

"Very astute of you. In fact, this is a scale model of the Straits of Messina and the area of operation for the Southern Legion. Plus, the eastern coastline of the island of Sicilia," explained the Tribune. "Think of it as the view a soaring eagle would have of the land and the sea."

"It's a map," blurted out Alerio. "I didn't recognize it. Everything is miniaturized like the toy Legionaries I had as a child."

"Exactly. Oh, wait a moment," Velius said as he walked slowly to a shelf and pulled down a big box.

He handed the carton to Alerio. Reaching in, he pulled out a handful of red triangles. Velius sidestepped around the table, placing the triangles along the eastern edge of the blue ribbon. Several times, he moved the symbols from one area to another. When he was satisfied with the placements, he returned to the box and pulled out a blue piece, a yellow piece, and a black disc.

The blue was placed on the lower end of Sicilia. The yellow on the far side of the island, and the black circle on the shore across the blue band from a group of red triangles.

"Red represents the Southern Legion along the coast of the Republic," he explained. "Blue is the City State of Syracuse. Black indicates Messina just across the strait. And the yellow is territory controlled by the Qart Hadasht Empire. Until yesterday, the Empire was the focus of my attention."

"Until yesterday?" Alerio questioned. "What changed?"

"Walk with me," Velius ordered.

The old Tribune circled the table, stopping to stare at a section for a moment before moving on to another area.

Alerio followed and felt foolish as he could have stood anywhere in the room and watched Velius move slowly around the big table. At the far end, where the Republic's land curved around to the east, Velius put his finger on the map.

"The town of Bovesia at the Kaikinos River," he said so softly Alerio could barely make out the words. "That's where the answer is."

"Tribune Velius. The answer to what?" inquired Alerio.

"Come please," Velius said. He walked to where two desks were shoved together. The extra space was necessary as the parchments and scrolls from the village at Occhio were stacked on the surface. "These are detailed shipping requests from Egypt to the Greeks. And, records of proposed payments from Egypt to the Athenians. All the documents are for the transportation of..."

Alerio waited for the Tribune to finish his thoughts. Except, he didn't. He just stood there staring at the stacks. Finally, Alerio couldn't stand the silence.

"For the transportation of what, sir?" he asked.

"Ah, now, young Lance Corporal Sisera, you have the question," Velius said. He looked up from the parchment and studied Alerio's face. "Can you find me the answer?"

"I suppose if I was stationed at Bovesia Garrison, I could ask around," volunteered Alerio. "You said your focus changed. Changed to what?"

"The Illyrians. The Athenians. And, the Egyptians," he replied. "Three potential enemies of the Republic that aren't even on my map."

Chapter 19 – Deception

Alerio was met in the hallway by the First Sergeant. Without a word, the senior NCO directed him into an office.

"Good morning, Senior Centurion Patroclus," Alerio said when he saw who was sitting at a desk.

"Sit down Lance Corporal," the officer instructed without looking up from a piece of parchment. "Are you familiar with the term deception?"

"Yes, sir. It's when I lower and wobble my left gladius. My opponent attacks thinking it's my weak side," Alerio offered.

"Isn't the left arm weak for all Legionaries?" asked the puzzled Senior Centurion. He looked up from his reading material. "I thought we trained everyone to only use the right?"

"Sir, if I may," broke in the First Sergeant to shortcut the dead-end conversation. "Sisera is a gladius instructor and is proficient with both arms."

"I see. The analogy is a bit basic but it's germane to the topic," Patroclus admitted. "The Southern Legion is stretched over seventy-five miles of coastline. Not only are we under strength and drawn out, there are mountains

70

separating our garrisons. We have no direct overland routes to reinforce any of our Posts. On top of that bowl of mush, we have known enemies across the strait and pirates and suspected enemies across the seas beyond it. That's the cold hard truth of our existence."

"Yes, sir. I understand," said Alerio.

"So, to keep our enemies on their heels. As a swordsman, you should appreciate that description. We practice the art of deception," explained the Senior Centurion. "Centuries and squads are shuffled regularly between garrisons. Frequent rotation leads our enemies to believe we have an abundance of Legionaries. That's our first deception, but we're adding another."

"What's the second deception, sir?" Alerio inquired.

"We're adding a squad early," the senior infantry officer replied. "Seventh and Eighth Squads will join Third Century within the year. As a bit of deception, we're activating Eight Squad early. And you are the squad leader."

"You've been assigned to Tribune Velius for a mission," First Sergeant Gerontius explained picking up the narrative. "He wants you in Bovesia with the freedom to move around. We need to appear stronger, so we've combined the two. Congratulations, Decanus Sisera."

"That's Centurion Narcissus' Century," Alerio stated. "Aren't they at Occhio."

"Third is moving to Bovesia once First arrives in about four weeks," Patroclus said. "First Sergeant Gerontius has your orders on his desk. And, Lance Corporal Sisera, I don't

71

know what you're doing for the Tribune but watch yourself. You'll be operating without a squad at your back. Dismissed."

Alerio gave a salute, turned and followed Gerontius down the hall to his desk.

"This is a letter to Tesserarius Cephas. He'll be posting duty assignments for Eighth Squad," Gerontius instructed as he slapped Alerio's hand with a rolled and sealed missive. "He'll have the duty covered with other Legionaries. Just show up, walk the post like a real squad leader, then go be a spy."

"First Sergeant, I didn't ask for this," explained Alerio.

"It's not you I'm angry with," Gerontius admitted. "It's the Senate, the politics, and the lack of resources for my Centuries that gets to me. Good luck on your mission and be careful."

"I always am, First Sergeant," stated Alerio.

"Careful isn't what I'd call taking on a ship full of Illyrians at Occhio," the First Sergeant commented.

"I had acres and acres of grain fields at my back," Alerio informed him. "At night, it's the safest place in the world for a farm boy."

"Get out of my office Sisera."

"Yes, First Sergeant."

Act 5

Chapter 20 – Mouth of the Kaikinos River

Five boats lay beached along the right side of the Kaikinos River. Three were large merchant ships and from the brace supports along the hulls, they were laden with goods.

The other two vessels were smaller intercostal transports like the one delivering Alerio to Bovesia Garrison. Used for moving goods between river settlements, the shallow draft merchants plied their trade up and down the coast. Never venturing far from shore.

***

Long before first light, Alerio had boarded the ship and met Captain Hadrian. The man was just a shadowy figure when they rowed away from Port Rhegium.

"Your ship seems low in the water," commented Alerio to Hadrian.

"We have a load of olive oil and those amphorae rest heavy on the old girl," the Captain replied. "Took them on the day before yesterday at Gioia Tauro. If all goes well, I'll trade them for furs at Bonamico. If I can add a few more products, by the time I get back to the Capital, the owner will make a tidy profit."

"Aren't you the owner?" inquired Alerio.

"Very few of the sailors and rowers own their ships," admitted Hadrian. "I get a bonus if the trip is profitable but I'm like the rowers, just an employee."

"Then why do you do this?" asked Alerio. "Surely there are less dangerous ways to earn your coin."

Alerio felt the vessel shudder as the rowers fought the northbound current along the shoreline. It smoothed out when they reached center channel of the Messina Strait. Catching the southbound current, the low laying ship moved on its own and the rowers relaxed.

"Ship the oars and lower the sail," Hadrian instructed the rowers.

One of the four crewmen climbed the mast and untied lashings. Hemp rope lines hung from the top and the other rowers used them to attach the bottom of the sail to the rails. The wind hit the linen cloth and the ship's speed increased.

"Dangerous?" laughed Hadrian once the crew had set the sail. "No Lance Corporal Sisera, this isn't as deadly as fighting in a shield wall. Here, hold this steady."

The Captain motioned for Alerio to take the rear facing oar. The handle vibrated from the force of water flowing over the submerged blade. Once Hadrian was confident Alerio wouldn't turn his ship, he stepped to a trunk secured to the deck rail. From it, he lifted an old leather belt with a gladius sheath attached.

"When I was a young man, I signed up for the Legion," Hadrian offered. "I was just out of training when my Century marched out to face an eastern tribe. Trained by

74

Greeks they were. Imagine me standing shoulder to shoulder with my squad mates and out marches a formed and orderly line of tribesmen. I was shaking in my boots. The squad leader called for a new formation and my Right-Pivot shifted just before our lines clashed together."

He stroked the hilt of the gladius and let a slight smile crease his sun-tanned face.

"The fates deem some for war and others for commerce," Hadrian suggested. "I was barely set in the new formation when the tribe reached us. On the first advance, I shoved with my shield, withdrew it, and ran out my gladius. Then things went terribly wrong. A spear smashed into the side of my helmet and this happened."

Hadrian gripped the hilt and pulled it from the sheath. The blade was snapped off leaving only a quarter of its original length. He stared at the straight, clean break and shook his head.

The blade, what was left of it, shined as if newly sanded and oiled. And the old sheath was just as well maintained. Obviously, Hadrian took pride in the weapon.

"You could get a new gladius," Alerio proposed.

"No, Decanus Sisera, while I lay on the ground, my squad stomped and pushed forward. When the second line passed over me, I was lucky to avoid their boots," explained the merchant. "The fates, lad, the fates decided my future right there on the bloody battlefield. The next time I strap on this gladius, it'll be for my funeral. Now give me back the oar. I get nervous when anyone but me pilots the old girl."

They sailed by Point Ravagnese and Occhio inlet. Later, they left the straits and followed the distant shoreline on an easterly heading. The sun was high when Hadrian pointed to a town carved and built on rocky hills above the beach.

"There's Bovesia. I'll have to drop you in the water," announced Hadrian. "I'm not making port here."

"Not too deep, I hope," replied Alerio.

"You're a Legionary. You know how to swim," commented the merchant.

"Not while carrying my gear," admitted Alerio.

"Oh, you youngsters. Back in my day, in the old Legion, we swam fully armored while holding our javelins in our teeth," boasted Hadrian.

"Really?" asked Alerio in amazement.

"Of course not, but it's how us old timers like to remember the past," Captain Hadrian said before shouting to his crew. "Roll the sail and man the oars."

Without the sail, the overloaded merchant vessel slowed and began to rock in the gentle waves of the Ionian Sea. Once the oars were dipped and put into use, the ship moved toward shore.

"Back-her-down," shouted Captain Hadrian.

The four oarsmen reversed strokes and the ship slowed. But momentum allowed it to travel enough that the merchant vessel gently nudged the sandy bottom.

"Hold water," he instructed and the transport stopped before running onto the beach. "That's as close as I can get you, Lance Corporal."

"It's close enough Captain Hadrian. Thanks for the ride," responded Alerio.

Decanus Sisera leaped from the foredeck and landed in waist deep water. Hadrian tossed down a bundle containing his armor, helmet, and gladii. As he waded to the beach, he heard Hadrian shout, "Stroke. Stroke. Get us away from the shallows."

By the time Alerio reached the shore, the transport was in deep water and turning eastward.

***

Alerio marched across the sand and gravel to a set of wide steps cut into a rocky hill. Twenty steps later, he came level with the first buildings of the settlement. The rest of the clay brick structures rose as the trading town stepped to higher and higher elevations.

"Beverage, Legionary?" asked a man sitting at a table outside one of the buildings. "Salt spray dries a man out something fierce."

Alerio started to pass by then remembered his assignment. Instead of climbing higher, he rested his armor and helmet package on the table.

"What have you got?" he inquired.

"Some watered wine and spring water," the man offered. "But the pride of my establishment is my beer. Best in Bovesia."

"Sold," Alerio said as he dropped four coppers on the table before sitting down. "Join me."

The merchant swung his legs off the table and stood. Alerio almost missed the markings. While the man wore sandals with thin tie straps, his ankles and calves were indented in wide, deep strips like the kind made by heavy military boots.

The man returned with two mugs brimming with frothy foam. Alerio took a sip as the man dropped into the other chair.

"Pholus, brewer of fine beer," the man exclaimed while lifting his mug.

"This far exceeds any beer we made on my father's farm," exclaimed Alerio as he wiped the foam from his upper lip. "Well done, Master Pholus."

Pholus beamed with pride and explained, "Greek copper. Instead of clay or wooden barrels, I brew it in top quality Greek copper."

"Is it hard to get?" inquired Alerio.

The man laughed, pointed out to sea, and rotated his arm a little to the right. "Greece is just over the horizon about seven days rowing and sailing," he said. "I bought the pot off a merchant and have been perfecting the mash ever since."

"Do you get many Greek ships here?" asked Alerio.

"Legionary. I can tell you've never been to Bovesia," the man advised. He took a pull from his clay mug. "Ships traveling up the coast to the east, heading for deep water going west, and those bound for Greece, Egypt, Qart Hadasht and other southern places stop here to resupply. Before heading out on a long sea voyage, or returning to the coast, they all stop at Bovesia."

Alerio thanked Pholus, hoisted his gear, crossed to the set of steps and began the climb to the second plaza level. A glance to his right gave him a view of the Kaikinos River. Its murky water ended a short way out into the blue water of the Ionian Sea. Fishing boats beached on the far side of the river rested near rustic huts of reeds and wood. Between the huts and boats were fish drying racks.

On the next plaza level, Alerio found merchant buildings. Nets, hemp rope, copper and metal goods were on display. He imagined there were other repair items inside. An enclosure holding five mules gave a hint as to how the sold merchandise got transported to the beach.

***

He located the crews from the five beached boats on the third level plaza of Bovesia. It was a mad jumble of activities. Smoke from roasting meat filled the air. The yelling of slightly intoxicated men and cheers from a number of games created a roar. Even a couple of bards, vying for the crewmen's attention and coins, sang or recited verses.

Alerio shoved into the crowd and grabbed a man.

"Where is the Legion garrison?" he demanded of the oarsman.

"Over the crest," the man replied before staggering away.

Alerio shoved aside a few more sailors, threaded an alleyway, and stepped to the back of the buildings. Down a narrow trail were two buildings and four tents. It was obvious from the indentions in the dirt that not too long ago four additional tents had also occupied the garrison space. A wall of thorn bushes surrounded the buildings, tents, and parade and practice field. Spying a Legion banner outside one of the buildings, Alerio headed down the hill.

Chapter 21 - Bovesia Garrison

"Tesserarius. Decanus Alerio Sisera, Eighth Squad, Third Century reporting in," Alerio announced while stepping up to a desk in one of the buildings.

"Since when does the Third have eight squads?" inquired the Corporal. "And where are your men?"

"They aren't due for several weeks," Alerio replied.

"So, what am I supposed to do with you in the meantime?"

"I'm a gladius instructor," Alerio informed the NCO. "It seems obvious to me."

"I'm Cephas. We'll put you with supply in building two until your tents arrive," the Corporal declared. "Go and settle in. You can introduce yourself at the morning formation."

***

While not large, the room in the supply building, behind the quartermaster's shelves, had a desk, a window, and a bed. All the comforts of a barracks, plus a bonus, it was a single. As Alerio stowed his equipment, he realized he was hungry.

After strapping the single gladius around his hip, he left the building. Beyond the briar bush wall, the trail headed up the hill towards the highest level of the town.

He noticed wooden stairs climbing the back of one building. The steps ended at a tall stand on the roof. Three Legionaries stood with their backs to the camp so they could watch over the town and the Ionian Sea beyond. A long trumpet rested beside one of them.

The festivities were still in full swing when he reached the top of the hill. Picking the least riotous dining establishment, Alerio pushed through the crowd onto the broad porch of the Columnae Herculis. Once he located a doorway, the hungry NCO entered the restaurant.

***

"Food in the dining room," a powerfully built man stated. He easily looked down on the top of Alerio's head. "You can drink outside."

81

Alerio studied the speaker. The man was tall and heavily muscled to the point a comparison with a bull wouldn't be out of line. From the callouses on his hands, Alerio figured he'd spent a lot of years pulling an oar.

"Food," Alerio advised the man.

"Over there," the waiter instructed by indicating a table across the room.

Instead of escorting him, the greeter walked away. The table was unoccupied and it's other three chairs moved to accommodate diners at larger tables. Not only was the small table empty, it sat between two large ones. The spot was perfect for a man who wanted to fade into the background and listen for information.

An unordered platter of lamb and vegetables landed on the table.

"I didn't order yet," Alerio advised the muscular server.

"You want the food or not?" the man asked as he began to pull the platter from the table.

"Stop. Lamb will be fine," Alerio relented. "You just caught me by surprise."

"Don't get caught by surprise in Bovesia," the giant suggested as he walked to a table near the front. The occupants didn't notice the server approach. They were too busy conversing through a window with a rowdy group of people on the porch. "Eat inside," the large man announced. He studied the table full of empty platters and half-filled mugs. "Drink outside."

With platters stacked in his big hands, the giant didn't see the fist. It slammed into the bottom of the platters driving them up and into his face. Two men swung from hip level as the plates fell away. Together, they hammered his grease and food scrap covered face.

Alerio chewed and watched the show. Figuring the big man could handle four sailors, he speared another bit of lamb and popped it in his mouth. His contented chewing stopped when a sailor drew a knife.

The knifeman circled the melee where his three friends were absorbing blows from the giant. As if to sneak away, the man bent down and crab walked around the fighters. His eyes, however, weren't focused on the exit.

Recognizing a man seeking a weak spot on a target, Alerio jumped from his chair and charged at the knifeman. As he approached, the sailor caught the movement out of the corner of his eye. The knife's point swept around and rose until it was aimed at Alerio's gut.

'In four steps, the Legionary will be impaled on my blade,' calculated the knifeman. 'Then I can cut the big Athenian.'

But the charging Legionary stopped at three steps and a shuffle from the knifepoint. The knifeman thrust the blade forward to close the distance. He got agitated when the hand holding the knife flared off to the side. When he pulled back his wrist, the stranger's wrist stayed attached to it. Jerking his arm up to disengage, the hand holding the knife, aided by pressure from the strangers' hand, rose too fast and

83

traveled too far. The knifeman had to rock his head to the side so the blade only nipped his ear.

Alerio had the knifeman's right arm up and out of the way. Just as he made a fist with his left hand preparing to drive it into the sailor's ribs, the knifeman collapsed. The blunt end of a herder's club withdrew over Alerio's shoulder. Turning to see who knocked out the sailor, Alerio came face-to-face with a handsome woman.

She was tall, with a cascading mane of wild black hair framing her face. But it wasn't the height or the hair that fixed him in place. It was the gold flecks in her brown eyes and the challenge in her stare.

"Out," she ordered. "No fighting inside."

Alerio's sense of what a fight was or wasn't didn't match the situation. So, he laughed. Her eyes narrowed and the herder's club rose from alongside her long leg. He didn't mean to look that closely, but her leather pants did nothing to hide her shape.

The shift from facing a knife brandishing sailor to facing a beautiful woman armed with a club was too much. Alerio doubled over with laughter while holding out a hand to stop her from hitting him with the club.

"Out," she insisted while pointing the weapon at the doorway.

From across the room, a familiar voice called out, "Need help Marija?"

"No. Hyllus and I have it under control," she replied to Corporal Cephas. Then to Alerio ordered. "Get out, now."

Tesserarius Cephas had just walked into the triclinium. Flanking him were two armored Legionaries. The three didn't look pleased to see the new squad leader facing off against Marija.

Alerio, from past experience, knew nothing good could result from confronting someone in a cafe. Pulling out a few coins, he dropped them on the table and headed for the door. Corporal Cephas' face was screwed down in an unpleasant expression and he didn't acknowledge Alerio's nod. As Lance Corporal Sisera approached the threshold, the giant came in from the porch. He noticed Alerio heading for the door.

"You. Finish your food," ordered the big man.

"The lady said to get out," Alerio explained.

"Woman. See this?" the giant asked while raising his arms to shoulder level and turning in a full circle.

"See what, Hyllus?" she asked curtly. Despite the short question, her face softened and the scowl lifted.

"No knife holes," he said lowering one arm and drooping it over Alerio's shoulder. "If it wasn't for him, there would be a hole. Or, a couple of holes. Did you see any?"

"No, I don't see any holes but that doesn't mean I wouldn't install a few myself," she replied. "All right, he can stay."

85

She made the pronouncement, marched to the back of the dining room, and disappeared through a rear door.

"Hyllus," the big man said to Alerio. "That's my woman Marija. We own this fine establishment."

"Lance Corporal Alerio Sisera," replied Alerio. "I've just reported to Bovesia garrison and stopped in for a bite. I can leave if it's going to cause a problem."

"Marija, you barbarian of a Macedonian, can the little guy stay?" shouted Hyllus.

Alerio had been called a lot of things over the years, but little wasn't one of them. However, after craning his neck to look up at Hyllus, he decided most people were little in comparison to the giant.

"Oh, he can stay you sweet talking Athenian. But you should take the next boat back to Greece," Marija bellowed from the back room. "Or, you can stop hanging around like a King holding court, and come back here and help me move this kettle."

"Duty calls. Go eat Lance Corporal," Hyllus said as he ambled towards the rear. "I'll bring you a honey cake for dessert."

Chapter 22 – Beaching Fees

Alerio had just taken a bite of lamb when Cephas and the two Privates approached his table.

"Good afternoon, Tesserarius," Alerio said in greeting. "You missed the excitement."

"Seeing you squared off with Marija was more excitement than I needed," Cephas admitted. "I was afraid you'd messed me up."

"How so?" inquired Alerio.

"There are two other restaurants in Bovesia. One is a glorified gambling hall, and the other is a favorite of oarsmen who like to wrestle," explained Cephas. "The Columnae Herculis is quiet and peaceful thanks to Marija and Hyllus."

"I can see the giant keeping everything orderly," acknowledged Alerio.

"Oh, he's tough enough but his wife is the dangerous one," Cephas said to Alerio's surprise. "I supposed you noticed the club and the leather pants? But did you pay attention to the short sword on her left hip? Most men miss that until it's buried in their guts."

"Never saw it," Alerio declared. "I was too busy laughing."

"Anyway, I use their dining room to meet with ship's captains and collect beaching fees," Cephas informed him. "They don't mind coming in here. Although they do mind paying the Republic's fees for stopping at Bovesia."

"Why would they pay?" asked Alerio. "They could pull into any inlet."

"Legion protection while docked," explained Cephas. "The beach, this town, and the supplies are guarded by us. Without the Republic, pirates would take over within a week."

"Sounds noble," Alerio ventured. "You know, keeping the trade routes safe."

"I never thought of it like that," Cephas confessed. Then he glanced around to watch a man come in from the porch. "Ah, my first merchant captain of the afternoon. Enjoy your meal."

While the Corporal, followed by his Legionaries, made for a table in the corner to collect a fee, Alerio looked down at his cold lamb and vegetables. He shoved the platter away. A glance showed him the restaurant was mostly empty, but the party on the porch was going strong. He was about to stand when two shadows fell across his table.

"Lance Corporal Sisera. This is my woman, Marija," Hyllus said.

The big man placed a plate holding a slice of honey cake on the table as well as three mugs of ale. Then, the big man pulled two chairs from the adjacent table and held one for Marija.

"I'm perfectly capable of getting my own chair," she complained but the tone didn't match the smile she flashed at the giant.

"Of course, you are, my sweet," Hyllus assured her as he sat in the other chair and picked up a mug. "To my savior."

"I thought you were with the sailors. When I came out of the kitchen it appeared you had a falling out with your crewmen and started a fight," Marija described while reaching out and laying a hand on the big guy's arm. "Hyllus explained that you came to his rescue. Thank you."

"Not much of a rescue; he had them handled. I just detoured the knifeman," Alerio remarked. Then he asked. "Where are you from?"

Chapter 23 – Divisive Politics and True Love

"I was an oarsman on a Greek ship," Hyllus started to say.

"Don't be humble. He was first oar on an Athenian Navarch's quinquereme," she boasted. "I have all his medals and trophies in a trunk in the back. Go ahead, love."

The big man waited a heartbeat to be sure she was finished before continuing.

"The Macedonians launched a fleet of warships and military transports," Hyllus told Alerio. "The army was bound for the coast between Thebes and Athens. The strategy was to march on Athens from the backside of our defenses. But we discovered their plans and our fleet met them in the Aegean Sea. By nightfall, their transports had turned back. Their fleet stayed to cover the retreat. During the naval battle, we captured the Macedonian General and their Navarch."

"Hyllus. Please," Marija uttered in exasperation.

"All right. As the First oar, once the ship-to-ship fighting started, I grabbed my shield and sword," the big man said haltingly as if speaking about himself was difficult. "I boarded the Macedonian flag ship and joined in the hand-to-hand fighting. I was swinging and blocking from behind my shield when all of a sudden, it ended. Somehow, I was in the lead. As the first fighter in the rank, the Macedonian General and Navarch surrendered to me. The rest of their fleet fled."

"We floated around for two days to be sure their warships didn't come back," explained Hyllus. "On the second day, a single Macedonian bireme rowed between our picket line. It seemed their King wanted his commanders back. My Navarch thought it would be fun to sail into their harbor and deliver them personally. So, we rowed in and my commanders left the ship to personally escort the Macedonians to their King. A squad of our soldiers was on the docks guarding the approach. I had nothing to do, so I grabbed a block of wood, my best knife, and I sat with them while I carved. Then the most beautiful woman in the world danced onto the pier."

Marija tossed her head back and released a full belly, open-mouthed laugh.

"I wasn't dancing. I was challenging the Athenians to come forward and fight," she asserted. "There they were, bronzed helmets and shields on my pier, on my ground, on Macedonian soil. I was prepared to push them into the sea or die on their spears."

"You were going to fight men in armor holding shields?" asked Alerio.

"I had my spear and my sword, so yes, I was prepared to fight," Marija confirmed. "My family are Macedonian nobles and warriors. While other girls learned sewing, I practiced with the sword and spear. The very thought of an Athenian warship at my dock was infuriating. I was about to attack when my father's personal guards arrived and held me back. While I argued and begged them to join me in the attack, this huge, half naked Greek steps from behind the soldiers. He struts up to me and hands me a carved piece of wood."

Marija stopped talking and turned to gaze at Hyllus with adoration. The giant returned the look. They stared long enough for Alerio to feel he was intruding on a private moment. Finally, they broke eye contact, and Marija's attention returned to Alerio.

"The nerve of this Greek to approach me and hand me a piece of wood. I had my arm cocked ready to toss it into the sea," she recounted. "Before I could launch it, the captain of my father's guard stopped me. Look, he said, it's you. I peered at the block. Carved into it was the likeness of a wild haired woman with a face I recognized. My face."

"I let my father's guards guide me away. As darkness fell, I slipped back to the docks," Marija explained. "The soldiers wouldn't tell me who the big man was who carved so delicately in wood. It wasn't until I began to yell at the Athenian ship that Hyllus reappeared."

"She was screaming something about wanting to see the savage who carved her image," Hyllus chuckled. "No one could get any sleep, so I went down to face the Macedonian banshee. I figured she assumed I'd captured her soul in the wood or some other mystical thing. I didn't take my sword and shield although a few sailors suggested it."

"So, there I was on the dock yelling over the armored line of men when he came strolling down the ramp," Marija cooed. "I didn't have my sword out so I don't know why he stayed behind the soldiers. I held out the carving and demanded to know where he'd seen me before. It was too fine and couldn't have been done in the short time I was at the pier. He insisted he did the carving while I was there and claimed he'd never seen me before. I challenged him to prove it."

"She didn't have a blade out, so I pushed through the guard line, and showed her my carving knife," Hyllus said. "We walked to a deserted section of the dock and sat down under a lantern. With our legs dangling over the water, I carved, and we talked until the sun came up."

"Unfortunately, he carved a mooring post so I couldn't take it with me when my father and his guards arrived," Marija complained as she took over the tale. "We jumped up. I told Hyllus, if we had a boat, we could run off together."

"What saved me was the arrival of my Navarch and his guards," Hyllus interjected. "During the standoff, I leaned down and kissed her. Then I ran for my ship."

"He kissed me. Right in front of my Macedonian father and his Athenian Navarch," Marija said with a sigh. "For decades, our people have been at each other's throats. Seeing two of their people in love didn't sit well with either of them. With the taste of his lips on mine, I floated between the armed men and headed home."

"But if you went home and he rowed out with his ship," Alerio asked. "How did you get back together?"

"A week later a boy delivered a carving to me. It was a scene of a merchant ship moored to a dock," Marija replied. "I recognized the dock area and when I went to investigate, there was Hyllus sitting on the foredeck of a merchant vessel."

"I resigned my position at the first commercial harbor," Hyllus voiced his side of the tale. "I caught a ride with a merchant and after a number of ports-of-call, we arrived at the Macedonian capital. When it sailed in the morning, Marija and I were on it."

"We couldn't stay in Macedonia because of Hyllus, or go to Athens because of me," Marija offered. "We got lucky when we found a ship heading for the Straits of Messina. Bovesia was the first stop after the ocean voyage."

"We got off the ship to stretch our legs," Hyllus described. "And never left."

"Do you still carve?" inquired Alerio.

Marija stood and walked to a shelf. From it, she plucked a small block of wood and returned to the table. She handed it to Alerio. As if cast in clay or painted by a master, Marija's face peered back from the carved block.

"Every shelf around the restaurant has carvings on it," Marija explained. "Birds, animals, Legionaries, ships and mythological creatures, all carved by Hyllus."

"It's why there is no drinking inside," Hyllus added. He collected the three empty mugs, the plate, and the platter. "Also, it cuts down on the fighting."

"Thank you for the drink, dessert, and most importantly, the story," Alerio said as he stood. "I need to go and get familiar with the rest of the town."

"Don't get caught by surprise," warned Hyllus as he walked away with the dishes.

Chapter 24 – Bovesia, the Steep and Narrow Way

Alerio dodged between the sailors on the porch and reached the street. A stroll across the plaza carried him to another restaurant and pub. Unlike the Columnae Herculis, oarsmen with clay mugs flowed in and out of the building at will.

A few doors down and closer to the stairs, he encountered another tavern and dining enterprise. From inside muffled voices rose in sudden outbursts before the low mumblings returned. It was a typical gambling establishment with dejected losers sitting on the porch in groups sharing their misery.

Just before stepping down onto the first riser, Alerio glanced over the rooftops of the buildings on the next plaza's level. Blue and gray water spanned the vista for as far as the eye could see.

While taking the stairs down, Alerio judged the width between the buildings to be about five shields wide. A squad of Legionaries could hold off an army on this walkway with a two-line formation.

The sun was low and most of the supply businesses had closed for the day. It made sense as the five boats on the beach two levels below had been there since midday. He meandered through the plaza looking at the merchandise and seeking someone to question. So far, Alerio was a failure as a spy.

He strolled down the stairs to the next plaza and thought about having another of the brews. But, he was full and the beer would lay heavy on his stomach. After crossing the plaza Alerio stopped at the top of the stairs and looked out over the ocean.

The sea rolled, birds dove at the swells, and clouds hung low on the horizon. Below, the five merchant vessels rested solidly on Bova Beach. Four of the firewatchers huddled together in conversation. One, however, was working on his ship's hull. An idea formed and Alerio turned from the stairs. He walked back to speak with Pholus, the vendor who sold the delicious beer.

***

"Thirsty duty," suggested Alerio as he approached the man working on the ship's hull.

A clay bowl half filled with melted tar rested on iron legs over a small wood fire. Before answering, the man shoved a dowel into a sack of hemp fiber. With fibers dangling from the stick, he dipped them in the clay bowl. The resulting messy clump was set against the side of the boat. With his other hand, the sailor used a wedge to stuff the tar coated fibers into a gap between the boards. Once the fibers and tar were spread along a crease, he picked up a hammer. Tapping carefully along the newly placed sealant, he drove the waterproof material into the crease to seal the hull.

"Not so much thirsty as frustrating," the workman said as he lay down the wedge and hammer.

"I'm new to Bovesia garrison and thought I'd get to know more about the ships that beach here," Alerio said while holding out the mug. "I'll trade you a beer for some information."

"Why not. I couldn't finish caulking this tub if the Captain gave me two full days," the man exclaimed as he took the mug of beer. "What do you want to know?"

Alerio studied the ship, and although not a sailor, he realized the hull had many warped boards. This vessel needed a lot more hemp fiber and tar treatment to keep out the sea water.

"Why can't you take two days to finish the repairs?" asked Alerio. "This seems like a safe harbor with food and beverage."

"It's a good port. I was surprised when the Captain said we'd row out at first light," the man stated between sips. "I was eating when he charged into the diner and whispered that I needed to finish what maintenance I could before dark. So here I am, slopping and pounding until the light fails me."

"What's your next port?" inquired Alerio. "Is it close?"

"No. We've got four days of rowing and sailing to reach Syracuse," the sailor reported. "It'll be good to get home. If Favonius grants us a steady west wind and we don't sink on the way."

While they sipped beer, the man and Alerio talked about trading between ports, what cargos his ship hauled, and the man's life as a sailor. All the while something was nagging at the back of Alerio's mind.

When the beer was gone, the man went back to caulking his ship and Alerio strolled over to the other four sailors standing watch at their boats. After a few sea stories, he crossed the beach and started up to stairs.

At the first level plaza, he returned the empty mugs to Pholus. When he stepped on the stairs, Hyllus' refrain came back to him, "Don't get caught by surprise."

Chapter 25 – Conjecture or Conclusion

Corporal Cephas had a look on his face as if he'd just bitten into a spoiled olive. He sat behind the desk in Second Century's office and glared at the source of his indigestion.

"A merchant wants to row out at first light," repeated the NCO. "I don't see a problem with him wanting to get an early start on a long voyage."

"It's not that they're leaving," explained Alerio. "It's the fact he hasn't completed repairs. Why would a merchant be in such a rush to leave Bovesia in a leaky boat?"

"Sisera, you've just reported in. After you've been here for a time you'll realize that all merchants, sailors, and oarsmen are crazy. Why else would they spend their days on the open sea?" questioned Cephas. "Look, with my Centurion at Headquarters with half the Century. And my Sergeant off training new Recruits, it leaves me in charge of the Second. I'm not about to round up five ships' Captains and grill them on why they do what they do. Go get some sleep. You're teaching a class in the morning."

***

The sky blushed pink but no light appeared over the mountains. Alerio had completed his calisthenics and was sitting on a barrel running a stone over the blade of his gladius.

"Second Century, on the parade ground for training," shouted Tesserarius Cephas when he marched from the Headquarters building. He glanced around as if looking for something. Then, he spotted Alerio. "I thought you over slept?"

"Good morning, Corporal. I'm an early riser," replied Alerio as he hopped off the barrel. "Ran sprints, did long jumps, hand balancing, and stretched already."

The sounds of men grumbling and putting on hobnailed boots came from the tents.

"Lance Corporals. Hurry them up," Cephas called out to his squad leaders. "You'll soon be burning daylight, and you know how much I hate waste."

A short blast from the trumpet rang out followed by four more individual notes.

"The ships have rowed out," announced the Corporal pointing to the stand on the rooftop of the building on the hill. "More will be rowing in this afternoon."

"Is that how it works?" asked Alerio.

"Everything at Bovesia is like the tide," described Cephas. "Ships roll in and roll out as steadily as the waves. When do you want to run the class? After the exercises or before?"

"Let's do the training first," replied Alerio. "That way, if I need to work one-on-one with some of them, I'll be able to pull them aside."

"Pretty confident you'll find flaws, aren't you?" asked Cephas.

"An Optio told me years ago you can always improve. If your technique is solid, then work on your attitude," replied Alerio.

By now weak morning light had touched the bare ground and Legionaries were emerging from the four tents. In tunics without helmets or armor, they lined up with their shields. A rank of five backed up by a rank of four. The squad leaders, who would be the fifth men in the second ranks, adjusted the rows before marching to the head of each formation.

"Second Century. This is Decanus Sisera, a gladius instructor," Cephas stated. "This morning he'll be running you through some drills."

Legionaries by virtue of their occupation and the training required to stay in the Legion were jaded, cynical, and suspicious. They didn't give respect. It had to be earned.

Cephas knew this and after announcing Lance Corporal Sisera, he drifted back to watch the entertainment and read a scroll; one of many he needed to review. Being a Century's Tesserarius and acting as the Sergeant was tough. Cephas had discovered that if he worked on small things while watching other things he could do twice the work.

"Who is your best swordsman?" Alerio inquired softly as if he were shy and unsure of himself.

An older Legionary stepped out of the ranks.

"That would be me," the infantryman boasted. He drew his gladius and swung it through the air as he strolled towards Alerio. "Where do you want me to strike you? Low so it hurts or high so it shows?"

Behind the man, laughter ran through the ranks of Legionaries. In the Legion, if you professed to be a specialist,

100

then by the gods, you'd better be extraordinary. Specifically, if you taught the gladius and shield. The weapons infantrymen used when they fought belly-to-belly against an enemy.

"That's an interesting question, Private," replied Alerio as he drew his own gladius. "Give me a second, please."

More laughter rose from the formation as the Private said confidently, "Take all the time you need, gladius instructor."

Alerio used a shuffling gate to cross the open ground to the hedgerows of thorn bushes. All the Legionaries watched as the Decanus reached into the shrubbery with his hand and the gladius. When he turned around, he held a long half inch thick branch. As he meandered back to the formation, he used his gladius to strip off the thorns. By the time he reached the Private, his blade was sheathed and he held the switch in his right hand.

"What's your name, Legionary?" Alerio asked while running his eyes from his own hand and up along the length of the thin stick.

"Private Lupus. Right-Pivot of Second Squad," the infantryman replied with a toothy grin. "Are you going to draw your gladius and fight? Or are you going to draw pretty pictures in the dirt with your stick?"

Corporal Cephas looked up from the scroll and shook his head in frustration. He was about to go rescue Lance Corporal Sisera and save him anymore embarrassment. He took a step when…

"Guard position," ordered Alerio while raising the stick to cross Lupus' blade. "Fight."

The first thing Lupus did was pull his blade far to the side so he could swing back and cut the ridiculous stick in half. Before he could chop it, the switch rotated downward and snapped forward whipping the Private across his stomach.

Lupus swung the blade back and leaned forward to reach the instructor. But, Alerio recovered the stick and bent at his waist to let the gladius tip pass harmlessly by. The stick though, snapped forward and slammed into the Private's right shoulder. Like the strike to the stomach, it wasn't debilitating. But, it would leave an angry red welt.

Private Lupus lost his temper. With the gladius held low, he stepped forward and shoved the blade towards the Lance Corporal's midsection. It was intended to be a killing move. The tip and the heavy blade behind it hurled towards Alerio's belly. Just before it ripped open his stomach, Alerio used the stick to shove the tip off to the side.

Stepping inside Lupus' guard, Alerio rotated the switch upward. With momentum, the branch came from overhead and slapped Lupus' left shoulder. Lupus shuffled back trying to get distance between himself and his tormentor. A single step at this close of a range and he could butcher the instructor. Alerio didn't give him the opportunity.

As Lupus stepped back, Alerio stepped forward staying almost chest-to-chest with the Legionary. While their torsos were mirrored, the stick was busy slapping the Private on the head and neck. When Alerio tired of the head, he began to slap Lupus' legs.

They had taken four steps when Alerio snaked a leg between Lupus'. A shove sent the infantryman down where he landed on his butt. To punctuate the lesson, Alerio placed the tip of the stick on Lupus' forehead and pushed. Second Century's top swordsman was forced to lay back and stretch out in the dirt.

"Never underestimate your enemy," Alerio announced while he walked to stand in front of the formation. Pointing back to Lupus, he continued. "Private Lupus' mistake was focusing on my weapon and not his training. The stick wouldn't have stood against his gladius if he had dueled with me."

Alerio gripped the branch in both hands. Raising it overhead, he bent the stick and it snapped with a loud crack. While demonstrating the weakness of the rod, he watched the eyes of the men at the side of the formation. That, along with listening, alerted him to when Lupus scrambled off the ground and charged at Alerio's undefended back.

Pivoting to his right, Alerio bent his knees while drawing his own gladius. Lupus' blade passed over his shoulder. But Alerio didn't remain stationary. He spun completely around and smashed the flat of his blade into the Private's back.

Lupus was driven forward two steps before he could regain control. Turning, he faced Alerio with his gladius in the guard position.

"Now, we'll fight properly," the infantryman growled between clinched teeth.

"First off, Private Lupus, I want to thank you for volunteering," Alerio complimented as he raised his blade. "You see, there is nothing to correct if there is no mistake."

"Your mistake, gladius instructor, was in facing off against me," Lupus spit back.

The blades touched for half a heartbeat. Before Lupus could set for his first attack, Alerio's blade twirled around his blade. In effect, it created a tunnel of spinning steel locking both blades in place. Lupus pulled back his blade trying to extract it. As his gladius withdrew, Alerio's blade jutted forward until the tip rested gently against Lupus' throat.

"Get back in the ranks, Private Lupus," warned Alerio. "Unless you prefer to bleed for your pride."

Lupus smiled and nodded his head as he sheathed his gladius.

"Thank you for the lesson, instructor," the Private said as he backed cautiously away from the steel tip of Alerio's gladius.

"Enemies of the Republic come from many tribes," Alerio informed the assembled infantrymen. "They may have simple primitive weapons, but remember this, it's their primary weapon. If you stray from your training and attack the weapon instead of staying with proven gladius techniques, you may end up dead. Do you follow me?"

"Yes, instructor," forty voices shouted back. Loudest among them was that of Private Lupus.

"Draw!" ordered Decanus Sisera.

He began walking between the ranks adjusting arm or leg positions. Once Alerio was satisfied, he had them pair off and begin gladius drills. Tesserarius Cephas rolled up the scroll and joined him.

"That was dangerous, going against a gladius with a stick," commented the Corporal.

"It only works one time," admitted Alerio. "After the demonstration, they'll know to stay with the basics. Lupus could have easily deflected my stick at any time. Instead, he lost focus and his attitude deteriorated."

"In your final analysis then, it is about attitude," ventured Cephas.

"After a certain skill level," explained Alerio. "Attitude is everything in a sword fight."

Chapter 26 – Over Confidence Kills

Most of the Legionaries were running sprints under the watchful eye of their Corporal. A few were off to the side with Alerio for additional gladius instruction. Although it was still early, the sun was climbing and it looked to be a beautiful day.

Alerio finished and sent the infantrymen back to their squads to join in the sprints. As the men raced back and forth, Alerio strolled to the edges of the garrison and peered down into the valleys. The side of the hill with the river he looked down on mud flats and brown water. On the other side of the Legion hill, farms dotted the landscape between crops of trees. He could tell the farmers were poor as none had oxen or horses to pull the plows. With a brother, son, or wife guiding the plows from behind, the farmers were harnessed up front so they could pull.

'It's a hard life,' he thought remembering his childhood and his father's farm. Then he glanced at the infantrymen who were sweating and sucking in great lungsful of air. 'Life is hard everywhere.'

Suddenly, the trumpet interrupted the sounds of men grumbling and breathing deeply. From atop the lookout stand, it blared out three long notes followed by two notes. Then, the trumpeter repeated the call.

"Second and Third Squads," shouted Cephas. "Grab your helmets, minimum armor, and shields. Take boat two. First and Fourth, full kit, cover the choke points. Move it, people."

"What's up Corporal?" asked Alerio once he'd covered the distance from the thorn bush wall to where Cephas stood.

"Three notes signify pirate or enemy warship activity off our coast," explained the Corporal. "Two means a merchant vessel is inbound. By repeating them, we know the ships are in contact or soon will be. I'm heading up to the lookout. Care to join me?"

"If it's all right with you, I'd like to go out with the patrol boat," Alerio requested.

"Get your helmet but leave your armor. You can strip off a helmet and shoulder armor and swim. With the side armor, you won't have time and you'll sink like a rock," advised Cephas. "Forget a shield, you wouldn't need it. Besides, this should be over quickly."

Alerio sprinted for his quarters. Once in his room he pulled on the shoulder armor and snatched up the helmet, then he paused. Draped over a peg on the wall was his dual gladius rig. He unstrapped his single gladius belt and placed it on the peg. As he rushed out of his room, he began tying the straps to secure the dual sheaths.

***

On the river side of the hill, Third Squad was queued up behind the remainders of Second Squad. The rest of the infantrymen were making their way down narrow plank walkways that doubled back three times before reaching a riverside pier. Two patrol boats lay at the dock.

Boat handlers had one boat untied and stood holding its lines. In the boat, another one sat at the rear. Before Alerio made it to the bottom of the walkways, the first Legionaries down snatched oars from a rack. They boarded the boat, placed their shields on the gunwale, and secured their oars in the oarlocks. Others filed onto the boat and repeated the activity. Alerio grabbed an oar as he passed by the rack.

The patrol boat had places for thirty rowers. Second and Third Squads manned twenty of them. The two boat handlers pushed off and jumped in adding two more rowers. It left the boat underpowered by eight rowers. When Alerio placed his oar in a notch, the boat was only seven rowers short of the maximum.

After a hard shove, the boat drifted away from the dock.

"Stroke, stroke, stroke," the helmsman called setting a steady pace.

Soon the patrol boat left the river and ventured into the open sea. Alerio peered over the aft section as he rowed.

"I can't see any ships," he said to the Legionary in front of him.

"No one in this boat can," the man replied with a turn of his head. "Look back at Bovesia. We're taking directions from the overlook."

Alerio twisted his head around and after being confused by the sameness of the shoreline, he located the town and the over-watch stand. A distant figure on the stand waved flags directing the patrol boat towards the unseen merchant and the warship.

They maintained the stroke rate until the beach and the first two levels of Bovesia vanished below the horizon. By then, the upper hull of a merchant vessel appeared. The helmsman angled the patrol boat to intercept the ship. As they drew closer, Alerio recognized the merchant vessel. He studied the rear deck as they drew closer, looking for Captain Hadrian at the rear oar.

"Hold water," directed the helmsman.

The patrol boat slowed and began to drift as the oar blades stayed motionless in the water. A sailor on the merchant vessel waved at the patrol boat and tossed down a line.

"Merchant. Are you in danger?" shouted Second Squad's Decanus.

"We're running from a pirate," the man called back. "It's just over the horizon."

"Private Lupus, take half a squad and show your shields," the Second Squad's leader ordered.

An odd feeling rolled through Alerio's chest. Something was wrong with this situation. He turned to the Third Squad's leader.

"Only five Legionaries to repel pirates?" he asked.

"We do this about every three weeks," the Lance Corporal replied. "Pirates chase a merchant. We row out, show some Legion muscle, and the pirates row away. We'll be heading for shore in a little while. Although…"

"Although what?" inquired Alerio.

"We're usually not this far out," the squad leader said while glancing in the direction of the invisible shoreline.

Thoughts screamed in Alerio's mind as Lupus and the four members of his squad gripped the rail of the merchant vessel. Unbalanced in the rocking patrol boat, they waited for a wave to lift them and reduce the six feet difference between the transport and the patrol boat. They wobbled and waited to scramble over the rail and onto the merchant ship. The troublesome ideas solidified when Captain Hadrian appeared on the foredeck.

It wasn't that the Captain looked out of place that far forward. Or, that the commander of a ship held his hands behind his back, and watched silently as Legionaries prepared to board his vessel. Or, that the sail wasn't unfurled when the merchant was supposed to be running from a pirate ship. All of these were clues. It was the gladius strapped to Hadrian's hip that brought the ideas together.

"Ambush," cried out Alerio as he stood from the rowing bench. He reached over his shoulders while running down the center of the patrol boat. Drawing the gladii, he repeated, "Ambush!"

At the raised curved bow of the patrol boat, he planted a foot, and launched himself sideways. The jump carried him over the gap and he landed, although wobbly, on the high rails of the transport. For half a heartbeat, he teetered on the gunwale.

A missed timed wave would have thrown him into the gap between the boats. But, the fates wanted to see a fight so the merchant ship rolled to its port side. Alerio was pitched into the air. Before landing on Hadrian's ship, he caught a bird's eye view of the cargo boards.

The cargo of amphorae were gone; replaced by ten Illyrians Pirates. Five were laying below the rail holding their long curved sicas ready to cut the throat of any infantryman attempting to board. The other five held bows in one hand and a handful of arrows in the other. Alerio crashed to his knees on the deck between the two groups.

Most fights were decided in the first three heartbeats of a conflict. The Illyrians, shocked by the sudden arrival of Alerio, squandered the first heartbeat. He didn't. Two of the pirates at the rail rolled away with deep slashes in their backs. On the second heartbeat, the Illyrians responded.

Alerio felt a burning in the side of his thigh. Despite the high angle of the arrow jutting from his leg, he stayed focused on the knife welding men. They were the bottle neck for reinforcements and the key to winning this battle. It's almost impossible for a man laying down to fight a standing man. Even when the upright fighter had to limp over to make the kill.

Three of the pirates were out of the fight when the next arrow pierced Alerio's side. In frustration and pain, he screamed, acknowledging Algea, the Goddess of agony. He so wanted to turn and slaughter the bowmen, but there were still two knifemen at the railing.

They cast glances at the Legionary carrying two gladii, but he was struggling to shake off the shock of being impaled by two arrows. Their job was to kill infantrymen as they boarded so they ignored him. The one behind them was the archer's concern.

Alerio fought off the haze that clouded his mind and limped forward towards the pirates. An arrow appeared in the deck in front of him. It came from between his legs. The archers were on their feet and Alerio expected their next arrows would be more accurate. Still, he closed the distance between him and the pirates at the railing.

On the third heartbeat, a shield came over the railing. Powered by a vaulting Private Lupus, it smashed into a pirate.

"Shield him," Lupus screamed as he plunged his gladius into the off balanced pirate's chest.

Two more Legionaries came over the rail. One joined Lupus as he stalked the final knifeman. The other placed his shield between Alerio and the archers.

When the fourth Legionary hit the deck, Lupus ordered, "Battle line."

As the fifth pirate from the rail fell from slashes to his face and torso, the five infantrymen linked shields.

"Advance. Advance. Advance!" shouted Lupus.

At first, the shields were thrust forward meeting empty air, and the gladii followed also striking nothing. On the third advance, the five Illyrian archers were hammered back against the port side rail. Trapped between the retreating shields and the limit of the vessel, they had no place to go when the blades came. The infantrymen carved into their flesh and all five archers were dead by the time they sank to the deck.

Alerio smiled as the archers died then his face contorted as his thigh cramped up and the pain in his side doubled him over. He crumpled to the deck.

Chapter 27 – Win the Battle, Lose the War

Alerio looked up to see Private Lupus and Second Squad's Lance Corporal standing over him. The stench of burning flesh clogged his nostrils. He winced as someone tightened a cloth around his leg.

"We cauterized your wounds after removing the arrows," the Decanus informed him. "It'll leave scars but we don't have anyone who can sew skin."

"When does your class on committing suicide begin, gladius instructor?" Lupus inquired. "Because I am going to request latrine duty that day."

"Nobody sane requests latrine duty," replied Alerio.

"Nobody sane attacks a ship load of pirates, alone," Lupus offered.

"I didn't know there were that many," admitted Alerio.

"How many is the proper number?" questioned Lupus. "I'm just trying to gage what level of madness you'd entertain."

Second Squad's Lance Corporal interrupted them. "Can you stand?" asked the Decanus.

"I can make it to the patrol boat," Alerio assured him.

"That's not going to happen," the Lance Corporal informed Alerio. "I mean; can you hold a shield? We have an Illyrian bireme bearing down on us and I don't think they'll be happy with the way you interfered with their ambush."

"I can hold a shield," Alerio ventured as he placed a hand on the deck and pushed to a sitting position. After pausing to let the spasms of pain fade, he added. "If someone can give me a hand up?"

Once on his feet, Alerio looked around for Hadrian. He located the merchant ship's captain sitting between two Legionaries. Both had their blades out.

"Lance Corporal. Why is the merchant captain under guard?" Alerio asked.

"He was armed and I figured he was part of the ambush," replied the squad leader.

"Pull the gladius and you'll see he was barely armed," Alerio stated. "If not for him wearing the sheath, I wouldn't have known about the Illyrians."

"Are you sure?" the Lance Corporal challenged.

"Absolutely. Besides, if we're going to have a sea battle," suggested Alerio looking out at the approaching bireme. "We might as well have an experienced sea captain at the helm."

The guards acknowledged the squad leader's signal and went to join their squads. Hadrian stood and walked to Alerio.

"The Illyrians asked, after killing three of my men, what I'd wear into battle," the merchant explained. "I told them my gladius. They never checked the blade."

"I'm glad you did," Alerio confirmed. "Any recommendations about the bireme?"

"We can't out run him but my ship is doubled hulled. He can't ram us without getting stuck. By the time he frees himself, we can be far away in the patrol boat," Hadrian proposed. "The tide is coming in. If we get movement towards the beach and move into shallower water, we'll at least limit which side they attack from."

"How would that work?" asked Third Squad's Lance Corporal.

"They need deep water to circle us," Hadrian explained. "Without depth or the knowledge of Bova beach, they'll fear running aground. So, they'll be forced to come along side us. We'll dictate which side by turning the other side to the shoreline. But we need to move and move now."

Ten Legionaries manned the patrol boat and four others rowed the merchant vessel. Lashed together, they were able to row and tow the transport closer to shore. When the squad leaders could make out individual faces on the Illyrian bireme, they had the patrol boat tow the transport sideways to the beach.

"A strong swimmer could make it," Lupus announced when he climbed from the patrol boat. "If he avoided the sharks and the Illyrian arrows."

Alerio looked away from the approaching warship and back at the shoreline of Bovesia. From this distance, he could see the beach, the steps, and the shields of Legionaries at the second level. Features on faces were blurred by distance, so it looked closer than it was. He started to disagree with Lupus.

"Shields up and form on line," a squad leader directed. "If they start with arrows, we don't want another Lance Corporal Sisera. Keep the shields tight."

If Alerio felt better, he would have resented the squad leader using him as an example of a mistake. As it was, he was using all his strength just to stand stooped over. There wasn't energy left for feelings.

Four infantrymen grouped on the raised platform shielded Hadrian and the rear oar. They fully covered that ten feet of the transport. The other eighteen Legionaries stood on the cargo boards along the port side rail. Between the height of the side boards and the shields, they presented a strong face to the approaching Illyrians.

"Where do you want me, Lance Corporal?" Alerio asked the squad leader.

"My shield and the other squad leader's shield are with the boat handlers," he replied. "That leaves one infantryman and us to replace any injured. You're the forth replacement. If it comes to that, pick up a shield and stand in line. Until then, try not to attract any more arrowheads."

The Lance Corporal walked away, no doubt to encourage his men, and Alerio looked around to see where he should go to get out of the way. He noticed Hadrian. The captain was waving to get his attention. Despite the pain, Alerio limped to the ladder and climbed to the platform.

116

"Captain. What can I do for you?" Alerio asked while holding his side.

There was no blood thanks to the hot iron poker, but there was pain. The agony distributed between the entrance and exit holes and the placement of the wounds in his thigh and his side. He chose to hold his side, because holding the thigh required him to bend and that aggravated his side.

"The satchel beside my trunk," Hadrian replied. "Bring it to me."

Alerio limped to the leather pouch. He almost screamed when he stooped to lift it, but after biting his lip, he walked it back to Hadrian.

"What's in it?" questioned Alerio. "Another relic with a storied history?"

"No, Lance Corporal Sisera. It's medicine to kill the pain," the merchantman replied as he fished around inside the satchel. He pulled out a small glass container with a waxed seal. "We keep it on board for when one of the crew is injured. In most of our ports-of-call, there are no doctors or spare crewmen. So, I kill the pain with this. Put your finger over the mouth, wet your finger with the potion, and place it on your tongue."

Alerio peeled off the wax, placed a finger over the lip and turned the bottle over.

"What's in it?" he asked as he lifted the finger to his mouth.

"Honey mixed with oils from the plant of joy," Hadrian explained. "It's Egyptian as is the glass. Take another three doses."

There were conflicting tastes in Alerio's mouth. The sweet honey swirled around while a thick bitter substance coated spots on his tongue. Focused on the flavors, he forgot his pain. It wasn't gone, but the sharp debilitating feelings had receded to a level where he could function. Except for the muscle in his thigh, which had damage that limited movement.

"What do I owe you?" Alerio asked as he straightened his back for the first time since the arrow penetrated his side.

"You saved the ship and my life. I would call that a fair trade," Hadrian stated, then asked. "What are the pirates after? Killing two squads of Legionaries isn't profitable. Not even if they sold you as slaves."

They both looked over the Legion shields at the pirate's bireme. It had stopped advancing and sat bobbing in the swells. A group of Illyrians stood mid-ship studying the merchant vessel and the Legionaries lining the rail.

"Whatever they wanted, it didn't include two healthy squads of Legionaries," offered Alerio.

Then he remembered a lesson from his formative years. The veteran Centurion and Optio had explained that it wasn't always necessary to defeat your enemy's entire force to take an objective. Sometimes it was more useful to simply lure troops away so they were unavailable to join the fight.

The Second and Third Squads had been lured into deep water and even though they survived the ambush, they were stuck and unavailable. But, unavailable for what?

After tossing off a salute to the merchant captain, Alerio hobbled to the ladder. Moments later, he had both squad leaders huddled around him.

"We're not the primary object of this exercise," he ventured. "The Illyrians just wanted us out of the fight."

"What fight?" Third's squad leader demanded. "As far as I can see, we're the only fight around."

"The gladius instructor is correct," Second Squad's Decanus countered. "Look at them sitting there like an eagle playing with a hare in an open field. If we break the shield wall and start rowing, they'll come swooping in and attack. If we stand firm, I have a feeling they'll just sit there until…"

"Until what?" insisted Third Squad's Lance Corporal.

Although far off and barely audible, the notes from a trumpet reached across the water from the observation stand at Bovesia garrison.

"Was that three notes or two?" inquired Alerio.

For some reason, he was having a hard time focusing on the faint sounds. The Lance Corporals were fine, even the pirate ship came in clearly, it just seemed to be too much trouble to concentrate on things far away.

"Silence," both squad leaders ordered.

The soft notes drifted across the water again.

"Two sets of three," Third's Decanus announced. "Definitely two sets of three."

"Hence, while we drift here with over a hundred and twenty Illyrians waiting to cut our throats and feed us to the sharks," Second's Lance Corporal reported. "Two more warships are heading for Bovesia."

"They've reduced the enemy by luring us away from the garrison," Alerio summarized. "What can we do?"

Chapter 28 – Invitation to a Massacre

"Let's invite them to come over and play," the squad leader for the Second suggested.

"On that warship, there are one hundred and twenty oarsmen, and the gods only know how many Illyrians soldiers and, of course, archers," the other Lance Corporal reminded him.

"Maybe. But we aren't the main target," replied the squad leader from the Second. "I think that ship is here to pick up their men after the ambush."

"Therefore, they are shorthanded and may be out of archers," Alerio suggested. "Let's test the premise."

Before either squad leader could object, Alerio had pushed between the shields of Private Lupus and another Legionary.

"Need a favor Lupus, and a hand," Alerio said.

***

The Illyrians watched as a bandaged Legionary was shoved up on the rail of the merchant vessel. From his perch, he made rude gestures with his fingers, hands, and arms. A grumbling ran through the oarsmen on the warship.

Illyrians prided themselves on being brave and they depended on the public's perception of them being vicious and fearless fighters. When the Legionary lifted his tunic and ground his hips at them, the entire crew was ready to mutiny. A couple of well-place arrows would stop the insults but their best bowmen had been on the merchant ship. Now the Illyrian Captain had to decide; attack, or follow orders, and make sure the Legionaries didn't reach the beach.

The Legionary on the rail extended both arms as if hugging the Illyrian crew. Then, he looked to the sky and laughed before his body leaned back and he toppled out of sight below the rail. Although an enemy and an irritation, the Illyrian crew gasped.

Alerio looked back and forth at the two kneeling Legionaries who cradled his body.

"How did I look?" he asked. "Were they mad?"

"Gladius instructor. The next time you give a class on taunting the enemy I'm going to ask for double latrine duty," Lupus said.

Once the Legionaries let Alerio all the way down to the cargo boards, he crawled behind the line of shields.

"They don't have archers," reported Alerio. "And from their reactions, I'd say the crew is really angry."

Second Squad's Lance Corporal looked off in the distance before snapping his head back and glaring at Third Squad's Lance Corporal.

"I say we move the line to the other rail and invite the Illyrians to the party," he snarled between clinched teeth. "We sit here and our brothers at Bovesia die. I'd rather fight. Besides, do you think they'll leave without setting fire to this oversize wine vat on their way out? I vote, we fight."

"Third Squad, step back to the starboard rail," their squad leader ordered. "Let's see if any Illyrians have the cōleī to come over and fight."

"Second Squad, step back," the other Lance Corporal instructed. "Up on the platform, maintain your position."

Both squad leaders threaded between the moving shields and marched forward to the now empty rail.

"Lance Corporal Sisera. Join us," they said in unison.

Alerio followed and soon the three junior noncommissioned officers were standing at attention with their right arms across their chests in a salute. Then slowly, they straightened their arms, keeping them parallel to the deck, until the three fists were pointing at the Illyrians.

A roar went up from the pirate ship and a few oars splashed in the water. Illyrian oarsmen jumped up and yelled at the NCOs. Yet, the Legionaries stood as still as granite statues.

The Illyrian Captain stalked the center line of his ship. As he prowled, he called out threats on a leather tube that was narrow on one end and wide on the other. Despite the verbal thunder, the only promise of lightning was from the three Lance Corporals standing defiantly, and unyielding, on the deck of the small merchant vessel.

"I think we look foolish," Third Squad's Lance Corporal said out of the side of his mouth.

"They don't think so," the leader of Second Squad whispered. "I'd say they've just about reached a boiling point."

"How long are we going to stand here? Until a sea gull drops merda on us?" Third Squad's Lance Corporal asked. "And what's to prevent them from ramming us with that huge copper mentula?"

"The merchant ship is double hulled," Alerio offered relaying information he'd gleamed from Hadrian. "The warship can ram us but he might get hung up. If that happens, we'll run for the beach in the patrol boat."

"Well aren't you a wealth of information, gladius instructor," teased Second's Lance Corporal.

As if a centipede suddenly awakened, the one hundred and twenty oars on the bireme lifted in a flurry before dipping into the water.

"Gentlemen. I believe our challenge has been accepted," the squad leader from Second Squad announced. Then loudly, so everyone on the merchant ship could hear. "Stand by."

Twenty-one hobnailed boots stomped the heavy cover boards making them rumble, and twenty-one voices replied, "Standing by Lance Corporal."

"Draw," he ordered and as twenty-four gladii were pulled from their sheaths, he added. "I'll command the aft section. Sisera, you've got the center and..."

"I've got the bow," Third's squad leader stated. "Good luck, Decani."

The Illyrian ship had drifted too close to come broadside so it first rowed away. However, after swiftly circling, the warship came at the merchant vessel.

***

Alerio stepped in front of the six Legionaries standing in the center of the cargo deck. They looked dejected and afraid while watching the warship bear down on them.

"We're going to die out here, aren't we?" asked one of the infantrymen.

"Illyrians are known to be tough fighters and there are over a hundred of them," another reasoned. "We're perfututum, for sure."

The Legionaries were thinking about the entire battlefield and mentally casting themselves into the morass of a defeat. They should be concentrating on the unit's area of responsibility, instead of potentially being massacred.

"Stretch your arms out to the sides," ordered Alerio. After the six men complied, he continued. "That is the width of your kill zone. In front of you are fifteen feet of deck, that's the depth of your kill zone. Just like a fight in an open field with a full Legion, you are only responsible for the Illyrians entering your kill zone. Now here's the best part..."

The six bent forwards hoping to hear some good news about this bad situation.

"The rail height of this merchant ship is nine feet above the water. She's empty and riding high," explained Alerio. "The bireme tops out at seven feet. So, just like an enemy crossing a trench, they'll stumble when they enter your kill zone. Here's another thing. I can guarantee you, they won't have cavalry."

"Unless they can ride seahorses," one of the infantrymen joked.

The six men laughed and some of the tension faded. Alerio marched to the last man in line. He locked eyes with the man before hamming a fist down onto the Legionary's right shoulder. Without a word, he continued to strike each of them while looking into their eyes. Sometimes the bracing effect of a leader comes from a steady presence rather than pretty words.

**

Grappling hooks flew across the open space and Illyrians sailors pulled hard on the lines. The warship and the merchant vessel drew together until they were joined as one platform on the open sea.

"Steady. Hold position," Alerio warned from behind the line of his unit.

While the bireme was a little over a hundred feet long, the merchant ship was only sixty. This funneled the Illyrian fighters, limiting the number who could cross over.

"Forward," Alerio ordered calmly as if it were a parade maneuver and not a march towards screaming pirates. "Advance. Advance. Advance."

The shields plunged forward followed by the stabbing of gladii. Once, and twice, then again, before Alerio ordered. "Four paces back."

The directions confused the six Legionaries. They had the enemy stopped at the rail and couldn't figure out why the Lance Corporal ordered a retreat. Two looked back.

"Do I look like an Illyrian sailor?" shouted Alerio. "Four paces back, now."

The fury in his voice overcame the confusion and the six stepped away from the line of bleeding and dead pirates.

"Mind your front. Steady," Alerio stated with a measured tone. More Illyrians jumped up on the rail, paused, and then stepped to the cargo boards. "Forward, advance. Advance. Advance. Advance."

Once the wave of attackers was chopped down, or injured and reeling from the Legionaries' assault, Alerio ordered. "Four paces back."

This time the six infantrymen followed directions. Peering over their shields, they immediately noted the reason for the withdrawal orders.

The first group of Illyrians had easily jumped the two feet up to the merchant ship. As more crowded forward, eager to get into the fight, they pushed those ahead, making them trip over the two feet difference. Now, as they fell over the rail, they had to scramble over the stacked bodies of their fellow pirates before facing the Legion shields and gladii.

"Forward. Advance. Advance. Advance," called out Alerio. His unit met and hacked into the newly arrived pirates. "Step back four paces."

A horn blared from the Illyrian warship and Alerio watched as heads disappeared below the rail. Shortly after, shields appeared over the grappling hooks and when the shields withdrew, the hooks were gone. The warship drifted far enough for their oars to dip, and the ship rowed away.

"Not so tough, are they?" Alerio asked of his unit.

Two infantrymen dropped to their knees from injuries, but as they collapsed, he heard them say. "Not so tough, Lance Corporal."

On the cargo boards of the merchant vessel, Legionaries bent to render aid to their wounded. Others bent to dispatch living Illyrians while another team tossed the bodies over the side.

Alerio stood tall and looked up and down the merchant vessel. Hadrian still manned the oar and all four of the Legionaries on the raised platform were uninjured. On the aft cargo boards, Second Squad's Lance Corporal was directing the clearing of the deck. Towards the bow, Third's squad leader was doing the same. Overall, the Legionaries had done well, Alerio thought. Then, his legs weakened, his mind went blank, and he tumbled to the deck.

Chapter 29 - The Battle at Bovesia

"Is he dead?" a Legionary questioned.

"No, the insane gladius instructor is resting," Private Lupus answered.

Alerio opened his eyes and peered up at the two infantrymen.

"I just needed a nap," Alerio lied. With his mouth dry and his lips so stiff he felt they would crack, he requested. "Water?"

An arm slid behind his back and lifted him to a sitting position. Alerio expected intense agony, but his wounds were numb and only throbbed with deep aches. A clay mug of water touched his lower lip and he grasped it with his hands and sucked down the contents. After two more mugs of water, Alerio took time to inspect his wounds.

Spots of red dotted the bandages on his thigh and side. It seemed, he had cracked the cauterized skin and blood was leaking through from the wounds.

"Want me to heat up the iron poker?" asked Lupus with a little too much enthusiasm. He pointed at the wet spots.

"No. No, but thank you," Alerio replied quickly. "They're just leaking. What did I miss? Did the Illyrians come back?"

"They're just sitting there licking their wounds like a mountain ram after a fight with a wolf pack," Lupus informed him. "And deciding if they want to come back for another kick in the cūlus from our lads. Oh, and those warships arrived."

Alerio followed the direction indicated by the outstretched arm. At Bova Beach, two more Illyrian biremes approached the shoreline.

As the warships neared the beach, a stream of citizens from the lower levels of Bovesia scurried up the stairs with boxes, amphorae, and bundles of their most valued possessions. On the second tier, Legionaries were stacked three-deep on the narrow stairs. Corporal Cephas had beefed up the choke point but had to break the line to allow the civilians to pass.

"Can they hold?" asked Alerio.

"For a while, maybe. But there are over two hundred fifty Illyrians about to come knocking on their door," Lupus replied.

"Reminds me of Thermopylae," Alerio said remembering lessons from when he was younger. "If we could get there..."

"We'd all die, gladius instructor," replied Lupus. "There's no way anything less than three full Centuries could face those pirates."

The oarsmen on the biremes stroked steadily as they approached the beach. Just before reaching the shore, they pivoted the warship, back stroked, and ran the aft hard aground. Ramps dropped from the rear sections. Then, nothing happened. No Illyrians came down the ramps, or left their rowing stations; no one moved around as if preparing for an attack.

From one of the ships, a body was thrown. It sailed through the air and landed like a sack of grain. There it lay; a solid unmoving lump. The body seemed to be a signal. Soon after, pirates began pouring down the ramps.

About half carried shields, armor, and swords while the other half came down bare-chested and armed with the wicked sicas and spears. Those would be the oarsmen. Once on the beach, the Illyrians from both warships gathered below the aft of one of the ships.

A man strutted to the steering deck and raised his arms. His mouth moved but Alerio being too far away couldn't hear the words. He noticed a dramatic lean forward by the assembled Illyrians when the man indicated the body.

Two pirates appeared dragging a third man up behind the speaker. The speaker pulled a long knife and stabbed downward into the prisoner's chest. A roar from the crowd reached Alerio and faded when the stabbed man was tossed off the vessel. He landed half on the beach with his hips and legs in the surf.

The speaker pointed up the hill at Bovesia. There was a pause then the Illyrians charged across the beach directly for the stairs and the Legionaries waiting high above.

Alerio cringed as the mob moved. He relaxed a little when they bunched up pushing and shoving while trying to gain the stairs. Their greater numbers looked more manageable once the Illyrians were compressed to five abreast on the risers. At the first level, they spread out but were again jammed together on the stairs as they approached Tesserarius Cephas and his infantrymen.

Blinking to clear his distance vision, Alerio strained to see details of the Legionary line. In the third rank, standing head and shoulders above any of the men stood Hyllus. On one arm was slung a huge bronze shield. In his other hand, he gripped a long spear. Alerio couldn't locate Marija but he was confident she was somewhere near her man.

The first rank of pirates approached the solid line of interlocking shields. They slowed, but the pent-up pressure from those following drove the first into the barrier. Alerio couldn't hear the command, it wasn't necessary. The shields thrust forward and were pulled back. When the gladii followed they sank into the chests and necks of the tightly packed pirates. Some fell, blocking the feet of the attackers Others, wounded or dead, were lifted by the throng and passed overhead and downward until there was room to throw the bodies off to the side.

While the Legionaries slaughtered those on the stairs, other Illyrians began to stack objects at the buildings. Once their hands reached the roof of a structure, the pirates began to climb up. Four infantrymen appeared on the roof and fought with the climbers. On the other side of the stairs, three Legionaries and Marija jumped and raced across the roof to engage other Illyrians climbing from the lower plaza.

The Macedonian innkeeper was a good as her reputation. Sweeping back and forth with a spear tipped by a sharp broad-head, she defended a section of the roof. The Illyrians trying to avoid the woman and her spear ran into the infantrymen. They took care of the wet-combat while Marija continued to herd newly arriving pirates into the shields and gladii. But more were crawling over the lip of the roof forcing Marija and her Legionaries to step back as they fought.

Below that fight, on the stairs, Hyllus jabbed his long spear over the head of a Legionary. With each thrust, an Illyrian fell out of sight and under the feet of his comrades. But here as well, the sheer number of pirates was taking a toll. The ranks of infantrymen were down to two lines of defenders.

On the other roof, one Legionary lay dead and the three remaining were almost lost in a ring of Illyrians.

A scream of frustration burst from Alerio. Hadrian and the Legionaries tore their eyes from the battle and looked at him.

"I can't just sit here floating around with my mentula in my hand," Alerio yelled. "They're getting massacred. I need to be there."

As he talked, Alerio struggled to his feet. Private Lupus rushed to his side.

"Gladius instructor. There's nothing we can do for them," the older Private stated. "If we were on that beach, we'd die as sure as a river trout meeting an ocean shark."

Alerio deflated and his shoulders slumped. As he raised his eyes to the battle at Bovesia, the trumpet from the stand rang out three sharp notes.

"What now?" Lupus complained. "More Illyrians?"

Chapter 30 – Ninety-Six Greeks on Bova Beach

Faster than the pirate's biremes, taller by several feet, and dipping one hundred and eighty oars on each stroke, the Greek quinqueremes sped towards Bova beach from the east. As they came near shallow water, one veered off and headed towards the warship guarding the merchant vessel.

Five banks of oars propelled the Greeks closer and closer to the pirate and merchant ship. The Illyrians sank oars and turned away from the charging warship. They rowed to open water with the quinquereme in pursuit.

"To the patrol boat," Third Squad's Lance Corporal bellowed. It seemed Alerio wasn't the only one frustrated by the situation.

Before anyone could move, the first Greek warship backed onto Bova Beach. Ramps dropped and armored men carrying large bronze shields descended. They didn't rush towards the stairs and the fighting.

The Greek ship kept disembarking men until two groups stood on the beach. From the ship, men passed down long spears and these were distributed to the men on the ground.

"There's only about a hundred of them," Lupus commented. "Just a fat Century's worth of fighters. Why didn't the other ship come in?"

The Legionaries', a second ago elated at the Greek's arrival, now sank into despair.

"It's a tight battlefield," observed Alerio. "The Greek Hoplites are renowned as close formation fighters."

"They may be good but one hundred against two hundred isn't great odds," commented Lupus. "They'll get swallowed up like a sparrow meeting a vulture."

Some of the infantrymen had legs over the rail and they paused on that perch. Others were crowded behind them. No matter where they were on the merchant ship, they shifted their eyes between the fighting at Bovesia and the Greeks on Bova Beach.

***

Four Greeks stepped out in line. They began to slowly shuffle towards the Illyrians. Four men from the other group also stepped off. Their long spears held up as if they each carried a flag pole.

The two groups of eight men continued to kick sand as they walked down the beach. Four more men joined the march, then four more until each group had forty-eight men in the loose, slow moving formations. To the watching Legionaries, the Greek formations weren't impressive.

The Illyrians had noticed the gathering of Hoplites on the beach. Almost three quarters of them broke from the fight with the Legionaries and rushed down to the beach to meet the new enemy.

"At least the Greeks have pulled Illyrians from the town," Alerio offered.

"That gladius instructor," commented Lupus. "Is a good thing. Even if the Greeks are going to die, their sacrifice will save infantrymen."

While the pirates moved into rough lines facing the odd formations, the Greeks continued to shuffle awkwardly forward through the rocks and sand. Legionaries marched, Illyrians swaggered, so neither side could figure why the Greeks couldn't pick up their feet.

The pirates didn't care, they yelled and broke into a hard charge. In response, the Greeks closed ranks until their formation shrunk.

"Those sailors need to come on line," suggested Private Lupus. "You can't swing a sword or defend with your shield standing in ranks."

The fastest of the Illyrians had covered half the distance to the Greeks. In a few heartbeats, they would barrel into the tightly packed masses and disrupt the formations.

Suddenly, all the Greek shields lifted and touched edges. Because of the density of the packed men, the shields ended up covering the formations from ground level to overhead, and down to the ground on the other side. Where the long spears had jetted into the air, they were now parallel to the beach aimed directly at the charging Illyrians. The awkward, shuffling steps allowed each formation to move steadily while keeping their shields together. They powered up the beach encased in a shell of shields bristling with spears.

"They look like armored porcupines," observed Lupus. "Kind of like our testudo formation."

"That Private is a phalanx and those aren't sailors," offered Alerio. "It takes a lot of training for Hoplites to get it right and to keep it tight in battle."

"How would you defeat that formation, gladius instructor?" Lupus asked.

"I would suggest you not stand in front of a phalanx," replied Alerio. "It's not fast but it would be a tough nut to crack. Give them room and chip away at the sides like cutting down an old oak tree."

"Couldn't have said it better myself," replied Lupus.

The first Illyrians to reach the Hoplites, zigzagged around the longest spears. But some of the shafts were drawn into the formation. When the pirates dodged the long spears, the short ones thrust forward impaling them on the tips. Others never made it to the short spears as the long spears swept sideways knocking the Illyrians to the ground. Those who fell disappeared under the bottom of the forward shields. When the phalanx formations moved beyond the spot, the bodies weren't recognizable as human remains.

The Illyrians continued to clash against the phalanx from the front. It seemed as if they collided with huge rolling boulders. Those not impaled, bounced off the shields and vanished under the steadily advancing phalanxes.

The Greek formations remained apart. Each clearing a section of the beach. Now, as Illyrians realized the moving fortresses couldn't be breached, they stepped out of the way and clustered between the formations. That's when each phalanx stopped.

For three heartbeats, the pirates stood between the massed shields. Puzzled by the lack of motion, they peered at each other or stared at the wall of shields. Then, the Greeks began moving again.

One step forward, two steps forward followed by a ninety-degree pivot. The two formations began closing the distance between them, trapping and mangling the Illyrians caught in the middle. Most Illyrians, seeing they again faced the front of the phalanx formations, broke ranks and ran for their ships.

The final few remaining between the phalanx-vice felt a slight relief when the shield-shell broke apart. It was a small moment, soon replaced by apprehension when a line of Hoplites stepped forward and drew their swords. They tapped their blades on their shields as a challenge.

Illyrians prided themselves on being aggressive fighters. They replied to the Greeks by rushing at the line of individual Hoplites.

Legionaries fought head-on even when in one-on-one combat. They were trained to keep the enemy in front of their formation. The Greek Hoplites, however, were fluid. They deflected with their shields and spun the Illyrians behind, or even over their heads. All the while, hacking and stabbing with their swords.

"At least they're not afraid to come out from behind their shields and fight," Lupus said as he hopped into the patrol boat.

Alerio prepared to follow but had to wait his turn. Balanced on the top board of the merchant vessel, he studied the fighting. After a final look at the fleeing Illyrians on the beach, he peered up at the Legionaries on the stairs.

Corporal Cephas had only five healthy Legionaries on the steps. On the roof to the right, two infantrymen stood protectively over two fallen comrades. Across the stairs on the other roof, Marija and a Legionary favoring a wounded leg, stepped back as four Illyrians dashed in and out attempting to inflict damage on the lone pair. The infantryman stumbled and dropped to a knee. Instead of deserting him, the Macedonian restaurant owner jumped forward using her body and spear to defend the injured Legionary.

The Illyrians facing the lone woman warrior turned to each other, nodded and tensed. One final attack and they could circle around behind the unit blocking the stairs. One more assault and Bovesia would fall.

Like an avenging Greek god, Hyllus leaped onto the roof. In five long strides, he joined Marija. The Athenian used his big shield to drive two Illyrians back while hoisting his sword high overhead. A powerful slash brought the blade downward and across the bodies of the other two. They stumbled away clutching gaping wounds to one's chest and the other's stomach. Hyllus and Marija advanced on the last two pirates.

Alerio missed the rest of the fight as he dropped painfully into the patrol boat.

***

"Stand by oars," shouted the helmsman, "Dip oars, and stroke, stroke."

The patrol boat glided away from the transport. The Legionaries were hot to join the fight. But, on the fourth stroke, three signals sounded the end of the battle for Bovesia.

Additional horns sounded from the Illyrian ships and from the Greek quinquereme. By the last note, the surviving pirates were flowing down from the stairs, or across the beach, and lining up at the ramps or climbing the sides of their ships. The Hoplites with no enemy nearby answered their own horn and jogged to their vessel.

Chapter 31 – Wayward Assassin

The patrol boat passed the two Illyrian warships. They rowed frantically in the direction of open water, and the Legion boat rowed just as sharply for shore. Further down Bova Beach, the Greek warship lagged behind, but not by much. Soon the quinquereme pushed off the beach and the five tiers of oars dipped. It was obvious from their immediate launch, they planned to chase down the Illyrians.

The patrol boat touched the shoreline and with the keel grinding on the sand, the twelve healthy Legionaries leaped to the beach. Alerio, along with the other walking wounded, rolled over the gunwales and waded slowly to shore. Despite their injuries, they pulled and shoved the boat up onto the beach. At least far enough so the severely injured wouldn't drift away.

Half the fit infantrymen bolted up the stairs to render aid to the town's defenders. The other half spread out on Bova Beach and began to relieve wounded Illyrians of their pain.

***

Alerio found a broken spear on the beach. Using it as a crutch, he limped to the body of the man thrown from the aft of the Illyrian warship.

A graying older man with a bald spot on the back of his head rested crumpled on the beach. Alerio rolled him over expecting to see stab wounds. When the body revolved, there were no indications of blade cuts. Confused, he placed the body back onto its face. Alerio lifted the man's tunic and upon closer inspection, he located a small hole. Less than a silver coin's thickness around, the puncture wound, off to the side of the man's lower back, was barely noticeable. He rotated the body again and studied the face. It was a good face, with ropy muscles beneath the deeply tanned creases. But, the skin had a yellow pale to it, which extended to the yellow tinting of the man's eyeballs.

A groan came from the side and Alerio turned to see the second man who was thrown from the warship. His hand reached out and clawed at the sand. For a moment Alerio thought he was attempting to crawl out of the surf. But the hand didn't stretch out. The fingers dug down creating a shallow hole.

Images of injured and dead Legionaries came to Alerio. He reached back and pulled the Golden Valley dagger. While he struggled to stand, the man's hand continued to scoop out sand and rocks. Clearly, the wounded man sought to dig a hole.

With his dagger in one hand, Alerio leaned on the crutch and limped to the man. Struggling against the pain, Lance Corporal Sisera dropped to a knee and rolled the digger over. A blade had entered the top of his chest muscle but was deflected by the ribs so it didn't penetrate into the torso. A small exit hole below the man's nipple showed the path of the blade. As if the Gods willed it, the man survived so Alerio could get revenge.

"This is for the Legionaries who go to the Fields of Elysium thanks to the Illyrians," Alerio swore as he raised the dagger over the injured pirate.

Alerio expected either rage or resignation from the Illyrian. He wasn't expecting to see the man smile. Slowly raising a hand, the man gently laid it over the blade of Alerio's dagger. With his other hand, the man began to pull up the leg of his worn, woolen pants. As he gathered the material, a sheath came into view. When it was fully exposed, the man flicked a strap and the blade holder parted revealing a black hilt with a yellow stripe.

Hidden on the inside of the man's thigh was a Nocte Apis; the blade of the Dulce Pugno.

The night bees were the exclusive property of the Sweet Fists, the assassins from the Golden Valley. For anyone, not a Dulce Pugno, to possess a night bee was forbidden; it was a death sentence for the person. The Sweet Fist, when they came to reclaim their Nocte Apis blade, killed everyone near the person possessing it.

The smiling, wounded man recognized Alerio's dagger and whispered, "Ally."

Alerio's dagger was a gift from the Dulce Pugno identifying him as an Ally of the Golden Valley. As an ally, the Sweet Fists wouldn't take a contract on him and he could go to any Golden Valley trading house for information or help. Alerio wasn't sure if being an ally also included him helping an assassin of the Sweet Fist by rendering medical aid and sanctuary.

"What have you got there, gladius instructor?" Lupus inquired as he strolled up and stood beside Alerio. He held a gladius coated in blood along the side of his leg. "Need me to put the dēfutūta Illyrian, out of his misery, for you?"

Alerio reached out and snatched the night bee while cuffing his own dagger. Although not of the exact same design, the handles and scrolling on the blades were close and anyone could see both blades came from the same metalworker.

"No. What I need is to get him off the beach and somewhere where I can clean his wounds," explained Alerio. "And that wine skin from around your neck."

"It would easier to kill him," replied Lupus. "And save the vino."

"I can't question a dead man," explained Alerio. "And I can't press for details if he gets the rot before I'm finished with him. Now, are you going to help?"

Lupus shrugged, walked to the water's edge and rinsed off his gladius. He dried it as he strolled back.

"Where do you want him?" the Private questioned as he placed the gladius in its sheath.

***

A short while later, Lupus went in search of a medical kit after laying the Sweet Fist on a flat rock at the base of the steep hill. Alerio lifted the assassin. Drops of wine trickled onto his lips and the man's eyes fluttered. He'd been beaten badly before the stabbing, but a quick test by Alerio failed to locate any broken bones. They were about twenty-five feet from the start of the stairs so Alerio wasn't concerned about being overheard.

"Return the Nocte Apis when I am dead," the wounded man pleaded.

"You won't die from the flesh wound. Unless it's from the embarrassment at being discovered, Sweet Fist," Alerio said. "You'll live."

"It doesn't feel so at the moment," the man mumbled. "I am Gilibertus. A trader from the Golden Valley. The Illyrians attacked the ship I was traveling on. They took me as an oarsman."

"Good story. Now Dulce Pugno Gilibertus, who stabbed you, and who is the dead man on the beach?" asked Alerio. Then, he added. "And how did you get caught? Your brothers and sisters are usually more careful."

Before the assassin could answer, Lupus arrived with a Legion medical kit and a bucket of water.

Chapter 32 – Acolyte of Angitia

Lupus built a fire and rested the iron tip above the flames. Once the iron poker glowed red, he pressed it onto the chest wounds. Gilibertus screamed and passed out. The smell of melting flesh hit Alerio's nostrils and he gagged. But Lupus inhaled deeply and his eyes glowed with delight.

"They always go out and miss the aroma," offered the Private. He lifted the iron to his nose and sniffed. "Don't you just love the smell of flesh cooking?"

"Why is it, Private Lupus, you are only a Private at your age?" asked Alerio trying to change the subject. "And don't tell me it's because you're incompetent. I saw you giving orders on the transport and leading the Legionaries in the assault."

"And I'm a fine swordsman. In spite of your cheating ways, gladius instructor," Lupus teased with a grin. "I'm from the central tribes of the Republic."

"When I was a small lad, my parents sold me to the temple of Angitia," explained Lupus. "The temple was always short of children. Oh, not because they abused us. On the contrary, as potential priests and priestesses, we were fed well, and taught letters and numbers. No, the shortage came because this sect of Angitia showed homage to the Goddess by handling her snakes. You've got to start a devotee young when working with living serpents. Unfortunately, not many of the children were granted the gift by the Goddess."

"Those without the gift, or lacking pure intentions, got bitten. The priests would hold hot iron pokers on the bite marks as a way to burn out the venom. After a while, I grew to love the smell. The aroma of burning flesh means a second chance. If the bite was only the result of impure thoughts, then the Goddess and the red-hot iron would allow the bitten to continue the training. If it truly was a lack of the gift, Angitia would take them from this world," the

Legionary explained. "I was kissed twice by Angitia's pets in my early years."

Lupus rolled up the left sleeve of his tunic. The scars looked as if candle wax had dripped down the back of his arm. He lifted the left side of his tunic displaying another line of melted flesh on his chest.

"Kissed twice by the Goddess and I lived because I have the gift. As I got older, I became exposed to more of the mysteries of Angitia. Beyond the public rituals of snake handling, the sect makes medicines from the venom. There was this little girl, like a sister to me she was. One day while milking a snake," he would have continued but Alerio's eyes opened wide. "Oh, you didn't know you could milk a snake like a goat or a cow. Yes, Lance Corporal, you milk them by placing the fangs against the side of a smooth clay bowl. Press down lightly and the snakes will eject a milky substance. It's used in many potions."

"This little girl hung around me like I'm her big brother," Lupus related. "One day while I milked a snake, she reached into the box with the other serpents. I heard her cry out. When I turned, she was withdrawing her arm from the box. There were three kisses from the Goddess on her tiny arm. It was early morning and none of the priests or priestesses were nearby. There was only one way to save my little friend. I had to burn out the venom."

Alerio watched Lupus' face for any sign of distress. There was none. The infantryman had stopped with a smile on his face as if reliving a pleasant morning on a farm. After a time, he resumed his tale.

"I kicked over a brazier, grabbed a piece of cloth, and picked up the hot dish," he explained. "But my little friend didn't have the gift. No matter how many times, or how hard I pressed the metal to her arm, the Goddess called her from this realm. When they found us, I was holding the lifeless form of my friend in my lap still pressing the cold metal to Angitia's kisses."

"Three snake bites to a child?" stated Alerio. "On the farm, we had grown men die from one bite. I can't see how a child could survive three strikes from three snakes."

"That's what the priestess said. But, I knew better. If the Goddess had given her the gift, my little friend would have lived," Lupus insisted. "I blamed the Goddess, and finally, my rantings got me expelled from the temple. With no other prospects in sight, I joined the Legion."

"You joined as a full-grown man," Alerio guessed. "That's why you're only a Private?"

"Ah, gladius instructor, you are kind like a dove in the meadow at first light," Lupus exclaimed. "I was eighteen when I joined the Legion. One thing being in a temple teaches you is focus. While the other lads in my training unit struggled to learn, I calmed my soul. A call to Angitia, like when I was preparing to handle the snakes, allowed me to open my mind to new things. Like a new unsullied scroll, I absorbed the lessons and graduated at the top of my class."

"A few years later, my Century marched north," Lupus declared. "By then I was a squad leader. When our Corporal fell and broke his foot, because I learned to write and do numbers at the temple, I was promoted to the position. We met the barbarians north of a large trading town. For five days, we engaged, rotated off the line, rested, and went back into the fray. For five days, we delivered death and accepted death into our ranks. By the time the savages vanished into the mountains, my Century had lost only ten of our eighty Legionaries. Other Centuries had suffered much greater casualties. Angitia watched over us is how I explained our low injury rate."

"You know what they say - never talk politics or religion around a campfire. Well, I broke the rule," admitted Lupus. "After announcing Angitia was the source of our luck, a few of my infantrymen challenged the assertion. Did I mention, we had consumed a large quantity of vino? We had. I went into the fields, and as I'd learned to do as a little lad, I gathered a sack full of snakes."

"You brought serpent into a Legion camp?" a horrified Alerio asked.

"Only ten, but five were babies. I was a little drunk. If I'd been clear headed, I could have found more," Lupus boasted. "I called the Century to attention and explained the gift of Angitia while the pokers heated in the fire."

"What did you do?" demanded Alerio.

"I had those brave enough, and with enough faith, put their arms into the sack," described Lupus. "Some emerged with no kisses from Angitia. Others were chosen and I placed the iron pokers on their kisses. The sweet smell of second chances filled our Century's area, and the hand of the Goddess moved through our ranks."

"How many died?" Alerio asked.

"The Goddess only took five," Lupus confessed. "We would have discovered how many more had the gift, but my Optio arrived, and stopped the ritual."

Alerio for the first time looked closely at the Legionary's eyes. They were open wide, and he stared as if looking into another world. In that look, Alerio recognized the fever of a true fanatic.

"I was transferred to the Southern Legion and placed in Second Squad," Lupus concluded. "Sadly, my Lance Corporal has an unnatural fear of snakes. Just the mention of serpents, or the Goddess Angitia, and he gives me extra duty."

Private Lupus packed up the iron poker and the ointments. He stood and looked down at Alerio.

"Don't tell him about our talk," begged Lupus. "If he finds out, he'll put me on latrine duty for a week."

Alerio let out his breath slowly as the infantryman strutted away. Then, Gilibertus stirred and he glanced over at the assassin.

Chapter 33 – City State Politics

Gilibertus groaned and asked for water. Alerio held the ladle to his lips while attempting to clear his mind of serpents.

"Will I live?" asked Gilibertus.

"You are cleaned, salted, burned, greased up, and alive," Alerio informed him. "All signs point to your survival."

"Then you are truly an Ally of the Golden Valley," the assassin declared. "How may I repay you?"

"Answer some questions," replied Alerio. "Who stabbed you? Who is the man on the beach? And how were you discovered?"

"The body on the beach is the former assistant Navarch of the Illyrian Navy," Gilibertus replied. "He died and a commander more in favor with Martinus Cetea took his place."

"How did he die? I examined the body and the only mark is a small hole in his back," explained Alerio.

"He is dead," was all Gilibertus would say.

Alerio recognized the evasion. The Dulce Pugno never talked about the target of a contract or the client who ordered the assassination.

"I assume the new assistant Navarch is the man who stabbed you," Alerio deduced, then asked. "How did they catch you?"

"Yes, the new assistant stabbed me after they found a deceitful note by my patron in the dead man's belongings. Just one person knew of my position as a rower on the warship," Gilibertus explained. "He has broken the contract and will suffer the penalty. But, you haven't asked the proper questions."

"What are the proper questions?"

"Why would the Illyrians attack Bovesia?" suggested Gilibertus. "And, why would the Greeks interfere?"

"I guessed the Illyrians wanted the supplies and Bovesia was handy," said Alerio.

"No, ally. The pirates are seeking a merchant ship," Gilibertus reported. "One sailing from Egypt to Syracuse to a Greek city-state. A ship with the ability to make common cause between Alexandria and Athens."

"Why would the Illyrians care if Athens and Alexandria signed a treaty?" Alerio questioned.

"As a kingdom, they don't. It's their benefactors who seek to interfere with the treaty," Gilibertus explained. "Think. Why would the seagoing Illyrians, who don't colonize, attack Bovesia? Unless paid to do so."

The assassin raised an arm and pointed out to sea. Three quinqueremes with light brown sails billowing in the wind floated across the horizon. Between the sails, and hull color, the three distant warships were identifiable as Qart Hadasht Navy.

"The Empire cares and their gold and trading agreements buy a lot of favors," proclaimed Gilibertus. "The Greeks also seek the merchant ship. It's why they came to your rescue; they want to keep Bovesia free, and under the protection of the Republic."

"I don't understand. Why is a trading treaty between Athens and Alexandria threatening to the Qart Hadasht Empire?" Alerio pondered.

"I only know what I learned while rowing on the Illyrian warship," admitted Gilibertus.

The trumpet from the watch stand blared. Three notes of three sounded, signifying the Empire warships were in the area. From high up in the town, Tesserarius Cephas called out for the infantry to form up.

"I have to go," said Alerio. "What can I do for you?"

"If you have coins to lend, I will signal for a fisherman's boat, and leave," Gilibertus stated.

Alerio reached under his tunic, pulled out the Nocte Apis and a coin pouch. After handing them to the assassin, he helped him stand. Gilibertus staggered up the beach towards the bank of the Kaikinos River. Alerio turned and limped down Bova Beach in the opposite direction. Pain radiated from his side and his thigh at the thought of climbing the stairs.

Chapter 34 – Reinforcements and Reports

The healthy Legionaries stood as if on parade across the stairs, and over the roof tops. Behind them, and hidden from view by the shields were the walking wounded. These

152

infantrymen tended their injuries. If the Qart Hadasht warships beached and attacked, they would be available to man the lines. Far behind the injured Legionaries, merchants and citizens huddled in groups.

Alerio, on the right roof top, leaned on his armor and wrote on a piece of parchment. Other than a smear of ointment and a change of bandages, he required no additional treatment. His helmet rested on his bent knee. A piece of parchment was wrapped around the back of the helmet to provide a writing surface.

"Writing your last will and testament, gladius instructor?" asked Private Lupus.

"No, a letter to my family," lied Alerio.

In reality, he was crafting a note to Tribune Velius. The information might be old stuff. If old, at least it would confirm what the spy master already knew. If new, it was information the planning and strategies commander could use to fill in his map.

"Stand down," announced Corporal Cephas as the sails on the warships disappeared over the horizon. "Looks like the Qart Hadasht navy took one look at you killers, urinated in their silk panties, and decided to go bother a softer port of call. Squad leaders, on me."

The trumpet blared again from the watch tower. The Legionaries on the front line had just hoisted their shields when the trumpet sounded. Everyone tensed and counted notes. When it passed three, they relaxed. At five they smiled, when five additional notes followed, they began to cheer.

"Mail and reinforcements," Tesserarius Cephas announced. "Let's get a squad on the beach and another on the stairs. Let's go people; the Legion isn't paying you to sit around wasting a perfectly good day."

***

By the time one squad was on the beach, and the squad members from another stood on separate steps, two Legion patrol boats came into view. The boats beached and seventy Legionaries waded ashore. Medics carrying heavy bags jogged straight for the steps.

"How did you know we needed medics?" Alerio asked a short time later.

"A Greek warship rowed into Rhegium and talked with the Colonel last night. We rowed out at dawn but Occhio was attacked so we stopped there. Not too much work for me. The lads saw them coming and rained arrows down on the Illyrians. After a skirmish, the pirates boarded their ship and rowed out. Then we headed here," the medic explained as he peeled back the dressing on Alerio's side. "Someone is good with the hot poker. A little more ointment and you'll be as good as I can make you. It's rest and time now."

A Legionary with two huge pouches bouncing on his thighs came up the stairs. He was delayed as the stairs were full of equally loaded down citizens making the descent. After he navigated the crowd and arrived on the upper level, he began to shout.

"Lance Corporal Sisera, Third Century, Eighth Squad," the man called out. "Lance Corporal Sisera?"

"Here. Over here," Alerio replied.

The mail carrier dropped a sealed parchment into Alerio's lap. After an exchange of coins, the man left with the parchment for Tribune Velius.

Alerio broke the seal and unrolled the letter.

Lance Corporal Alerio Sisera, 3rd Century, Eighth Squad
Greetings, hopefully, this missive finds you in good health.
There is a town on the Kaikinos about eight miles upriver.
I would appreciate a report on the mood of the Republic's
citizens from Passomasseria. Specifically, concerning
any contact with foreign agents. With great
anticipation, I await your report.
Tribune Velius, Southern Legion Planning & Strategies

"Lupus. What's the best way to get upriver?" Alerio called over to the Private.

"How far up?" Lupus asked. "To the split, or higher into the mountains?"

"To a town called Passomasseria," Alerio said.

"It's about eight miles," Lupus explained. "Our patrol boats can make the trip. Much beyond there and you'll need a trapper's canoe. Or you can hike, but it's steep trails and high plateaus most of the way. Oh, that's right, you have an arrow hole in your leg. Forget the hike."

Alerio struggled to his feet, which wasn't as difficult as bending over to pick up his armor and helmet. Finally, when

155

he had the gear in hand, he went in search of Tesserarius Cephas.

He located the Corporal, the Century's seven squad leaders, and their Centurion who had accompanied the reinforcements. They were meeting in the command building. Alerio found a bucket, turned it over, and placed it under the awning of the porch. He sat down stiffly to wait for the staff meeting to conclude.

***

"Lance Corporal Sisera. There are easier ways to catch flies," said Corporal Cephas.

Alerio, squinting through his eyelids, saw the Tesserarius and the Centurion looking down at him. Apparently, he'd leaned his head against a porch post, and fallen asleep with his mouth open.

"Sorry, sir," he replied while attempting to stand.

"As you were," commanded the infantry officer. "The medics have you on light duty. You should be in your quarters resting. But, I'm glad to find you here."

"Why's that, sir?" Alerio asked.

"Two of my squad leaders and my Corporal seem to have developed an obsession," the Centurion replied. "They can't stop relating tales of bravery, cunning, and acts of outright stupidity by one Lance Corporal Sisera. Seeing as you saved the lives of my Legionaries while, somehow miraculously surviving, I wanted to thank you."

"I was just doing my duty, sir," Alerio responded. "But, if you're feeling generous, I have a favor to asked."

"What is it gladius instructor?" the Centurion inquired with a broad smile. From the look and mention of his title, Alerio knew Cephas had related the stick versus gladius story.

"I have to go to Passomasseria for Tribune Velius," Alerio said. "A ride would be appreciated."

At the mention of the planning and strategies officer, the smile vanished.

"Here's the truth Lance Corporal. The Illyrians could return at any time," the Centurion explained. "I can't spare a single man, let alone twenty to row you up the river for a spy mission. Besides, you are on light duty. If I let you go off on a mission before being cleared by medical, I could end up on the Colonel's merda list."

"But sir," Alerio began to protest when Corporal Cephas stepped between him and the officer.

"Stand down, Lance Corporal," the Tesserarius ordered although Alerio was still sitting. "Go get some rest, and we'll revisit the topic in a few days. Do you understand?"

"Yes, Corporal," Alerio said meekly.

The Legion demanded discipline, and the punishment for any infraction could be brutal. Even if the offender was a hero, the questioning of a Centurion once he rendered his decision, could include digging trenches, cleaning out latrines, beatings with a staff, running to full exhaustion, or

157

other difficult tasks. As Alerio was wounded and unfit physically to perform extra duties or to withstand a caning, the most likely penalty would be lashes from a whip.

The Corporal had just saved the hardheaded young Lance Corporal from a world of hurt.

If Alerio had the time to ask, Cephas would have told him, "It would be a waste to have a Legionary damaged more than Sisera was already." Not because he was overly fond of Alerio. It was simply, Corporal Cephas hated waste.

The Tesserarius and the Centurion walked off and Alerio stood, but he was bent over. Inching around until he could get both hands on the porch post, Alerio walked his hands up the beam until he stood upright.

Limping slowly, he made it to his room in the supply building. After stripping off his shoulder rig, and slinging his dual sheaths over the wall peg, he sat on the edge of the bed. A grunt escaped his lungs as he leaned down to loosen the straps on his hobnailed boots. Once he kicked them off, he fell back on the bed. The day's events faded, and sleep came fast to the weary Lance Corporal.

Act 6

Chapter 35 - Rest and Reputation

A night, a day, and half the next night passed before Alerio stirred. Still half asleep, he rolled over on his right side. Pressure caused the wounds to throb, and the pain jolted him fully awake.

Crawling weakly out of bed, he inched across the floor to his personal pack. From it, he pulled a narrow bundle of silk. After unrolling the twelve feet of fine material, he measured a section and sliced off a length. The longest piece was tightly wound around his waist. The shorter piece he used to wrap his injured right thigh. Next came his boots. Then after slipping on an old tunic, he left the room.

***

Tesserarius Cephas completed his written reports, did the Century's accounting before getting a little sleep. He woke well before dawn. It was another day he would also act as the Century's Optio.

"Century. On the road for exercise," he called out while lighting a lantern. "Lance Corporals, get them up and out. Now people."

From out of the dark, a stumbling figure emerged. He was breathing heavily and seemed to be favoring his right leg. The Corporal watched as Lance Corporal Sisera hobbled into the lantern light.

The Decanus placed both hands on his knees and, between clinched teeth, said, "Good morning, Corporal."

"You are up early," Cephas noted. "How are you feeling?"

"Like I have arrow holes in my body," Alerio, still short of breath, blew out.

"You're supposed to be on light duty," Cephas advised. "Not hobbling around my camp in the dark. I'm surprised the sentries didn't challenge you."

"They didn't need to. I found each of them," admitted Alerio.

"You could have just found the acting NCO of the Guard," Cephas explained. "He would have alerted the guards to your presence."

"But then, I couldn't have begged dried goat's meat off the guards," said Alerio.

"Hungry, were you?" asked Cephas.

"I still am. But the meat will hold me until after class," Alerio declared.

"You really want that ride to Passomasseria, don't you?" suggested Cephas.

"I have orders and if the only thing holding me here is medical, I have to prove my fitness," Alerio stated. "It's going to be a basic class. No fancy dueling for me."

Cephas shook his head at the stubborn weapon's instructor. Then, he faced the squad tents.

"Lance Corporals. If daylight touches my heels, and everyone isn't on the street," shouted Cephas at the tents. "I'll have seven squad leaders digging new latrines. Now people!"

"What did I miss yesterday?" inquired Alerio.

"While you were malingering in bed all day? Not a lot. We haven't had any merchant ships or warships come in," Cephas reported. "And Hadrian hired a crew of fishermen and sailed east for Crotone."

Alerio smiled. It seemed Gilibertus, the assassin from the Golden Valley, had found a ride home.

A Lance Corporal came from the direction of Bovesia. He entered the garrison at a dead run heading for one of the dark tents.

"Trouble, Sergeant of the Guard?" asked Cephas.

The acting SOG slid to a stop and faced his Corporal.

"No, Tesserarius. I wanted to finish rounds before checking on my squad," the squad leader replied.

"You're Right-Pivot should have them up," Cephas scolded. "Shouldn't he?"

"Lupus is a sound sleeper," Second Squad's Lance Corporal replied. "I'm just checking to be sure the squad is up."

"Get them on the street," urged Cephas.

The Decanus ran into his squad's tent. Soon shouting and a few thuds drifted to Alerio.

"Make it a short class," ordered Cephas. "We're running double guard duty and everyone is busy."

"It will be, unless there are issues," promised Alerio.

***

The sun was barely over the mountains when Centurion Laurens, Second Century's commanding officer, strolled onto the practice field. He'd been up early and having finished his reports, he decided to check on his Legionaries.

As Laurens walked to where Tesserarius Cephas oversaw the wrestling, he glanced at the gladius posts. Five infantrymen were standing in a tight formation and attacking three practice posts with wooden gladii. Behind the line, a man with a silk wrap on his leg leaned between the ranks and adjusted arms, feet, and even the head angles of the five.

"Who is running gladius drills," asked the infantry officer as he approached the NCO.

"Lance Corporal Sisera, sir," replied the Tesserarius.

"Shouldn't he be on light duty?" inquired the Centurion.

"According to Sisera that is light duty," Cephas responded. "At least that's what he claimed this morning after his run."

"I'm beginning to see why our squad leaders are so taken with him," the Centurion commented. "All right, once he's cleared by medical he can go on his spy mission. However, we can't spare rowers. He'll need to find his own way to Passomasseria."

"I'll let him know, sir," Cephas replied.

***

Alerio had picked five Legionaries who failed to advance with authority. After adjustments, they were sharp and precise in their shield and gladius movements. They stood facing the instructor.

"Delivering a unified first strike to the enemy puts them on notice that they are about to have a very bad day," Alerio said to the five sweating infantrymen. "If you lag behind those around you, the enemy will see you as a flaw in the line. It gives the enemy hope. And, the one thing a barbarian warrior doesn't have when facing a squad of Republic Legionaries, is hope. We fight as a unit. We kill as a unit. Understand?"

"Yes, instructor," the five responded.

"Dismissed. Stow the training gladii, and go check in with your Decani," Alerio ordered.

As the five jogged away, Alerio placed his back against a training post. He hurt from running and teaching. Plus, he was dirty and hungry. Across the training ground, the Century had installed a vat that was kept filled with river water by a bucket brigade. It wasn't very far, but to the injured and exhausted Alerio, it seemed a long way.

Chapter 36 – A Proper Meal

Alerio knew Centurion Laurens and the medic were watching him. They appeared to be in deep conversation on the porch but when he left the supply building, they followed him with their eyes. He was cleaned and shaven, and wore his dress tunic with the Lance Corporal band, the instructor brooch, and the Legion Raider silk over his shoulder. Although he looked fit, he worried about making it up the steep trail to the town.

Gritting his teeth and bracing his back, Alerio marched up the hill. He only stumbled once near the top. It wasn't until he rounded the corner of a building, that he let the pain and cramping show. Now out of sight of the infantry officer and the medic, he leaned against the wall, moaned, and began massaging his thigh.

Once the muscle loosened up, he straightened his back and jerked down the hem of the tunic. With all the dignity he could muster, Alerio limped across the plaza and entered the Columnae Herculis.

"Lance Corporal Sisera," shouted Hyllus in surprise. "We thought you were dead."

"No, I'm still alive," stated Alerio.

"Don't let him fool you," Marija said while leaning around the doorframe from the backroom. "He checked with Corporal Cephas three times about your condition."

The big man smiled and pointed at a corner table, "Sit little man. I'll fetch you a meal worthy of an Athenian Hoplite."

"Does it take a lot to feed men who stand mentula to cūlus when they fight?" inquired Alerio.

"You refer to the phalanx, of course," said Hyllus after pausing to think about the description. "You try holding an Athenian shield in place while jabbing with a long spear. All the while you're blind to what's going on outside of the shell and the commanders are shouting orders. And it's hot with all those bodies pressed close together. We call it the love machine. Delivering a perfututum to our enemies where every we go."

"I thought you were a rower?" ventured Alerio.

"When I was younger, I served with a phalanx unit," Hyllus described. "But I was so tall, they placed me in the center to keep the shell balanced. Let me tell you, there's a lot of gas expelled in those formations. Do you know what happens to hot, smelly gas?"

"Not really," admitted Alerio.

"It rises to the highest level of the phalanx," Hyllus declared. "So, I joined the Navy to breath clean sea air."

"Is pork and onions all right with you, Lance Corporal Sisera?" Marija yelled from the kitchen.

"Sounds delicious," replied Alerio.

"It'll give you gas," warned Hyllus. "But Legionaries fight in lines, so it's doesn't matter. I'll get your food."

Alerio sank into the chair and spread out his legs. His thigh appreciated the position as the muscle loosened, and he relaxed. When the meal arrived, he cut fast, and chewed slow, savoring each bite.

Marija limped up to the table. A bandage, wrapped around a shin gash, caused the limp.

"Were you injured in the fighting?" Alerio questioned.

"An Illyrian dove under my blade and sliced me," the Macedonian replied as she pulled out a chair and sat. "Can you believe it? I don't know what he expected me to do, fall back or collapse."

"What did you do?" Alerio inquired.

"I buried my blade in the back of his skull," Marija replied with a smile. "How are you, archery target? Or, should I call you ambush bait?"

"I assume, you heard about the action on the merchant ship," Alerio said. "Why would the Illyrians attack us? And why did the Greeks come to our rescue?"

"I can tell you why the Greeks got involved," Hyllus said as he crossed the dining room, pulled out a chair, and sat. "Athens depends on trade and shipping. Our Navy is the biggest in the region and we've been fighting the Illyrians for decades. Bova harbor is the closest landing to the Greek coast for ships heading to your coast, to Rome, Syracuse or Qart Hadasht ports. If Bovesia were taken, it would disrupt our trading. At least until your Legionaries took it back."

"What about Macedonia?" asked Alerio looking over at Marija. "Do their traders pass through here?"

"A lot more than before. We've had trouble with that upstart king in Egypt," Marija explained. "Can you imagine that ungrateful wretch, not bowing to his rightful king."

"The king of Egypt needs to bow to another king?" Alerio said as he choked on a piece of onion.

"Why the king of Macedonia of course," Marija informed him. "After all, he is a descendent of a Macedonian General. One of our great King Alexander's military leaders. The king of Egypt is a Macedonian and must acknowledge the fact. Isn't that right, Hyllus?"

"We've been over this, many times love," the big man spoke slowly as if his words were footsteps, strolling on bird's eggs. "Egypt has coins from their fertile grain fields, a navy, and an army. I really don't think he owes allegiance to Macedonia after all these years. Like Athens, Egypt is a free state."

"Nonsense, King Alexander claimed Greece and all the lands to Egypt and beyond for Macedonia. Athens participated in the conquest," Marija insisted. "Why can't you see the truth?"

"Because the only reason we sent cavalry, men-at-arms, and coins to your Alexander was to prevent him from turning his army around and marching back," explained Hyllus. "Threaten any city with a quarter million-man army and bend over, because the city will happily kiss your cūlus rather than be destroyed."

"You just can't see reason," an exasperated Marija said. She stood and began limping away. After a few steps, she stopped and turned around. "One day, Macedonia will sail on Egypt and take back what is ours."

Hyllus waited until she vanished into the back room.

"Alerio. Do you have a woman?" he asked.

"No. One day perhaps, but not now," Alerio replied. "Why do you ask?"

"A warning. Do not lose your heart to a Macedonian she-devil," the big man said. Then he winked and added as he stood. "No matter how exciting she is."

Chapter 37 – The Healing Properties of Work

Alerio spent the next four days pushing himself to show his fitness to the medics. Except for the mission from Tribune Velius, he had no other duties. He stayed busy with gladius training infantrymen in the mornings and working with Tesserarius Cephas and Centurion Laurens in the afternoons.

Late on the fourth day, Alerio stepped back and dropped his guard. The Centurion's gladius swept up from hip level. It carved a path toward Alerio's chest. Just before the blade could score a touch, Lance Corporal Sisera pivoted around. Letting the tip pass his side, he spun while raising and bending his arm. When the elbow was two inches from the officer's jaw, Alerio halted the motion. Dropping his arm and turning to face the Centurion, he explained.

"Barbarians don't duel, sir," Alerio informed the infantry officer. "They're fluid. It's fine, even preferable, for a Legionary to square his shoulders to the line of attack. For a Centurion, without a shield and fighting companions, you need to stand sideways in a sword fight. That will allow you forward and reverse movement to defend against an attack like the spinning back elbow. Plus, it makes you a smaller target for enemy arrows and spears."

"Speaking of arrows," the officer commented while he sheathed his gladius. "I see your leg is better."

"Yes, sir," Alerio stated. He lifted his left leg and pivoted on his right. "I'm fit for duty."

"Or, a reconnaissance mission I assume," Laurens stated. "I still can't free up rowers. Even though only a few merchants are sailing, we need to be on guard. Believe me, the entire Republic and many foreign powers are screaming for Illyrian blood. My last message from Rhegium was to stay at full readiness. I can release you to full duty, but transportation is on you."

"Thank you, sir," Alerio said. "I'll figure something out."

***

Throughout history, there were two military truths. One was Sergeants, Optios, Sminias, NCOs, or any other name you called noncommissioned officers, they ran the army. Another truth, if you wanted to know the easiest way to circumvent a regulation, avoid a duty, or find transportation outside of official channels, you spoke with the oldest Private in the unit.

"Lupus. I need transportation to Passomasseria," explained Alerio.

"We could steal a patrol boat," suggested the Private. After seeing the look of horror on the Lance Corporal's face, he added. "Or, I could have one of my fishermen friends row you there."

"You have friends among the fishermen?" Alerio inquired.

"Sure. I go to their village and clear out the snakes during my off-duty time," Lupus informed him. "You see fish parts draw small rodents and the favorite food of serpents are small rodents. One draws the other like dung beetles to a pile of merda."

"I'll pay for the ride," offered Alerio.

"No need Lance Corporal Sisera," Lupus assured him. "They owe me as I can't eat, or take, all the fish they offer in exchange for my services. What they don't know is, I always leave a few of Angitia's beauties for the next hunt."

At the mention of Lupus' goddess, his eyes clouded over and his face went slack. Alerio waited for the seizure to pass.

"Tomorrow morning at first light?" asked Alerio.

"Meet the boat at the Legion dock. Someone will be there," Lupus promised.

Chapter 38 – The Mists of Kaikinos

The weather had been hot and dry since Alerio arrived at Bovesia Garrison. When he left the supply building, he assumed the moon had set. Then he realized the moon was still up but hidden behind a thick layer of clouds.

He could, as all farm boys, smell the promise of rain in the air. Plus, a heavy mist covered the Kaikinos River. Alerio's field of vision shrunk on the stroll down the rickety ramps into the gray fog.

The two Legion patrol boats bobbed gently in the flow of the river. At the end of the dock, he located fingers and a hand through the fog. They clung to the wooden planks of the pier. As Alerio drew closer, the mist parted revealing the hand's connection to an arm, a shoulder, and finally to a hooded man sitting in a wide flat-bottomed boat.

"Are you my ride to Passomasseria?" asked Alerio.

No reply came from the man. But the hand pointed to the front of the boat and the head nodded. Alerio had his dual gladius rig and a few articles of clothing in a bag slung around his neck. He'd left all the legion gear in his room, taking only rough woolen civilian clothing. A sprinkling of raindrops hit his head and, after climbing into the rocking fisherman's boat, he pulled out his cloak. The rain did nothing to dissipate the fog.

The hand pushed and the boat drifted away from the pier. A splash announced the dipping of the rear oar and the fisherman began a slow, rhythmic back and forth motion with the oar handle. With what appeared to be little effort, the fishing boat nosed into the fog, creeping steadily northward.

Alerio could tell the boat tracked close to the river bank from the occasional low tree branch that appeared overhead. From what he could see of the river's center, logs and leaves flowed by swiftly in the current. The floaters let him know why the fisherman stayed near the bank.

***

A long time later the boat cut across the current and at the opposite bank the fisherman ran it aground. The wood scraped on the gravel riverbed.

"You leave here," announced the fisherman.

"Is this Passomasseria?" inquired Alerio.

"There," the man indicated a direction upriver. Then, he advised. "In the mountains, it rains. Kaikinos rises."

"What does that mean?" demanded Alerio.

"I'm going back to Bovesia. You walk, or return with me," stated the fisherman.

"How long will it take me to reach the town?" Alerio asked as he slung the strap over his shoulder and stepped out of the boat.

"As long as it takes," replied the fisherman. Then he warned. "Stay away from the river's edge."

The boat now lighter by the weight of one large infantry NCO rose and lifted off the riverbed.

Alerio watched as the boat turned, and was soon swallowed by the fog. He looked around. To his left, the land rose and became studded with small trees and brush. The gravel bed where he stood allowed for good footing, and although the gray mist limited his visibility, he could see it was mostly flat. With the river on his right, the Legionary began walking northward on the gravel surface.

He noticed a few pebbles rolling into the river at the edge of the flat ground. Guessing it was normal when the current flowed that fast, he ignored them.

After walking for a while, he encountered a stream cutting across his path. Rather than wade the swollen tributary he headed inland and climbed the bank. Under the grass and shrub trees, the ground was damp and soggy. By the time he struggled to higher ground his sandals and lower legs were covered in mud. Luckily, on the bank, he found the stream narrower and easily jumped. After circling a boulder and slogging through more sticky mud, he dropped back down the bank to the gravel of the sand bar. The walking was easier even though the river's edge seemed closer.

He climbed twice more and was forced to leap wider raging streams. Each time he noticed the ground ran flat for a few yards from the riverbank. Then, the flat ended at steeply climbing ground. At each crossing, the ground ended at higher and higher walls until they became cliffs. Following each traverse of an overflowing creek, he climbed down to the gravel bed at the river.

***

Where it had misted before, rain now fell in fat drops that clinked on the gravel and plopped in the river water. Overhead the charcoal clouds hung low as if trying to blend with the ground fog. Alerio pulled his hood up and leaned forward as he marched northward into the storm.

His world shriveled to the soreness in his thigh and side, and the worry about locating Passomasseria before nightfall. Along with the weather, his attitude grew as dreary as the day.

Yet, he trudged onward remembering the words of the Sergeants from Legionary training.

"Your first enemy isn't over the next rise. Your body can take the punishment. It can take more then you believe. No, the enemy isn't an unknown barbarian. It's that voice inside you screaming about pain, fear, and hunger. Give in and die. Ignore it and survive. Conquer it and thrive. Because, your first enemy is your mind."

Further upriver a strange noise jerked him out of his stupor. For two heartbeats Alerio couldn't understand the rumbling. It was as if a hundred supply wagons, pulled by runaway horses, bounced along a rocky road.

He discovered the source when the river leaped up and slapped his knees. Before he could react, a wall of water rose out of the fog and engulfed him.

***

Submerged, choking, and tumbling in the raging water, Alerio felt helpless. Ever since he outgrew being a timid farm boy being chased by older teens, he had depended on

174

his strength and skills to survive. But, his was no match for the power of the water. It bent him, twisted him, filled his nose and mouth, and confused his mind. For a heartbeat, Lance Corporal Alerio Sisera surrendered to his fate.

"Your first enemy isn't over the next rise. Your body can take the punishment."

The words cut through the lethargy, focusing his mind, and energizing his limbs.

Alerio fought the tumbling water to pull his knees and elbows in close to his body. Tucked as he was, he rolled faster without any idea of direction. Up, down, the location of the surface or the riverbed was impossible to judge.

"Your body can take the punishment. It can take more then you believe. No, the enemy isn't an unknown barbarian."

His legs shot out and he began a swim-kick. Along with the legs, he thrust out his arms. Like a water wheel in a stream, the raging water turned his body end-over-end. On the second rotation, his legs touched the riverbed and he kicked off. With lungs screaming for air, he burst through the surface and gulped down a deep breath.

"It's that voice inside you screaming about pain, fear, and hunger."

Before the water sucked him down again, he spied the shoreline. Underwater, in the turbulence, he kicked and angled for the riverbank. Fighting the current that attempted to pull him to the center of the river, he swam. He floundered in the rolling water and was bent sideways. Yet, he kicked and swam some more.

"Give in and die. Ignore it and survive."

Another breath and a view of the bank gave Alerio hope. With energy waning and his body failing, he remembered.

"Conquer it and thrive."

Alerio's face broke the surface. Rather than lifting it as a drowning man would, he turned his head to the side and inhaled deeply. Legionaries learned to swim. Some better than others, but all Legion infantrymen could swim. For the next six heartbeats, Alerio kicked hard and stroked powerfully until he felt his heart would burst.

One hand touched dirt. Then his other hand gripped the base of a shrub tree. Alerio's arm acted as a fulcrum and his body swung in an arc until it slammed into the riverbank. With the last of his strength, he clawed at mud and reeds while pulling his body clear of the water.

With the side of his face pressed against the mud, he whispered, "Because, your first enemy is your mind."

When his breath returned to normal, Alerio rose to his knees. His face was hot from the frantic swim and he tilted it skyward to feel the rain. Glancing back, he noted the water lapping at the top of the riverbank. Realizing the river could rise more, he looked to the line of steep hills in front of him.

They were almost cliffs and as exhausted as he was, he knew climbing was impossible. Dragging his feet to the base of the cliff, he walked along the rocky face looking for access to higher ground. Fifty feet from where he emerged from the river he came upon a break in the cliff face. A rushing creek created a mini waterfall; the heavy flow rushed from the saddle between the hills, over the riverbank before disappearing in the boiling river water. Spying a ledge on this side of the rapidly flowing creek, he stepped on a large rock and placed his hands on the sheer rock face.

Gazing up he located foot and hand holds and began to climb. Three small outcrops later he rolled onto a ledge. Far below, the river rose and its fast-moving water flooded the ground between the riverbank and the base of the cliff.

Exhausted, Alerio pulled the strap over his head and jerked up his hood. Using the pack as a pillow, he curled up in the cloak and went to sleep.

Chapter 39 – Strangers in the Rain

It was near dark when the sound of voices awakened him. Peering from under the hood, he almost called out. But the two men standing on the other side of the stream were too well armed to be farmers, hunters, or trappers.

They carried short Greek style swords on one hip and long fighting knives on the other. Both were muscular and wore thick soled, high sided sandals on their feet. Although not in uniforms or armored, they looked as if they would be comfortable in military garb. It was also in the confident way they carried themselves, and the thick set of their shoulders. Alerio remained hidden and watched.

The men stopped at the edge of the saddle and one pointed down at the flooding river.

"Like I told you. We'll not hear from the Sergeant tonight or tomorrow," he announced.

"How could you be so sure?" asked the other.

"I watched the clouds close in on the mountains," the first man explained. "It's been raining up there since yesterday. All that water has to go somewhere. And there it is. No way he can get here from Bovesia unless he can walk on water."

"I've seen the Sergeant do a lot of things since joining the Syracuse Raiders," the second man said. "I wouldn't doubt he could. But, you're right. We'll let the lads relax tomorrow."

As the men turned, the first one said, "It's a shame we can't go into Passomasseria. I'd like a proper drink."

"What? The Sergeant's excellent beer not good enough for you?" asked the second man.

"I said a proper drink. You know, wine," came the reply as the two marched away from the river. "I still don't see why we don't clear out that town. There's no sense in leaving an enemy at our backs."

"Is that a military strategy, or your opinion as a wine drinker?" asked the first man.

The rest of the exchange got lost to distance, the gurgling creek, and the rain. Alerio sat up and watched as the figures disappeared into the mist.

Slipping the pack over his shoulder the Legion NCO stood stiffly and walked to the back edge of the ledge.

Although barely visible, he could make out the imprints from the men's sandals in the mud on the far side of the creek.

He was still wet from the river. So, when he jumped off the ledge and began to slide down the cliff face of the saddle, it didn't matter. He splashed down in the creek. Six unsteady steps across allowed him to climb from the swollen stream. Once on the path, he dropped to his knees and examined the sandals' prints.

Lads born on farms hunt game for recreation and to supplement the family's diet. Alerio recalled the tracking skills from his childhood and set off after the strangers. They weren't hiding their footsteps, which told Alerio this wasn't the primary path to their camp. If it was, they would have eradicated their footprints to confuse an enemy. And although the rain smeared their tracks, they didn't seem concerned about an attack from this direction. The washed-out sandal prints and the fading light forced Alerio to stop frequently and feel for the imprints.

At a fork in the trail, Alerio squatted again to study the signs. The tracks headed off on a lower path. Glancing at the higher path, he noted it led into the hills.

Suddenly, his hunter's instincts raised the hairs on the back of his neck. Rather than stand Alerio remained low and crept forward. The men's tracks ran true for a few feet before one turned right scuffing the mud. Now facing off the trail, the sandals' imprints shuffled under a bush, before turning to rejoin the other set. The man had either relieved himself, or he'd spoken to someone in the bush. Maybe a sentry?

Alerio pondered this as the defused light of a cloudy evening finally faded. In the dark, he waited and listened trying to form a plan.

The sneeze was soft and the noise almost blended with the sounds of raindrops on leaves. If Alerio hadn't been listening he would have missed it.

The sentry was located off to the right of the lower path. But he was posted too far from the trail to engage an approaching enemy. Alerio sneaked back to the fork in the trail figuring to avoid the guard's notice.

He then went in the opposite direction and followed the high path. It rose, zigzagging back and forth as it climbed the steep hill. At an overlook that faced the lower trail, he slowly unslung the strap and eased the pack under a bush. Ignoring the cold and dampness he crept back to the fork in the trails.

***

If the listening post was guarding a secondary approach to the strangers' campsite, the sentry's relief, if any, would come from the direction of the main encampment. Alerio waited until the wind gusted before sliding under a bush and carefully crawling further off the trail. Then he waited.

He fought the shivers for fear the shaking would attract the guard's attention. He kept his breathing shallow for the same reason. As Alerio lay against the damp earth, he recited the training Sergeants' mantra, "It's that voice inside you screaming about pain, fear, and hunger. Give in and die.

180

Ignore it and survive. Conquer it and thrive. Because, your first enemy is your mind."

Just when Alerio began to doubt his tactics, brush to his left and behind the sentry began to shake and snap. Bodies were coming and as the noise of their passing came closer, Alerio crept forward.

He had waited a relatively short time and this was another clue to the make-up of the strangers. Rebels, highwaymen, barbarians, and marauders, didn't maintain regular guard rotations. This group was bringing a relief for the sentry.

Not only was a relief coming, but a supervisor accompanied the man. Only one entity had the discipline to protect their men from mental and physical fatigue by regularly relieving them – these men were part of a disciplined military unit.

Recalling the earlier discussion by the two strangers, Alerio reached a conclusion. The reference to Syracuse raiders didn't mean they were pirates or marauders. Rather it referred to a detached military unit. And, if a Sergeant was in charge, they would be on a mission. Armed with these thoughts, Alerio no longer doubted his tactics.

He crawled forward, using the noise of the approaching relief and noncommissioned officer to cover his movements. "Now, all I need is a more accurate count," he thought. "And get back and report the unit to Centurion Laurens at Bovesia Garrison."

Alerio paused when the three men met and whispered to each other. As the NCO and the off-duty guard backtracked through the bush Alerio fell in behind them.

***

The camp was composed of three ten-men tents with shielded lanterns marking the entrance to each shelter. As the off-duty guard disappeared into a tent, the NCO tapped another man on the shoulder. They walked into the bushes to Alerio's right.

While creeping back from the edge of the clearing, Alerio smiled. Now, he knew the strength of the Syracusan unit and the locations of their sentries. By splitting the distance between the listening posts, he was able to safely move back to the trail.

Alerio retrieved his pack and hiked up the winding path. Although tired, he couldn't rest on this side of the hill. It was one of the many problems with night maneuvers. A dark hiding spot in the night might turn out to be clearly visible to your enemy in the light of day. Moving slowly, he felt for the path with his feet until the ground leveled. When it began to fall away he located a thick bush and crawled between the branches.

Sometime in the early morning, the rain stopped. The silence woke Alerio. He listened for footfalls in the dark. When none came, he fell back to sleep. A sharp rock and the arrow wound in his side rousted him at dawn.

Chapter 40 – Hamlet on the Hill

The foothills before him reached higher elevations at each peak as they stretched out toward the mountains. Green covered most of the lower portions with clumps of small trees in spots. Where it wasn't grass, it was bare rock. Just as Lupus had described it, the landscape consisted of high hills. And, almost as if Mars had used his gladius to slice some of the tops off. But the plateau areas were serrated, not smooth.

After shaking the leaves from his cloak, he slung it over the pack and marched down the first hill. In the back of his mind, he worried the Syracuse NCOs might send out a patrol at first light. He couldn't afford to be seen, so even though the path was treacherous, he rushed to the valley below.

Two rabbits squatted, chewed, and watched him cross the valley floor. They rightly didn't consider him a threat. In his present state of mind, he wasn't. But, he hoped a few of their cousins, over the next hill, had the same relaxed attitude. Moments later, his attitude was no longer relaxed.

***

Alerio found himself sweating and kneeling in a clump of trees. On the hill where he spent the night, stood four men. They'd appeared when he was halfway up the hill. The soldiers had stopped to take in the vista before glancing down into the valley, and scanning the far hillside; that saved the Legionary. Catching a glimpse of their heads as they crested the hill, he ran for the trees.

His stomach grumbled when the four sat down, pulled strips from pouches, and began gnawing on the dried meat. In Alerio's mind, he went to an extreme and envisioned them chewing on fresh beef. It was more likely dried goat but, if you're going to be envious, you might as well make it worthwhile.

A root dug painfully into one knee and his back ached from remaining stooped. Alerio thought seriously about standing up and calling the four over. He wondered if they would share a few meat strips before the fight?

What saved him, was the appearance of a fifth man. The man must have been their squad leader as the four jumped to their feet. He wasn't happy and demonstrated it with a few explicit hand gestures. After the display, the five disappeared behind the summit of the hill.

Alerio waited a short time before standing and continuing his march upward. His stomach grumbled, overriding his worries about the soldiers. Instead, he worried about not seeing rabbits on the far side.

Thankfully, there were rabbits. After several well thrown rocks, Alerio had food. Unfortunately, all the kindling and potential firewood were soaked from last night's rain. He cut down a sapling and stripped off the branches. With three fat hares hanging from the pole, Alerio crossed another valley and climbed the next slope.

***

Heavy clouds rolled in and hung low hiding the sun and threatening more rain. Alerio's direction was generally northward. But with all the climbing, traversing, and crossing low lands, he didn't have a fix on his location. Somewhere off to his right, he was sure, the Kaikinos River ran fast and full. Behind, the Syracuse military unit and ahead lay the town of Passomasseria. He craned his neck to look up at the next steep grade. Glancing down at his feet, he put one in front of the other and struggled up the slope.

He was sweating and his right thigh throbbed by the time he reached the top. It was the steepest climb yet. Across the flat, he reached the far crest. Alerio peered down on a cliff face. No boulders clung to the bare granite; only sharp outcrops broke the vertical surface. Except for a narrow ledge ten feet down and far to his right, there were no handholds or spots to place his feet.

The smell of burning wood drifted on the midday breeze. Alerio set down his pack and the rabbits and got down on his knees. When he leaned his body out over the cliff, the odor grew stronger. Judging it to be coming from his right, he gathered the stick and pack and followed the edge in that direction.

As he walked the line of the cliff, giving wide berth to several crevasses, the narrow ledge rose. Fifty feet later, it became reachable. Alerio stepped down on the narrow path.

**

Some places required him to turn sideways and inch around outcrops. Then, the path would widen and he could face forward. At the outcrops, he noted chisel marks. They showed someone had carved the path in the granite at least

185

in some places. Twice the path entered large crevasses where steps were carved in the stone. At these, he was forced to turn around and back down. Blind to the front, he felt with a toe before easing his foot to the next rough-cut step.

The path, ever descending, led Alerio lower and lower along the cliff face. Below him, a green boxed in valley ended at a sheer wall. At multiple places, runoff flowed over the end of the canyon forming a rushing stream that cut through the center of this small sliver of fertile land. As he progressed, the smell of burning wood grew stronger.

***

Alerio crept into another crevasse, turned, and began backing down. But these steps were steeper than the others. Also, they wrapped around the far side of the fissure's edge. He descended the steps as they coiled around while facing the treads. The path and cliff face behind him were out of his sight.

"It'll be a quick death, falling into the valley," a voice at Alerio's back stated. "Or, you can go back the way you came."

Straining to look over his shoulder at the speaker, Alerio saw the deeply etched skin around the eyes of an old hermit. But his initial thought rang false. For one, the man's beard and hair were trimmed and neatly combed. The beard had leather strips woven into the gray hairs. Also, his bare arms were corded with muscles, and although the flesh was loose as you'd expect on an older person, the muscles were those of a well-conditioned fighter.

Alerio noticed the muscularity because the man stood erect and held a bronzed tipped spear in his hands. The shaft was polished and greased as if it had just come from an armory. And the tip's buffed and sharp edges displayed no tarnish or marring.

"It's a long climb back," Alerio commented. "I've rabbit to share."

"What makes you think I eat rabbit?" asked the man.

"Everyone likes roasted rabbit," suggested Alerio. "And to be truthful, I don't think my leg can make the climb without a rest."

The old man leaned forward and squinted. After a pause to examine the bright pink scar on Alerio's right leg, he straightened and inquired, "Where did you pick up the wound?"

"An Illyrian pirate arrow," Alerio replied. "While protecting a merchant ship."

"Name," demanded the hermit.

"Lance Corporal Alerio Sisera, Third Century, Eighth Squad," Alerio reported. "Of the Republic's Southern Legion."

"All right Lance Corporal Sisera, come down," offered the old man. Then he warned. "Go for a weapon and I'll run you through and throw you over the side."

"Not very trusting, are you?" Alerio observed as he took the last five steps to the path. Once on solid footing, he slowly turned around.

The narrow path ended five feet behind the old man. There, it widened to a broad and deep ledge. Big enough to accommodate a walk-in hut with a thatched roof pinned to the cliff face. A porch extended the footprint of the hut. Neatly organized around the hut were a weaving stand, a cooking pit, a tool and work zone, and a small grazing area with three sheep and a goat.

The oddest area was a sand pit with wood poles jutting from holes in the granite wall. Each pole was a different length and stuck out over the sand at various heights. Alerio had never seen the type, but he identified it as a weapon's training pit.

"You have a training area," noted Alerio. "I don't recognize the origin."

"And you have a good eye," the old man said with pride in his voice. "It's modified a bit but, basically, it's the design we use in Sparta."

"So that would make you, what?" asked Alerio.

"I'm Helicaon, the Spartan," announced the old man.

Chapter 41 – The Spartan

While Alerio turned the skewed rabbits over a fire, he asked, "Helicaon. How far is it to Passomasseria?"

"North of here but you can't get there," the old warrior said. He reached down and turned three yams that lay in the hot ash.

"Can't get there from here?" repeated Alerio.

"If you climb back up, head west for a few days, then hike into the high hills; you can come at Passomasseria from the northern approach. You'll reach it in a week," instructed the old man. "Or you can wait for two days until the river goes down. Then you can walk to it in a day and a half using the river bank."

"So, it's not far?" Alerio guessed.

"Not most of the year," the Spartan replied. "But in the fall and spring, the river swells, the creeks rise, and you can't get places. It's best to stay put."

They were sitting on wooden benches on opposite sides of the cookfire. The Spartan, with the butt end of his spear on the ground, nestled the shaft in the crook of his arm. Alerio knew the old man, although sitting relaxed, could bring the tip down in less than a heartbeat.

"I'm going to pull my knife to test the rabbit," Alerio alerted his host.

"Of course, you are," the Spartan remarked. "The yams should be ready, as well. I'll get plates."

While the sheep remained in the small pen, the she-goat had wandered over and stood beside the old man. When he stood and walked into the hut, the goat tagged along.

"She's been with me since she was a kid," the ancient Spartan commented as he reemerged from the hut and handed Alerio two clay plates. "We found this valley and built a home here. Away from people, civilization, slaves, and war."

"Sounds idyllic, if not a little lonely," Alerio said as he laid slices of rabbit on a plate and handed it to the old man. "Don't you miss conversation?"

"Sometimes," he admitted while placing a baked yam on Alerio's plate. "but then I remember why I chose this life."

"Why did you?" inquire Alerio.

"I've been in military training, or in a Spartan mess on active duty since I was seven years old," the Spartan related between bites. "Five years ago, my fifteen brothers sailed with King Areus to fight in Crete. At fifty-nine and seven months, I was nearing retirement. They elected me to stay in Sparta to supervise work on our barracks. And, to audition new recruits from those graduating from the Agoge."

The Spartan picked up the yam and bit off a chunk. He chewed hard as if the soft vegetable was tough. It wasn't the food that was tough, it was his story.

"Let me tell you, sleeping in a bed and eating regular meals maybe decadent, but after fifty-two years of living the life of a Spartan soldier, I couldn't complain. One day, word reached Sparta that King Pyrrhus had landed on our coast," he said. "The king had just returned from the kick in the cōleī your Legions handed him in the Republic. Still, he commanded a twenty-thousand-man army. Our emissaries met with the king. He assured them that his only intention was freeing a few cities west of Sparta."

The old man picked up a piece of rabbit, inspected it, then plopped it into his mouth. He shook his head and frowned.

"When Pyrrhus' scouts began marching towards Sparta, our emissaries went back to see him," Helicaon explained. "Same merda. By then his vanguard was headed north up the Eurotas River directly at our city. He wouldn't have tried it if our army had been there. With our forces fighting in Crete, and other units posted elsewhere, we weren't prepared to defend Sparta."

"But you are Spartans," Alerio stated. "I've been told one Spartan is equal to seven warriors. Well, maybe not Legionaries, but seven of anybody else's soldiers."

The comment earned Alerio a sideways look from the Spartan. Before continuing, Helicaon pulled out a comb and began running it through his long gray hair.

"Twenty-thousand warriors, plus Pyrrhus brought elephants," explained Helicaon. "Big animals that can crush a phalanx, or break through a stockade barrier. One day, I'm feasting and watching teenage soldiers trying to impress me with their bravery. And the next, the peace of the city gets shattered. At first there was panic, however, our former queen Arachidamia called everyone to the city center. Spartan women will not flee, she declared. They would assist in the defense of the homes. Now, here's the issue. The job of Spartan women is to stay fit and to birth new Spartan warriors. If Pyrrhus captured our city and sold our women into slavery, Sparta would cease to exist."

"Couldn't you just stay put, and defend your city's defensive walls?" Alerio suggested. "Why take the field against a larger force?"

Helicaon nodded sadly as if addressing a young soldier who said something so inane, it had to be a misunderstanding.

"Have you ever heard, Sparta doesn't have walls?" Helicaon asked. "Because Spartan soldiers are her walls?"

"No. But, oh I see," said Alerio as the realization dawned on him. "Sparta doesn't have defensive walls. What did you do?"

"I had a choice. As a veteran, I could have taken command of a section. Surrounded myself with inexperienced, but eager young men, and orchestrated their deaths," Helicaon explained. "Or, I could help dig the city's defenses and leave myself free to fight where I was needed. Less glory, but what does an old man need with glory. A blanket on a cold night, a few scraps of food at midday, and the occasional mug of wine are all I require."

Alerio glanced around the neat and orderly compound. Helicaon was playing the stoic Spartan. Yet, his life as a hermit was as regimented as a Legion garrison.

"I chose to help with the defenses. There I was, an experienced Spartan warrior with a shovel and a spade, surrounded not by blood thirsty barbarians, but by women and old men," Helicaon said with a gleam in his eyes. "At first I didn't know how to act. Women; I've never been around them. Soldiers, teenagers, boys sure, I know how to deal with them. But women?"

"I kept to myself as I dug and I noticed the women maintained a distance from me," Helicaon admitted. "But, some of them seemed to be in shock. Their homes and lives were threatened. A hoard of warriors was camped a bow's shot from where we worked. We could hear the elephants snorting and calling out as the afternoon wore on. Suddenly, I got angry. In a Spartan unit, heroics were just as contagious as fear. And I had fifty-two years' experience with motivating troops."

"You didn't whip them, did you?" asked Alerio.

"No Lance Corporal Sisera. That's the Legion style of getting results, from what I've been told," Helicaon replied. "No, I called the women together and told them Spartan women were now the walls. I challenged them to come home with their shovels or on them. I used every rousing speech I could think of and then I placed them on line."

"Isn't it with your shield or on it?" asked Alerio. "A Centurion told me the women of Sparta say that to their men before the army marches off to war."

Helicaon smiled and shrugged but didn't reply to the Legionary.

"We started at the edge of our city. The front line dug a level and moved forward. Behind them, another line dug another level and you know what I found out?" asked Helicaon.

"No, Spartan. What did you learn?"

"Women are easier to motivate than men," he said. "Not only that, they don't have to be coached on how to work together. No matter, at what age you start boys, the toughest part is to get them to act as a single unit. Women understand strength in numbers and they dug all night in unison. By morning, we had a deep defensive trench in front of King Pyrrhus' army."

"Soldiers can jump trenches," ventured Alerio to Helicaon's delight.

The old Spartan held up a finger while gripping his side. His laughter was infectious and Alerio joined him in the mirth.

"Did I say something funny," asked Alerio when he managed to catch his breath.

"The trench those women and old men dug ended up being eight hundred feet long. It was six feet deep and nine feet wide," bragged the Spartan. "Not only couldn't Pyrrhus' army jump the trench. Neither could his elephants."

"But they could attack through or around it," Alerio suggested.

"It felt as if we had dug almost to Hades. For Pyrrhus' troops, who went down into that trench and faced our young fighters on the rim of the other side, it was Hades. While we dug the trench, other veterans dug shallower trenches on the flanks and buried wagons," reported

Helicaon. "In one night, a city without walls sprouted defenses that halted an army."

"So, you stopped King Pyrrhus and his troops?" guessed Alerio.

"Unfortunately, it wasn't that easy," Helicaon informed the Legionary. "While the main body attempted to attack across the trench, a man on a big horse led two thousand warriors in a flank attack. They roped two wagons and managed to drag them out of the dirt. Then, they rushed through the breach and attacked the heart of Sparta. I belted on my sword, collected my shield and spear, and started for the center of the city. But a young veteran named Acrotatus stopped me. He had collected around three hundred Spartans. If you know history, three hundred is a rather special number to us."

"I've heard the story of Thermopylae," stated Alerio. "Three hundred Spartans held off thousands of Persians at a narrow pass."

"Well, we didn't have a narrow pass, but Acrotatus had a plan. Remember, I told you bravery and cowardice are contagious? Well, in most armies, the brave charge ahead while the fearful lag behind," explained Helicaon. "Acrotatus led us down backstreets, through depressions, and we emerged behind the enemy force. We hit them in full throat with every fiber of our hearts, and every skill a Spartan can bring-to-bear. We hit their rear rank and true to form, the fear spread as we hacked and chopped into their weakness. Soon we were fighting for our lives as the enemy fought us while trying to escape the city."

195

"And the siege ended?" asked Alerio.

"No. That was the first day. Once Pyrrhus called his army back to camp, we reset the wagons and prepared for day two," Helicaon said. "On the morning of the second day, Pyrrhus ordered men to run forward and toss dirt into the trench. When our women proved to be experts with rocks, arrows, and spears, he had to send units into the trench to attack. As they attacked, the dirt carriers ran forward; not only with earth but with the bodies of their dead. Soon part of the trench was a partially filled graveyard. I stood on the bank all morning chopping and yelling encouragement to the young men on either side of me."

"You didn't come off the battle line at all?" questioned Alerio.

"I stepped back to drink and eat, but once I was nourished, I returned to the fray," the Spartan said. "You see, we veterans were few and most of our defensive line was made up of young men not old enough to join a mess. By the afternoon, Pyrrhus' men had filled in a wide ramp and the fighting at that section became intense. It was off to my right in an area where our veterans had fallen."

"Suddenly, the enemy charged that part of our line. With the pressure lifted at my location, I stepped back to have a drink. Then Pyrrhus himself forced his horse through his own ranks," the Spartan recalled. "I tossed down the wineskin, grabbed my spear, and ran towards the fighting. As I jostled through my countrymen, the king led his troops through the gap. He charged into Sparta trailing ranks of his fighters. It looked bad for us. Without experienced units, our defenders were rushing around without discipline, and I couldn't push my way to the invaders. Out of frustration, I drew my arm back and launched my spear."

Helicaon's mouth twisted to the side and, for a second, he seemed younger than his years. He shook his head in agreement with his unspoken thoughts and inhaled deeply.

"The spear arched into the sky. At best, I hoped to hit one of the enemy soldiers," Helicaon explained. "The shaft tilted and the bronze tip angled downward. It struck perfectly and sank deeply into the flank of Pyrrhus' horse. The King toppled to the ground and his troops, seeing their leader fall, panicked. A group formed a protective wall around their king. Our archers and slingers, mostly women, rained rocks, arrows, and spears down on the King's defenders. Many fell but they managed to fight their way through the gap taking their ranks and their King with them. We rallied and closed the gap."

"Pyrrhus pulled back his army and sent an emissary forward," the Spartan boasted. "He explained that seeing as how our ranks were decimated, and Sparta's defenders couldn't possibly hold out against another attack, we should surrender. He demanded that Sparta herself lay down her shield in defeat. I sometimes wonder why Kings and war chiefs don't bother to learn history. We sent the emissary back with the roar of every citizen in his ears, daring Pyrrhus to come, and try to take our city."

The Spartan put away his comb and stretched his back. It cracked and he lowered his head. In almost a whisper, he continued.

"Early the next morning, I staggered, sore and weary, to my place at the ramp. Our lines were slim and the boys on the rim could barely stand let alone hold their shields. Across the trench, Pyrrhus and his army gathered in ranks. I could see the confidence in their swagger and in the casual way they stood around," Helicaon explained before raising his head. He faced flushed and his shoulders straightened. "Then a horn sounded. From the river, at first, a flash of scarlet, then another, and suddenly, two thousand Spartans, in perfect ranks marched towards the city. Units, disciplined and experienced, divided up the defensive sectors. Our brave, but outmatched youths were replaced by hardened veterans."

"I located my mess and fell in the ranks," Helicaon explained. "They'd rowed all night from Crete and, although tired, they were ready for a fight. Pyrrhus obliged. Unlike the last two days, when his troops attacked and our defenders simply fought to hold on, they met two thousand angry Spartan veterans. Men who don't just hold positions. They faced men who killed and took ground. It was only the twenty-thousand-man army that saved Pyrrhus. By the afternoon, the King was moving his army away from Sparta. Even as they retreated, Spartan soldiers killed his rearguard and marched after him."

During the tale, Helicaon had jumped to his feet. He jabbed at the air with his spear almost as if he were still with his messmates defending Sparta.

"That's a good story," Alerio complimented. "But it doesn't explain why you left all that to become a hermit."

Helicaon sat down on the bench and smiled.

"Well, remember the women from the trench," Helicaon said. "It seemed they liked being near a veteran who saved their lives and homes. Unfortunately for me, I was inexperienced and indiscriminate. I liked being near them, a lot of them, and some of them were married and all had fathers. So, I retired with beautiful memories, and fled Sparta."

Alerio studied the old Spartan. After visualizing him thicker with muscle and seven years younger, he accepted the explanation. To change the subject the Legionary looked around the compound for something else to talk about. His eyes settled on the sand and poles of the training pit.

"The sand, I understand. It's good for the legs," Alerio commented. "But the horizontal logs, their different heights and lengths, I can't see the benefit."

Chapter 42 – Secrets of Spartan Warfare

"How would you train against the logs?" asked Helicaon.

Alerio walked to the pit and stood in front of the butt ends of the logs. At first, he attempted to strike the logs with his hands. But the distance between the targets defeated his attempt at hand-to-hand combat.

Spying what he needed at the cooking area, Alerio strolled there and selected two thick sticks. Back at the training pit, he swung both striking the logs in turn. Soon he had a rough rhythm going as his sticks rapped against the logs.

"They are a little far apart for gladius training," Alerio said as he lowered the sticks.

"Do you know why the Spartans are such feared fighters?" asked Helicaon.

"Because you train your whole life to be warriors," replied Alerio.

"There is that, but being warriors is a requirement for our survival," explained Helicaon. "You see, our slaves outnumber my people. In order to maintain control, we have to be feared. It's also why Spartans don't surrender. Where would we go if we are fighting on our own land."

"It makes sense," Alerio confirmed. "And Spartans certainly have a history of holding a line and turning a battle."

"Yes. Military discipline starts at seven years old," Helicaon stated. "But our reputation comes from more than Spartan training. We study war and we study our enemies. And most of all, we study our enemies' weapons and tactics."

Helicaon disappeared into his hut and emerged with a long pole.

"Your Legion javelins are about this long," he said placing a hand on a short section of the pole. Then he shifted his hand to the end of the pole and added. "The Athenians use a longer spear. Like this."

After sliding his hands to a length somewhere between the javelin and the long spear, Helicaon began twirling the pole overhead as he stepped into the training pit.

"Each Legionary carries three javelins. Wastefully, you throw one or two before engaging in a skirmish," Helicaon said as he slid his hands choking up on the pole. He began poking at the logs. As if he held a short javelin, the Spartan demonstrated the straight forward thrusts used by the Legions. Rapidly, he worked back and forth striking each of the logs several times.

Then, he slid his hands to the rear of the pole and began efficiently poking at the log ends. "The Athenians and others, like the Syracusan, use long spears. Very effective for keeping the enemy off the shields of their phalanx."

Even while holding the long, unwieldy spear, Helicaon managed to rapidly tap each of the logs. He had effectively demonstrated skill with both the Legion javelin and the Athenian spear.

Abruptly, he stopped and moved his hand to a section between the long spear and the shorter javelin. Now, he moved the pole as if it were a long sword. Helicaon smashed the pole's tip between the logs so fast that the end of the pole blurred.

"How do you think King Leonidas and his three hundred Spartans fought off thousands of Persians?" asked Helicaon. "By poking at them with long spears? Or throwing away javelins and jabbing at them with the remaining ones? No, Legionary. Spartans fight smart with no wasted movement."

While Helicaon talked, his pole's tip swung rhythmically between the log targets. If the Spartan were standing in a battle line, he would effectively be striking multiple members of an opposing force. Alerio visualized a line of Spartans with bronze-bladed spears slicing and killing many times their number.

"We study our enemy and we train so, in fact, one Spartan is equal to seven other warriors," Helicaon bragged as he pulled the pole back and rested the butt end on the sand. "We know how our enemies move. We practice countering their maneuvers and drill against their weapons. It's why Spartans are the best fighters in the world."

"You haven't faced a Legion," advised Alerio.

"Not yet. Then again, you haven't expanded off your shores," pointed out Helicaon. "Your Legions have been too busy consolidating the Republic's territory. But you realize by now, Spartans are watching and studying your tactics."

"Speaking of watching. I witnessed an Athenian phalanx chew through a hoard of Illyrian pirates last week," mentioned Alerio. "How do Spartans defeat a phalanx?"

"We match them shield for shield in our own phalanx," replied Helicaon. "Unless there is a narrower battlefield nearby. Then, we lure them into tighter quarters. Hills and uneven ground are best. Barring that, we open a hole in our battle line and let them in. Then when the phalanx turns to attack one side of our broken line, we attack their rear. The problem is if they have elements behind the phalanx, you've opened a gap in your line for them."

"So, you'd need reserve units to reestablish the line," questioned Alerio.

"Now you're thinking like a Spartan," Helicaon said. "I believe you need to rest. I noticed you favoring your leg when you were showing off with the two-sword demonstration."

"One thing the Spartans may not realize, yet," Alerio informed him. "Legionaries don't rest until their blades are sharp and their equipment is serviceable. I'm going to clean and sharpen my gladii before I rest."

"If I were in Sparta, I'd pass that bit of knowledge along to my messmates," proclaimed Helicaon. "But I'm not. They'll have to learn it on their own. But, it's a good idea, I'll get out my sword and oil it as well."

"Now you're thinking like a Legionary," said Alerio as he walked towards where he left his pack and harness.

Chapter 43 – Mission Focused

Alerio rolled over and tossed back the hood of his cloak. A fire crackled softly in the cooking area. On the far side of the flames, Helicaon sat combing his hair and beard. The old man looked so relaxed and uncaring, it was easy to forget the spear and sword propped up on the logs beside him.

Last night, the Legionary and the Spartan had compared their respective armies. Both militaries demanded tough training and cleanliness. However, where the Legion depended on a show of ordered shields to awe an enemy, the Spartans went the opposite direction. In the dawn before a battle, the enemy would first see the Spartans sitting around grooming themselves. To the enemy warriors, who strutted around trying to shore up their courage before attacking, the sight of Spartans silently combing their hair, trimming their toenails, or calmly brushing their scarlet cloaks, was confusing and intimidating.

Alerio commented that he should have marched into the Syracusan Raider camp and announced himself while combing his hair. They both laughed because Alerio's hair was cropped closely to his scalp and he was cleanly shaven. And, because intimidation required more than just showing up, and posturing in an enemy's camp.

"Bread?" asked the Spartan as he tore off a chunk and held it out.

Alerio shook the dew off his cloak and spread it out on a rock before reaching out and taking the bread. Above, stars were visible in the narrow patch of sky above the Spartan's valley.

"You didn't make this here," ventured Alerio as he sat on a bench.

"No, I go to Passomasseria or Bovesia a couple of times a month," Helicaon replied. "Although Bovesia is my favorite. Before buying my supplies, I stop at the Columnae Herculis for a meal. Hyllus' lamb is the best I've ever tasted."

"I've grown fond of Hyllus and Marija," Alerio admitted. "And of Pholus' beer."

"Who is Pholus?" Helicaon asked.

"The beverage merchant on the first level," explained Alerio. "In the small shop on the first plaza to the right of the stairs."

"I was in Bovesia two weeks ago and that shop was empty," Helicaon said. "He must be new."

Alerio thought as he chewed. If the shop was empty fourteen days ago, when and where did Pholus brew his beer? It takes four weeks or so for the mixture to ferment. He'd have to ask Pholus when he got back to Bovesia.

Before Alerio could say anything else, Helicaon's goat came from around the animal pen chewing on a short branch.

"The water is receding," exclaimed Helicaon.

The Spartan hadn't moved. And from the cook site, neither man could see the river or the valley below the ledge.

"How do you know?" Alerio inquired.

"She's chewing a sprig of mint," explained Helicaon while pointing to the goat. "It grows in the valley so the water level must be dropping."

"Does that mean I can get to Passomasseria?" Alerio inquired.

"Why is it you are so set on getting to Passomasseria?" replied the Spartan.

"I've got a Tribune who wants to know if the citizens are loyal to the Republic," explained Alerio. "Or, if they've seen any strangers in the area."

"I was in Passomasseria last week. I needed a pouch of salt. The goat found my old one and chewed the leather and ate the salt," Helicaon said as he reached out and patted the goat's side. "So, I hiked up and spent the night. If there was any treason or disloyalty to the Republic, it would have come up in conversation. As for newcomers you, Lance Corporal Sisera, are the only one to have seen three squads of Syracusan Raiders in the vicinity. That sounds like strangers to me."

Alerio stopped chewing and let the bread hang suspended between his fingers. Reporting the squads to Bovesia's Centurion was far more important than checking on the citizens at Passomasseria. He had been focused on his mission and missed the ramifications of an enemy force behind the Legion Garrison. The Legionaries were capable of defeating the Raiders unless…

"Helicaon. I've got to get to Bovesia and notify the garrison," Alerio exclaimed.

"We can't go anywhere until the sun comes up and we get a look at the river," Helicaon replied. "Finish your bread and at sunrise, we'll go and see."

Chapter 44 – The Raging River

Alerio could tell why the Spartan wanted to wait for daylight. The path down to the valley was more fit for a goat than two humans. Even Helicaon, who was familiar with the trail, turned and walked backwards down a few of the steep and twisting sections.

At the bottom of the granite wall, they stood on top of a hill. Deeper in, the valley rose gently on either side of a rushing stream. Unlike the hill where they stood, the ground was green with grass and dotted with olive and lemon trees.

"On the other side of the trees is my garden," explained Helicaon. "The flood waters never get much higher than this mound."

Without another word, he led Alerio down to a path between their hill and another. As they walked, the roar of the river reached them. Alerio noted the fresh gravel, sand, and dirt under their feet.

"Yesterday, this was under water," explained Helicaon. "You wouldn't want to have been here."

"Or, out there," Alerio said as the river came into view. A shiver ran through his body as he recalled his struggles in the flood waters.

The river was flowing along the high banks, leaving a strip of land between the river and the curve of the cliff where it left the valley. Helicaon marched along the damp ground until they came to a crop of trees nestled in a crevasse.

Suspended behind the tree trunks, and up under the branches, was a small boat. Its leather sides crinkled from being in the river and drying afterward. Alerio could see the leather hull was coated with oil to preserve the exterior of the skin.

"What kind of oil?" asked Alerio as he and the Spartan approached the boat.

"Fish oil," Helicaon replied. He reached overhead and slapped the taut leather. "It's plentiful and a side benefit from catching my own food. Press out the oil and eat the rest, just like you do with olives."

Alerio studied the lines above the boat. He could see how one man could pull the boat out of the river, up the bank, and around the trees before pulling it out of sight and above the flood waters.

"Can it carry two and my pack?" asked Alerio.

"She can but not until the waters calm," Helicaon informed him. "It'll be tomorrow before we can paddle to Bovesia."

"What do we do in the meanwhile?" Alerio questioned.

"Help me harvest food from my garden," Helicaon replied. "After a heavy rain…"

Alerio interrupted, "A lot of the crops will be beat down. If we don't pick the vegetables, they'll rot in the mud. My family owns a farm. My father taught me farming."

"Excellent. Maybe you can show me a few farming techniques," suggested Helicaon. "Because my family also owned a farm. But, my father didn't teach me about farming. He instructed me in the use of a shield and a spear."

Act 7

Chapter 45 – Bovesia Garrison

Tesserarius Cephas stretched his arms over his head in the predawn. It was quiet and he relished the stillness. The rain, from the day before yesterday, had passed and the sky was cleared. For a moment, he enjoyed the stars in the night sky. Over the last three weeks, he'd been busy standing in as Officer of the Guard, writing reports, replying to one of the many requests from Southern Legion, setting the Legionaries daily assignments, and making sure the Centurion was satisfied with his work.

A blush of pink appeared over the eastern mountain.

"Second Century. Lance Corporals, get them on the road," he called out. The peace of the morning was broken. "You are wasting my day. And you know what I hate?"

From the seven tents, voices called back, "Waste."

Cephas smiled at the reply.

The ground had mostly dried, so he'd keep the physical training simple. For his own good, the Corporal ran with the infantrymen. After enough laps to equal ten miles, he called the squads to a halt.

"The rain held up the transports so today is going to be busy," he warned. "I want those on patrol to look lively. If you're on a post, stand straight. If you have no assignment, we have garrison repairs. I want every citizen who sees a

Legionary to know that if the pirates return, they are going to get chewed up and spit back into the ocean. Decani, on me. Century dismissed."

The Legionaries broke ranks and headed in different directions. Only six Lance Corporals converged on their NCO. The seventh and last squad leader was walking the guard posts as Sergeant of the Guard.

"I'm not jesting. The citizens need to know their Legion will protect them," Cephas informed his squad leaders. "We were attacked and the town is wondering if Bovesia is safe. They are wondering if we are capable of repelling another attack. Well, when they see a Legionary, I want them to be awed by the man's military bearing and his confidence. If I am not awed by every one of your infantrymen, I will replace their squad leader and the punishment will put the slacker in medical. Do you understand?"

"Yes, Corporal," the six squad leaders replied.

Second Century's Centurion strolled out from the command building. As he approached the group, all of the NCOs turned to face their officer.

"Good morning, Centurion Laurens," Cephas said as he saluted. "Any orders?"

"Illyrian pirates have been ravishing the coast for years," Laurens offered. "The only thing stopping them from taking over a seaport, like the Sons of Mars did to Messina, is the Legion. This is the first time in recent memory they were bold enough to attack a major garrison. If they did it once,

211

they may do it again. Keep your men on their toes. Dismissed."

As the squad leaders walked away, Laurens held up a hand to stop Cephas.

"Corporal. I didn't want to worry the men. But you should know," the Centurion said. "Reports from Rhegium state that Qart Hadasht may be behind the Illyrians' aggressive posture. They didn't say what the Empire is after but I can guess. They want Bovesia. From here, they'll control the south entrance to the Messina Straits, all shipping for fifty miles up the coast, and transports from the west. It's a valuable piece of real-estate for the Empire. And, Corporal..."

"Sir?" asked Cephas.

"They can't have it," Laurens stated.

"No, sir. We'll be ready for them," Cephas assured the infantry officer.

"I'm counting on you," the Centurion said. "I'd like to have our Optio and three more squads of Legionaries, but I don't. Luckily for the Republic, and me, I have you. Dismissed."

Cephas saluted, spun on his heels and marched away. The last three weeks had been a grind. Not only was he balancing the Century's books and the Republic's fees, he was the Century's acting Optio. He'd been feeling the pressure until the words from the Centurion. Now, he had a spring in his step, and he mumbled. "Bring on the Illyrian pirates."

Then he remembered the fighting last week and how his command had nearly been overrun. He deflated a little and prayed to Clementia for mercy from his utterance.

Unfortunately for the overworked Tesserarius, Mendacius heard his prayer. The God of trickery responded by twisting the plea to Clementia for mercy.

From the watch tower, the trumpet blared and everyone in Bovesia froze in place and listened.

Chapter 46 – Any Less Would Be Insulting

From high overhead, the Legionary on the trumpet let out two long blasts. A merchant ship was inbound. The town relaxed. Then, the horn sounded three long notes. No one panicked. One foreign warship posed no threat for the Legion garrison. When the trumpet followed the foreign warship warning with two more three-note announcements, merchants closed up shops, citizens gathered valuables, and everyone crowded the steps. Soon the plaza on Bovesia's third level resembled a street carnival; without the festive attitude.

The inbound merchant ship, under full sail, didn't slow. She rammed the beach and the squad of Legionaries on the lower level heard the keel snap. Her passengers were tossed forward and one sailor flew over the bow and crashed on the gravel of the shoreline. Ramps dropped and four large men carrying a huge chest rushed to the beach. Hastily following them, a swarthy man in an ornate robe scurried off the ship. Next off came a man in billowing pants. He had to look around a stack of scrolls, cradled in his arms, to navigate the ramp.

"I will see the man in charge," the robed dignitary demanded in a broken accent.

The squad leader selected a Legionary to guide the foreign party. As they started up the steps, the merchant ship's crew strolled down the ramps. After walking around their broken boat, they too took the steps to the upper level.

***

"What have we got, Tesserarius?" Centurion Laurens asked as he rushed from between buildings.

"They look Egyptian, at least their clothing is, sir," Cephas replied. "And three warships. You can just see the tops of their sails on the horizon."

"They seem to be converging from three directions," Laurens observed. "There's only one reason for that and it's not good."

"No, sir. It's not good," replied Cephas. "They were herding the merchant ship to Bovesia."

In short order, the warships rowed close enough to be recognizable as Illyrian biremes. The garrison of eighty-six Legionaries, of which seventy were heavy infantry, one a Tesserarius, and another a Centurion watched as the ships drew near the beach. On those ships were roughly three hundred and sixty rowers, plus an unknown number of archers and warriors from the Kingdom of Illyria.

"I'd guess four hundred," offered Centurion Laurens.

"Give or take a few squads," Cephas said then added. "Any less and it would be insulting."

The Centurion glanced over at his Corporal before shifting his gaze back to the three warships.

"Sir, I have to check our placements at the choke points," Cephas described.

"Of course. I'll wait here and speak with our guests," Laurens said while pointing down at the entourage climbing the steps. "And Corporal, you are correct about the pirates. Any less would be insulting."

"Yes, sir," Cephas said. He saluted before marching away.

Chapter 47 – Defensive Lines

Tesserarius Cephas placed one squad of his heavy infantry on the steps at the second level. With two lines of shields, they would hold the choke point. On the building roofs on either side, he placed two squads. If the pirates attempted to climb onto the roofs again, they would meet more than a handful of defenders. After placing another squad in reserve, he sent the seventh back to patrol the garrison grounds. With the garrison set on a high hill and a single goat trail on the north end being the only access, a squad of heavy infantrymen was about the correct level of security. Plus, he would rotate them with one from the plaza defenses later.

Luckily, he had a senior and a junior medic. They selected a covered porch at the rear of the plaza and commandeered it as the medical triage zone. After selecting two stretcher bearers from the boatmen, Cephas sent the support personnel back to man posts at the garrison. They would maintain the guard if the roving squad was required to defend the town.

While the Tesserarius organized the infantry, Centurion Laurens greeted the visitors from the wrecked merchant vessel. After a few words and polite curtsies, he escorted the robed man and his party to the Columnae Herculis.

'Let the officer play diplomat,' thought Tesserarius Cephas as he reexamined his defensive formations.

***

Fortunately, the pirates settled for landing and camping on the beach. The three ships' Captains erected tents in front of their warships while their crews crowded around campfires close to the tents. The only exception was the Illyrian infantrymen. Each ship carried a squad and these thirty men set up their own camp on the beach at the bottom of the steps.

For half the day, Cephas strolled from squad to squad as if he didn't have a care in the world. After checking to be sure the men ate and drank, he would say a few encouraging words before moving to the next squad. Specifically, he repeated an opinion about the pirates: Most were rowers and not professional soldiers. They couldn't possibly defeat the heavy infantry of the Legion. After the motivational talk, he moved to the next squad. His tour found him standing on the stairs talking with the men posted at the narrow point when a trumpet blast. It sent shivers down everyone's spine.

The tower signaled the arrival of another warship. Soon after the trumpet fell silent, the sails of a fourth pirate bireme appeared on the horizon.

Cephas climbed to the plaza level and marched onto the rooftop of a second level building. All of the Tesserarius' inspirational words crumbled as the warship backed onto the beach. Rather than set campfires, the one hundred and twenty rowers followed the squad of Illyrian soldiers down the beach to the bottom of the step.

***

Although the Corporal couldn't hear the words, the pirate's actions were recognizable. A big man stood on the beach while a team put up a pavilion larger than the tents of the other three ships' captains.

Cephas knew he was important, not only from the size of his tent but from the actions of the three Illyrian captains. They marched from their areas directly to the important man.

When the four were standing together, the leader began pointing and shaking his finger at the Legionaries manning the steps. The other three shook their heads in response and shrugged as if to say no, or not me, or more likely, not my crew.

Cephas glanced around for his Centurion. Other than the few times the officer came out to check on the Century's positioning, he was in a conference with the visitors from the merchant ship. Now with over five hundred combatants clustered on the beach, the Corporal needed the weight of an infantry officer to help calm the Legionaries. Plus, he wanted a second opinion on the argument he'd just witnessed.

Chapter 48 – Under Water and Under Cover

Helicaon sat in the back of the leather boat and guided it through the waves. The river was still torrid, and Alerio felt every jerk, rise, and fall as the Spartan guided the small boat down the fast-flowing river.

"How far to Bovesia?" Alerio asked as he turned his head to look at the Spartan.

"Not long in this soup," replied Helicaon. "It'll calm down where the river widens."

***

They bounced and swayed until the cliffs below the garrison came into view. Then, as if they navigated a different river, the current slowed. Where mudflats had been before the flood, now the far edge of the water stretched almost to the fishing village. Farther in the distance, where the Kaikinos joined the Ionian, the normally gentle flow was a churning and rolling mass of fresh water tumbling into the salty sea.

Helicaon guided the boat to the pier and Alerio stepped from the boat directly onto the wood of the dock.

"Hold the boat," ordered Helicaon as he reached out a hand to hold the craft steady.

Once Alerio had a firm grip, the old Spartan joined him on the platform. Together, they lifted the leather boat and placed it on the pier.

"Where are the patrol boats?" Alerio wondered out loud.

"Probably on Bova Beach," offered Helicaon. "They're too big to easily hoist out of the flood water."

Alerio slung his pack over his shoulder and along with Helicaon, they started up the ramps.

"Gladius instructor," one of the boat handlers at the top greeted him. "If I were you, I'd get back in the boat and paddle away."

"Why? Is it your night to cook?" Alerio teased back.

"No, Lance Corporal. It's the ten thousand Illyrians on the beach," the Private dropped his voice to stress his point. "They're everywhere."

Alerio glanced over the Legionary's shoulder and scanned the Legion Garrison. A roving patrol walked casually along the perimeter and men stood post at guard positions. That looked normal, but, a second glance revealed no other personnel in the camp.

After pulling his dual rig from the pack, Alerio tossed the bag to the ground.

"Keep an eye on that for me," he said as his arms slid into the rig.

Once the two gladii hilts settled on his upper back, Alerio sprinted for Bovesia. In his mind, he envisioned a battle with pirates flowing over the rooftops and up the stairs with a thin rank of infantrymen on the plaza fighting to hold back the pirates. He hit the path and made short work of the incline. He didn't break stride until he reached the back of the buildings. No sounds of gladii clashing or the screams of dying men carried from the plaza. At the mouth of the alleyway, he stopped.

A few infantrymen stood sentry on the rooftops and on the stairs, while their squad mates lay napping, or squatting around cooking pots. On either end of the plaza, citizens and merchants sat in groups talking excitedly. There was no carnage.

Alerio strolled to the center of the plaza searching for Centurion Laurens. He didn't see the officer, but he did spot Corporal Cephas. The Tesserarius stood staring down at Bova Beach. Turning to the shops, Alerio peered at the groups of civilians still looking for the Century's officer.

Hyllus stood on the porch of the Columnae Herculis. When he spotted Alerio, the big Athenian waved in greeting. Each table on the diner's porch was full of people leisurely drinking vino. The Centurion wasn't among them. Alerio did recognize one familiar face.

Pholus, the vendor of excellent beer, sat at the last table with a seat facing the plaza. He lifted his clay mug in salute. Alerio nodded at the vendor, spun, and walked to the other side of the plaza. There, he continued his search for the infantry officer.

When Alerio reached the end of the level and his patience, he decided to speak with the Corporal and let him pass along the report to the officer. As he turned, he noticed Pholus sauntering towards the Legionary sentries.

It was the first time he's seen Pholus walk any distance. The beer vendor didn't stroll, he marched, and the strap marks on his lower legs, the type made by wearing military boots, were more pronounced in the afternoon light.

Pholus peered between two legion shields. After violently shaking his head at what he saw on Bova Beach, the vendor turned slowly and tilted his face upward. At first, Alerio thought the man was checking the weather. But, Pholus didn't search the sky for thunderheads. He seemed more focused on the watch tower.

"Corporal Cephas. A word," called out Centurion Laurens as he emerged from the Columnae Herculis. He left the porch of the restaurant and started across the plaza.

The Tesserarius turned and took two steps towards his commander. Suddenly, Pholus ran at the Legion officer. Cephas shouted a warning but the officer was slow to react. Before he recognized the danger, Pholus arrived at the Centurion's side holding a knife.

Twice, the long blade of the sica pierced the Centurion's abdomen. On the third thrust, Pholus left the hilt protruding from the bleeding wound. Vital organs deep inside Laurens shutdown from the trauma and the Centurion died before Pholus reached the sentries on the roof.

He shoved aside the shields, made it to the edge of the roof, then paused to look down to judge the distance.

"Sergeant Pholus," cried out Alerio.

The vendor slowly lifted his head and turned towards Lance Corporal Sisera. A smile came to his face. He slammed a fist into his chest in a salute before leaping out of sight. The next view of Sergeant Pholus of the Syracusan Raiders was him skipping down the stairs to the lowest plaza.

"A beer vendor. What a great cover for a Syracuse Raider NCO renowned for his beer," Alerio chastised himself while sprinting to join Cephas. "I should have put it together."

Centurion Laurens was rolled onto a stretcher and the bearers carried him to the medical area. The senior medic frowned at Cephas as he scooped the Centurion's helmet from the pavers.

"Like it or not Corporal, you are now the acting Centurion," the medic stated as he brushed the dirt off the horsehair comb that ran across the top of the helmet. He offered the helmet to Cephas and added. "May Mars help us. But, most of all, may the God of war help you."

With those words reverberating in Cephas' ears, the medic went to check on the infantrymen. Cephas stood gripping the officer's helmet between his hands. Alerio waited until the medic was out of hearing range before whispering.

"Commander. Are there really ten thousand pirates on the beach?" Alerio asked.

"Not near that many. Only about five hundred and twenty-five," Cephas assured him. Then he stopped and asked in puzzlement. "Commander?"

"Garrison Commander. We can't have a Tesserarius running a battle," explained Alerio. "Congratulations on your promotion."

"No matter how short lived," Cephas mumbled. Then, he perked up and looked around to see who could have heard his comment. Seeing no one except Lance Corporal Sisera, he asked. "How was your trip to Passomasseria? Did you learn anything."

"Pholus is a Sergeant in the Syracuse army. He has three squads stashed in the hills north of here," stated Alerio by pointing to the Captains on the beach. "You've got an enemy force to your rear. And speaking of Pholus, he noticed something on the beach that got him upset. Then he eyeballed the tower before stabbing Centurion Laurens. Any idea of what caused his reaction?"

"Maybe it was the inaction of the pirates," Cephas offered. He began to walk away with the Centurion's helmet tucked under his arm.

"Commander. If you please," Alerio suggested while pointing at Cephas' Legion helmet. "The men need to know who is in charge. If they sense weakness in their command structure, you'll have a mutiny on your hands. Besides, you'll need to fill in your chain of command and the helmet will identify you to the infantrymen and the civilians."

Cephas reached up and hooked a thumb under the brim of his Legion helmet. After peeling it off, he replaced it with the Centurion's head gear.

"Squad leaders. On me," he called out before turning to Alerio. "Where do you fit into my chain of command, Lance Corporal Sisera?"

"I don't really know your men or the Decani, so make me a Tribune," suggested Alerio.

"Are you that useless?" inquired Cephas.

By then, six confused Lance Corporals had arrived.

"Commander Cephas. Permission to inspect the garrison perimeter, sir?" Alerio asked.

"Granted," Cephas said realizing Alerio had announced his title and new responsibilities to the squad leaders.

"Thank you, sir," Alerio said while rendering a cross chest salute.

Cephas returned the salute and before he could open his mouth, First Squad's Lance Corporal asked a question.

"Commander Cephas. What's the plan, sir?" the Decanus inquired.

All the Legionaries present witnessed the salute, and those nearby heard the squad leader's use of the title. As if

Averruncus' hand had passed over the plaza, the tension at witnessing the death of their infantry officer faded. Although Illyrian pirates still threatened to attack; the God who prevents calamity along with the installation of Cephas as the Garrison Commander averted a disaster. The Legion the infantrymen had a new leader. One they trusted.

Chapter 49 – False Assault

Alerio jogged to the roving squad in the garrison and called to their squad leader.

"We have an enemy force of thirty Syracuse soldiers to our north," he said pointing to the far-off hilltops.

"We always keep watch on the goat trail and the paths leading to the base of the hill," the Decanus assured him. "We haven't seen any sign of movement in the trees or around the farms."

Alerio glanced back at Bovesia. From here, no sound, other than the trumpet high up in the tower could reach the far end of the garrison. Certainly, no signal from the beach could be seen either. A messenger could go from the beach to the hills in the west. But it would require circling a swamp, and climbing hills far to the west before trekking back to a point north of the garrison.

"If they join the Illyrians on the beach, it's just more warriors against our main body," Alerio considered. "But, if they come at our backdoor and in the dark climb the hill, they will be a problem. Alert the other sentries."

"We always share intelligence, gladius instructor," the squad leader assured him.

Alerio agreed with sharing information. He informed them of the Centurion's death and the elevation of Cephas to Garrison Commander.

"Are there really ten thousand pirates on the beach?" a Private asked.

"Commander Cephas says it's more like five hundred and twenty-five," Alerio replied.

"Is that a lot?" a very young Legionary inquired.

"Anything less and it would be insulting," his squad leader answered. "Fall in. We've got rounds, and we're wasting daylight."

As Alerio jogged back to Bovesia, he reflected on his fear that Corporal Cephas wouldn't be accepted by the Century as the officer in charge. It was groundless. The Century already respected the Tesserarius' leadership style.

Alerio reached the plaza to find Commander Cephas deep in conversation with Hyllus and Helicaon.

"You've no room for foot work for your infantrymen on those steps," Helicaon the Spartan pointed out.

"I know Hyllus speaks highly of you, old man," Cephas said. "But I don't have the manpower to start a construction project."

"Hyllus and I will start it," Helicaon volunteered. "We'll need a few men for the installation."

"Fine. Get it to where I can see the value and I'll give you the labor," Cephas agreed. He acted as if he was beat down from arguing with the Athenian and the Spartan.

"What's with them, Commander?" Alerio asked as he fell in beside Cephas.

"I never realized that being an officer meant that everybody and their brother came at you with big ideas," admitted Cephas. "And, like a magistrate, you have to waste time weighing and judging the merits of each."

They arrived at the edge of the roof. From the vantage point, they looked down on the two lower plazas and Bova Beach. Standing at the large pavilion were the three Illyrian Captains. They faced another Captain and the Illyrian Sergeant. Pholus stood shoulder to shoulder with the large Captain, as if they stood against the other three.

"That's why I think Pholus acted," Cephas offered. "The pirates have been here all day without advancing. I think they are…"

Cephas stopped talking when he noticed Alerio shaking and staring daggers at the group on the beach.

"Lance Corporal Sisera. You seem as if you're staring into the mouth of Hades," offered Cephas.

"Oh, excuse me, Commander. In a way I am," Alerio exclaimed. "The big man next to Sergeant Pholus is Martinus Cetea, Navarch of the Illyrian Navy."

"That explains who ordered four warships to attack here," Cephas suggested. "But it doesn't explain why. It's something beyond the value of treasure from the merchant ship."

"Merchant ship?" questioned Alerio.

"While you were upriver, an Egyptian merchant was herded here," Cephas explained. "It's odd. They could have boarded her at sea and taken the treasure. It's almost as if they wanted the merchant's cargo here. But, I can't figure out why."

"Someone planned this operation," Alerio remarked. "The Syracusan Raiders were inserted weeks ago. This is the second time Martinus Cetea has attacked the Republic. He sailed into Occhio village and captured a treasure and an Egyptian in a gaudy robe from another merchant ship. There can't be enough gold and jewels in one chest to make those ventures profitable."

They were interrupted by several blasts from a trumpet on the beach. In response to the signal, the Illyrian soldiers picked up their shields and shuffled into ranks at the bottom of the stairs.

"Standby," Cephas shouted.

"Standing by, Commander," came the response for the Legionaries on the third level.

As the Illyrian soldiers moved into position, Cephas pointed at the beach.

"They don't seem pleased," he said as the three Captains stomped away from Navarch Martinus Cetea and Sergeant Pholus.

Their shoulders were slumped, their feet pounded the sand, and their chins were tucked into their chests; obvious postures of unhappy men.

"Attacking a prepared Legion Century isn't their usual fare," ventured Alerio. "Don't pirates favor soft targets like undefended merchant ships?"

"True. So, who wants this fight?" asked Cephas. He stepped behind the double line of shields. "Lance Corporal Sisera. Grab a shield and a javelin from the medical area. We've stacked extra gear there. Back up Third Squad on the stairs. I've pulled their squad leader and made him my Optio. Procopius, his Right-Pivot, is a good man, but it's his first time in command."

"Yes, sir," Alerio said.

Lance Corporal Sisera was frustrated at not having time to go to his quarters to collect his armor. But Illyrian soldiers were already marching up the steps. The few arrows sent down by the Legionaries impacted uselessly against their shields.

***

After grabbing a helmet, a shield, and three javelins, Alerio jogged down the staircase and joined Third Squad on the steps. On either side, the buildings created close-in walls that bracketed the infantrymen.

"What are you doing here, gladius instructor?" Procopius, the temporary squad leader, questioned. "Don't think we know how to hold a shield wall?"

"I'm sick of teaching," confessed Alerio as he leaned back against the side of a building. "I asked Commander Cephas where he put his sheep, and where he put his wolves?"

"And what did he say?" another infantryman asked.

"He said you can stand on a roof and repel pirates," Alerio replied. "Or, you can join my best on the stairs. Then he warned me..."

Heartbeats ticked by. When it appeared Lance Corporal Sisera wouldn't finish his thoughts, someone asked, "Warned you of what?"

"That if you fight your way into Hades with my wolves," Alerio replied. "You better have the cōleī and the skills not to slow them down."

The nine men around Alerio straightened their backs.

"Third Squad, Second Century, standby," Procopius shouted.

"Standing by, Decanus," Alerio and the infantrymen responded to the acting squad leader.

"Wolves?" another Legionary asked.

"That's what Commander Cephas said," Alerio replied.

"Third Squad, brace," Procopius shouted.

To Third Squad on the stairs, in the space between the buildings, where the walls created a canyon, the plaza to their front disappeared. The iron shields, helmets, and spears of Illyrian soldiers replaced the view of clay pavers and shops.

The attackers slammed into the Legion shields. They were stopped as if they ran into a granite wall. Spear and javelin shafts poked back and forth between the lines. Men screamed, urinated themselves, released watery merda and dropped, either dead or injured.

A spear jutted under a shield and a Legionary's ankle shattered. As he collapsed from pain and loss of support, he was pulled back off the front line. Another Legionary stepped forward to seal the breach.

Alerio help throw the injured man to the stairs behind the second rank. While stretcher bearers climbed down to pull him out of the canyon, the battle continued.

Frustrated by the necessity to hold the stairs and not advance, Alerio retrieved a second javelin. He began to growl as he thrust both weapons at the shields facing the first rank. Suddenly, the remaining eight Legionaries defending the stairs picked up the animal sound. No longer screaming or cursing, Third Squad reached into their guts and uttered piercing howls. Along with the sound, they gelled into a unified killing machine.

From unaligned strikes, they began to deliver blows in unison. Almost as if controlled by a single mind, the infantrymen on the stairs hammered the Illyrians. Unable to withstand the cohesion of the javelin thrusts, the soldiers of Illyria made a fatal mistake. They stepped back half-a-step.

"Front rank, draw," shouted the inexperienced squad leader.

Five javelins fell to the ground and five gladii snapped from the Legionaries' sheathes.

"Advance and step back," he ordered.

The front rank of Third Squad shoved with their shields, and for the first time since the assault started, they took the fight to the enemy. Five gladii found room between Illyrian shields and five soldiers dropped to the pavers. While they fell, the five Legionaries stepped back between the building walls. As they sheathed their gladii, javelins were handed to them and Third Squad reset preparing for another assault. The attack never came.

The Illyrians grabbed their dead and wounded and retreated down the steps on the far side of the plaza. When the last shield vanished below the top riser, Alerio looked around to see smiling faces under the helmets.

"Wolves in Hades," he announced.

Third Squad responded with howls.

"Lance Corporal Sisera. If you are finished entertaining Third Squad," Cephas said from plaza level at the top of the stairs. "I'd like a word."

Alerio winked at the blood splattered infantrymen and slapped Procopius' shoulder.

"I've got to go. Third Squad, it's been a pleasure," Alerio said as he started up the steps. Then he paused and turned to face the temporary squad leader. "Procopius, for a jumped up Right-Pivot, that was a gutsy move calling for an advance. You should know, you can be my squad leader any day."

Procopius nodded in recognition of the compliment. The six healthy infantrymen of Third Squad roared their confidence in the temporary squad leader. Procopius answered them with a growl.

***

At the top of the stairs, Alerio joined Cephas as they both gazed up at the burning watch tower. Flames leaped from the wooden platform while smoke rose high into the air.

"Would you call that a signal to the Raiders?" questioned Alerio.

"The whole attack was a farce," Cephas explained. "Their soldiers focused on the stairs. It was an attempted break through but not the purpose of the attack. Behind the soldiers and a few pirates, their archers loaded up arrows with flaming pitch and targeted the tower. So, yes, it's a sign to the Raiders."

"You said only a few pirates, sir?" asked Alerio.

Someone handed him a ladle of water. After rinsing out his mouth, Alerio took a drink before pouring the rest over his head. As the water dripped off him, it ran red. Alerio spit into the bloody water on the pavers before looking at Cephas.

"They have over five hundred pirates on that beach," Cephas responded. "Yet, only about a hundred accompanied the soldiers."

"Let me guess, Commander. Most of the pirates came from Martinus Cetea's ship," ventured Alerio.

"All right, what are you getting at?" inquired Cephas.

"I don't think those three Illyrian Captains want to be here or in this battle," Alerio suggested. "They aren't committed. The only two that seem to want this are Martinus Cetea and Pholus.

Lance Corporal Sisera's eyes closed and he inhaled deeply. Thinking he was exhausted from the fight on the stairs, the Garrison Commander started to excuse him.

"Give me five men and I'll remove the Navarch," Alerio stated.

"There's no way I can spare a single Legionary," Cephas declared. "I've got to protect Bovesia and guard the garrison."

"You know Commander, you've been in charge for less than half a day," teased Alerio. "And you already sound like an officer."

"It's making decisions that affect the future of too many people," admitted Cephas. "It makes you over think everything."

"You told me earlier that the reason for the garrison was to protect the town and to keep the beach safe," Alerio reminded him. "Now, you have a force moving in from your rear and a larger force to your front. Why protect the garrison when you have limited resources?"

"You are suggesting, I desert the garrison, and consolidate my forces in defending Bovesia?" Cephas exclaimed. Before Alerio could say anything, the Commander held up his hand for silence while he thought. After a long pause, Cephas nodded and asked. "What do you need to cut the head off the Illyrian snake?"

"Private Lupus couldn't have said it better himself," replied Alerio.

Chapter 50 – The Difference Between Mad and Daring

The sun dipped low and as it faded below the mountains to the west, a column of Legionaries marched from Bovesia, trekked the hill to the garrison, and then, loaded down with supplies, reentered the town. Other than those on watch at the north end of the garrison, and a few on the rooftops and stairs, everyone else hauled, toted, or pulled equipment.

After his fourth trip, Alerio went looking for Helicaon. He found the Spartan hammering a chisel through the end of a log. Two others lay nearby, already notched.

"Building a Spartan training pit?" Alerio asked as he sat on one of the logs.

"No, Lance Corporal Sisera. I'm building a stand," the old man said as he tapped out a slice of wood creating another notch.

"For where? I don't think the Commander will start rebuilding the watch tower just yet," ventured Alerio.

"When you fight on uneven surfaces, you're limited in your footwork," the Spartan explained. "Grab a couple of logs and follow me."

They had to squeeze by the squad guarding the stairs but once on the last step, Helicaon lay down his log. He picked up a stick squared on the sides, and fit the stick into the notch on the log. After another square stick was placed in the notch on the other end, he and Alerio picked up the log.

The log fit snugly between the walls with the sticks resting on the step two tiers higher. When they fitted two more logs on top of the first, the stack created a short wall between the steps and the second level plaza.

Commander Cephas arrived and after consulting with the Spartan, he directed men to fetch dirt and begin filling in the space behind the short wall. Soon, there was a flat surface from the top of the log wall back to the height of the third step.

"Now you have a fighting platform," Helicaon announced. "When the Illyrians come back, you'll be fighting down at them and they'll be straining to reach up and fight you."

"I'm surprised you went for it, Commander," Alerio observed as Helicaon directed the dumping and compacting of the dirt.

"Lance Corporal. If you ever have a command, I hope you remember this," offered Cephas. "Out of all the bad ideas offered, one will save the lives of your men. Hopefully, you will recognize which one. Speaking of bad ideas, how is your plan shaping up?"

"Just waiting for it to get darker, sir," Alerio said. "Lupus assures me he can hunt in the dark. Helicaon has volunteered to row. And I found four archers who are good swimmers. How about my diversion?"

"It's odd. I told the squads about your mad idea. After talking to them, except those defending the stairs, and Third Squad, who I excused," Cephas said. "They all volunteered. Then, Third Squad growled at me and demanded to spearhead the diversion. They mumbled something about wolves in Hades. Any idea what that's about?"

"Not a clue, Commander," replied Alerio.

***

Lance Corporal Sisera climbed the stairs and crossed the plaza. At the alleyway, he found Lupus squatting against the wall.

"We'll find out who has the gift tonight," the Private said. He raised his face in the lantern light. His teeth and eyes reflected the light making him seem to be made of glowing eyes and sparkling teeth.

Before Alerio could respond, four men came out of the darkness. They rattled, not from their armor. They wore none. Rather, they rattled from the bundles of arrows slung around their necks.

"Lance Corporal. When do we leave?" one asked. "Because, if we're going to the Fields of Elysian tonight, we'd like to have a hot meal and a mug of vino first."

"Make it two mugs," advise Alerio. "The water will be cold."

The four walked away in the direction of the closest pub. After they left, Alerio looked around for something to do. Although it was dark in the shadows, the sky still held the last vestiges of daylight.

Alerio sat down next to Lupus and rested his head on his knees.

"When I was a lad, three bullies beat and robbed me almost every day," he said. "I got lucky and learned the gladius. If it hadn't been for them, I might still be on my father's farm. This time of year, we make cider and butcher hogs."

"Feeling melancholy and homesick?" asked Lupus. "Missing the ole hearth and home?"

"No, Private. There is no place I'd rather be than here," Alerio replied. "Because the farmers at Occhio aren't having a good year. And I plan on butchering the hog who ruined it for them."

***

A long time later, as full darkness closed in around Bovesia, Helicaon came out of the darkness. Spying Lupus and Alerio, he squatted down in front of them, pulled out a comb, and began running it through his hair.

"Nervous old man?" Lupus asked.

"Not since I was eighteen years old and stood in my first shield wall," Helicaon declared. "It's when I learned to depend on the men on either side of me. I feared for their safety. I fought hard so they would live. Me. I was too busy fighting a naked brute with bad breath, and worst body odor. But I did learn one thing."

"What's that?" asked Lupus.

"Well, it was raining and cold but my savage didn't seem to feel it," Helicaon explained. "At first I thought he was drunk on beer or wine. But as we fought, I noticed the water beading on his flesh. When the battle line passed us, I was alone with him. It was the last time I was afraid. After I killed him, I moved up with my messmates. When the battle ended, I went back and checked the brute's pouches."

"What did you find?" Lupus said.

Helicaon put away his comb, reached into a big pouch, and drew out a large wrapped mass. He tossed it to Alerio.

"What is it?" Lance Corporal Sisera asked as he peeled open the goat skin wrap. After sniffing, he jerked his head back and coughed. "That's foul."

"It's bear fat and pine tar," Helicaon stated. "Waterproofs your skin and helps keep you warm."

"Repels friends and foe alike, I'd venture to say," Alerio observed. "Does it work?"

"In that battle, the rain was mixed with sleet and snow," Helicaon said. "And we were fighting on a frozen lake. What do you think?"

"Think about what?" an archer asked.

He and the other three came into the lantern light.

"I'll show you at the dock," Alerio informed them as he stood.

***

It took the infantrymen guarding the alleyway a while to move the upended cart and pull back the boxes to open the barricade. Once Alerio and his six-man detail were through, the obstacles were restacked.

The detail marched down the path and across the ground to the top of the cliff. Taking the ramp slowly in the dark, they descended to the pier.

"That's a tiny boat," Lupus whispered as he felt the leather of the craft. "Are you sure it'll carry us?"

"If you don't want to ride," one of the archers offered. "I'll trade places with you."

While the two talked, Helicaon tied a long hemp rope to the frame of his boat. After securing it, he began measuring out lengths and tying loops. After each loop, he measured another section and tied another loop. When he reached five, he handed the last coil to Alerio.

Alerio stripped off his woolen clothing, bundled them up, and tossed them into the small boat. With the loop hung over his arm, he produced the ball of bear grease and pine tar. With a swipe of his hand across the mixture, he began to rub it on his skin.

"That stinks, Lance Corporal," one of the archers observed. "But if it'll keep me warm, I'll take some."

As Alerio and the archers smeared their bodies with the grease, Lupus and Helicaon hoisted the boat and set it in the water. They climbed in and Alerio and the naked archers sat on the edge of the pier gripping the coils.

"Kick but don't swim with your arm," warned Helicaon. "When we get to the other side, get out of the water, and rub your limbs to keep warm. Once we're out to sea, it'll warm up a little."

"What's a little?" an already shivering archer questioned.

"Not enough to notice because by then, you'll be too cold," the old Spartan advised.

"Go," Alerio ordered as he slid off the dock and into the cold river.

Lupus and Helicaon began digging in with their paddles. The operation depended on crossing the river quickly. If the swimmers were in the icy mountain runoff for too long, they would drown. Or, become so cold as to be useless for their part of the mission. So, the paddlers matched powerful strokes and the line tightened and soon they were dragging five kicking and shocked Legionaries behind the small leather boat.

Chapter 51 - Angitia's Beauties

Alerio shivered and rubbed his arms and legs. In the distance, he could see fires at the fishermen's huts. The draw was unmistakable. He had to fight the urge to run naked through the brush and throw himself on the warmth of the fire.

"Think warm," suggested Helicaon. "When I was a boy in training, we were taken to the highlands in the winter. Twice a day, we bathed in the mountain streams. The only thing that worked was thinking warm thoughts."

"I'm thinking warm all right," one archer declared. "I'm thinking about killing you all and burning your bodies."

"Anger works as well," added Helicaon. "But the heat of passion burns out fast and leaves you colder."

A breaking of branches announced Lupus' return.

"Twenty-five of Angitia's Beauties," Lupus declared as he held up two withering goatskin bags. "The goddess will be pleased tonight."

"Back into the water lads," Alerio said with false enthusiasm.

"Did I tell you that I hate you, Lance Corporal Sisera?" an archer stated.

"Right now, Legionary, I hate myself," Alerio replied.

The hemp line went rigid and the five swimmers waded in and began to kick as the rope pulled them through the frigid water.

***

Between the shivers, the weakening kicks of their legs, and the endless flow of water across their faces, the five swimmers barely noticed when the water went from turbulent to simply swelling. From killer cold to just cold, they transcended from the Kaikinos River to the Ionian Sea. Far out, the boat turned until they were towed parallel to Bova Beach.

Alerio caught a glimpse of the first Illyrian bireme, the second and the third. His confidence climbed, if not his temperature, as they passed the fourth. One feature stood out. Along the beach, campfires burned brightly offering warmth. Fortunately, he knew the warmth came with death at the hands of the pirates. So, he clung tightly to the loop and kicked as best he could in the cold water.

Eventually, as do most uncomfortable situations, the end came in sight. The boat turned and the swimmers could sense the water warming as they neared the shallows.

Helicaon and Lupus climbed stiffly out of the boat. Their arms were dead from the rowing and their hands refused to grip when they attempted to pull on the rope. All five swimmers were dead weight and none helped by kicking. The Spartan and the Legionary had to force their hands to close and their shoulders to haul on the line. The swimmers were barely moving when they were reeled in from the sea.

Chapter 52 – Wine for Warmth and a Mission

Alerio was the first swimmer to revive. He accepted a drink of strong wine as a dry woolen shirt was thrown across his shoulders. Weakly dragging the shirt off his back, he slipped it on properly. It took concentration to pull on the wool trousers and even more to tie the string belt. Then, he pulled on his hobnailed boots and went to check on the archers.

One was sitting up but shivering violently.

"Get up and walk around," Helicaon ordered. "Don't think about it, just get up, shake your arms and walk around."

The Legionary finally climbed to his feet and began to move. Another archer crawled to his knees and looked up at Alerio.

"Sisera. Remember when I said I hate you?" he asked. "Well, now I hate you even more."

"I was right behind you in the water," Alerio informed him. "The best part of the swim was when you peed in the water. For a fleeting moment, I was grateful for your warmth."

The archer stared at Alerio for a few heartbeats. Then, he climbed to his feet and stepped up to face Alerio. After a pause, he threw his arms around Lance Corporal Sisera.

"That was some adventure," he whispered. "Let's go kill some pirates."

"First, we need to have everyone fit," Alerio stated.

The other two archers were slow to come around. Prolonged cold effects people in different ways. One couldn't stop shivering and was curled into a ball and crying. His fellow archer just sat with his head bowed. Unmoving or unable to move, he seemed lost in his own mind.

"What about those two?" asked Lupus.

"If they don't come around soon," Alerio responded. "We'll have to leave them."

The Spartan took the wineskin and approached the unmoving Legionary.

"See here lad," the old man said as he sat and draped an arm over the archer's shoulder. "You have a mission and I have wine. And I promise you don't have to go back into the water."

"I thought I was going to die," the archer mumbled.

"You almost did. But now you're safe on dry ground," Helicaon assured him. "I'm thirsty. Wine's a good way to rinse the salt out of your throat. Here, join me."

The old man took a drink than pressed the wineskin into the hands of the archer. Slowly, the Legionary lifted his head and drizzled a stream into his mouth.

"I may have had better wine," he whispered. "But I can't remember when."

"Get dressed," ordered Alerio. "You may die tonight but you won't have to get wet to do it."

"I'm fit Lance Corporal," the archer assured him as he stood and took some more wine. "But, let's never do that swimming thing again."

"Not in this lifetime," Alerio assured him. "Get dressed and move around. You'll feel better."

"And that leaves one," observed Lupus. "Any more tricks from you, old man."

"Just one," Helicaon said. "Throw him into the water. If he wants to live he'll swim back to shore. If not, he'll die. In either case, you'll know where he stands."

One of the archers was kneeling next to the curled-up Legionary. As he patted the man's shoulder, he whispered, "Lance Corporal Sisera. Can we start a fire? We can't see the pirate's campfires from here so they shouldn't see ours."

"The Illyrians on the first level plaza will see it," Alerio said to him. Then, he knelt and placed a hand on the curled-up Legionary. "I'm not going to throw him in the water. We'll leave him here with Helicaon. Collect your equipment and let's get moving."

"I'm not staying here and missing the fun," the Spartan announced. "Your lad will have to fend for himself."

After Lupus removed his squirming sacks, the three fit archers grabbed their bows and bundles of arrows from the boat. Alerio plucked his dual rig from the bottom and slung it over his shoulders. It wasn't surprising when Helicaon reached in and pulled out a gladius.

"Are we ready?" asked Alerio.

"Hold on," Lupus begged. "Almost done."

The Legionary stood away from the rest. Higher up the bank, he was lost in the moonlight shadows and the dark of the steep hill.

"All set," Lupus said after a while. "Let's go see who is blessed with Angitia's gift."

Alerio led and the others followed him towards where the pirates were camped.

Chapter 53 – Wolves in Hades

As the evening deepened into full night, all the civilians and a few of the Legionaries on the plaza slept; except for those on guard duty, and three squads. Those infantrymen sat around cook fires sharpening their gladii, or eating, or mending their equipment. Garrison Commander Cephas finished another round of checking on the night guards and walked wearily to where the squads sat.

"Go in, raise Hades, and get out," he ordered. "I need every one of you for tomorrow's fight. Understood?"

Squads Four and Five replied, "Yes, Commander."

The Third Squad growled.

'I'll have to ask them about that when this is over,' Cephas thought as he walked away.

He went to the first man on guard duty and told him to wake up a friend. They were encouraged to have a conversation; not too loud, but enough so the voices created noise from the plaza. After giving the same instructions to the other men on guard duty, Cephas went in search of one of the bards. He figured a ballad couldn't hurt.

***

Squads Four and Five descended the stairs to the second level plaza. Once on the plaza, they separated and silently searched the area for any hidden pirates. After making sure the level was clear, the squads took up positions on either side of the stairs leading down to level one. A Legionary separated from the ranks and walked back to the stairs.

"Clear," he whispered to the eight-man assault squad waiting there.

Third Squad filed down from level three and crossed the plaza. No one spoke, or stomped, or rattled their equipment. There were pirates snoozing on the stairs; along with about thirty-five Illyrian soldiers sleeping on the plaza below.

The assault squad stopped and stood perfectly still. Some of their eyes fixed on the quiet and motionless beach below; others cast further down the beach to the fires near the large pavilion.

Above them on the third level plaza, Legionaries talked and a bard sang a melancholy love song about Cupid's love for the beautiful princess Psyche. Third Squad stood between the low noises from above and the silent Illyrians below.

Chapter 54 – The Navarch Pavilion

Alerio tapped the three archers on their shoulders before pushing them to the top of the beach. Higher up, where the beach met dirt, they heal-and-toed it forward until they could see to the front of the pavilion. Sleeping forms sprawled around two low campfires. Both were close to the large tent's entrance. From the high ground, the multitude of campfires caused the rest of the beach to resemble a starry night.

The archers stuck out an arm to be sure they had the proper distance between them. Once satisfied they had elbow room, the three slowly unslung the bundles from their shoulders and squatted down. From the sacks, they extracted arrows, one at a time. As each arrow emerged, the bowmen stuck the arrowhead into the dirt to their front. When they had one hundred twenty arrows placed, the archers strung their bows and waited.

"The Goddess beckons," Lupus whispered from behind Alerio.

"Then answer her call," he urged.

There was a shuffling of feet on the sand and Alerio caught a quick glimpse of a form at the edge of the pavilion before it vanished.

The archers noticed the movement as well. In response, they stood, set their feet, and plucked the first arrows from the soil.

An apparition materialized from around the pavilion. A naked man glistened in the night except for the dark strip that coiled around his body. Above the shoulders, a cobra's head turned rapidly from side to side, as if excited about discovering humans on the beach.

"Snakes. Snakes on the beach," screamed the apparition as it raced from campfire to campfire. "Who is blessed with the gift? Serpents from the Goddess."

At the first pair of campfires, the spirit dropped snakes on the chest of two sleeping men.

One assaulted man felt the squirming immediately. He brushed the snake aside and jumped up yelling, "Snakes. Snakes on the beach."

The brushed aside serpent landed on another sleeping pirate. He cried out and leaped to his feet yelling, "Serpents, serpents. Serpents on the beach."

Both men were swept from their feet when arrowheads pierced their necks. As the others pirates around the campfires tossed back their blankets and rose, arrow shafts appeared in their chests. They fell back onto their blankets.

The action played out around campfires radiating out from the pavilion. A snake landed, was slung onto a mate, and men jumped up shouting about snakes on the beach. The Legion archers dropped several of the first group. But the cry of 'snakes' and the panic spread rapidly beyond the campsites targeted by the spirit. It spread so fast; the archers couldn't keep up with the targets.

As with all surprise attacks, those initially affected were afraid and vocal which spread confusion to their neighbors. Eventually, the farthest away, and unaffected were able to sort out the chaos. Soon they would discover the archers and the attack would end with the death of the Legionaries.

Except, from the plaza and the beach near the stairs, Illyrian pirates shouted warnings about an attack from the Legionaries. The attack-cry rolled from the stairs, down the beach, and through each of the unaffected campsites. Midway to the pavilion, the attack-cry clashed with the snakes-on-the-beach cry. In the confusion, pirates had to choose. Chase after an unknown and naturally feared foe, like snakes or attack a solid, recognizable enemy. Thusly, the snake-cry was forgotten and the pirates, grabbing knives and swords, ran for the stairs and the fight on the plaza.

No one noticed the apparition when it stumbled. His words so garbled, one would have to be very close to hear his voice.

"Goddess Angitia. Come and take me from this realm," he mumbled. The last two snakes were held up as offerings. Both hands and arms bled from fang marks. He stopped and gazed at the puncture wounds. "Take back your gift, my Goddess, and carry me home."

With those words, the apparition dropped to his knees. Slowly, he toppled face first into the hot coals of a campfire. The last sensation of his troubled life was the aroma of a second chance. For Private Lupus, there would be no second chance; his Goddess reclaimed her gift and carried him from this realm.

Chapter 55 – Steps into Hades

Third Squad couldn't understand the words. The cry of the pirates from the beach was too far away making it an undulating roar. Yet, they understood the meaning. Eight shields lifted, and the men howled while running down the steps to the lower plaza. To distract from the beach action and help alert the Illyrians to the attacking Legionaries, Fourth and Fifth Squads yelled at the top of their lungs. Despite the noisy display, they maintained their positions.

As Third Squad descended the stairs, two abreast, the Legionaries slashed and hacked the pirates sleeping on the steps. At the first plaza level, they slowed and came on line.

"Advance. Advance," shouted Procopius, the acting squad leader. "And yell. Let the perfututum Illyrians know, they've entered a wolf's den."

The shields shot forward. A few soldiers and pirates who were awake and standing died.

"Pivot right," Procopius shouted and the line swung to face Illyrians scrambling to pick up their shields. "Advance. Advance."

The unprepared Illyrians fell wounded or dead to the clay pavers of the plaza.

"Turn about," Procopius ordered. Each Legionary spun in place to face the enemy behind them. "Advance. Advance."

Sweeping back across the plaza, the Legionaries collided with the shields of Illyrian soldiers. In addition to the professional warriors, the plaza was filling with pirates and rowers from the beach. After glancing at the crowded stairs, where men pushed and shoved to get at the infantrymen, Procopius decided Lance Corporal Sisera had enough of a diversion.

"Right face and run," Procopius shouted as he moved to the front of the line.

Two Legionaries fell and were swarmed by sica wielding pirates. With his shield swinging back and forth, the temporary squad leader protected the remaining five members of his squad as they raced for the stairs.

The plan was to form a shield wall and back up to the second level plaza. If Procopius lost any more men, there wouldn't be enough of Third Squad left to seal the steps.

"Welcome to Hades. Greetings from the wolves," Procopius screamed as shields and spears battered his lone shield. He stepped back and stumbled. The Illyrians sensing a kill moved in on the off balanced temporary squad leader.

Suddenly, a wall of Legion shields closed down in front of him. Fearing Third Squad was sacrificing themselves for him, he screamed, "Step back."

A hand slammed into his shoulder armor and he turned to see Fourth Squad's Lance Corporal with his face an inch away.

"You haven't been a squad leader long enough to order my men around," the NCO challenged. "Now. Hit the steps so my lads can step back."

Procopius paused on the steps to look down on the plaza. Fourth and Fifth Squads were stacked in two ranks. In front of them were hundreds of pirates and two squads of Illyrian soldiers. The engaged Legionaries slammed their shields forward but didn't follow with a gladius strike. For this maneuver, they used the space created by the thrusts to step back before bracing for another assault.

Disengaging with the enemy while collapsing their formation to mount the steps was going to be a problem. The pirates massed on the plaza created constant pressure against the Legion ranks. Again, the Legionaries shoved forward with their shields, but the space opened and closed almost as rapidly as the shields created it. A battle of attrition spelled doom for the Legion squads.

"Procopius. Would you like to join us?" a voice rang out.

The temporary squad leader spun around to see Commander Cephas standing at the top of the stairs. Around him, on the second level plaza, were the remaining members of Third Squad and a half squad of additional Legionaries. Procopius sprinted up the steps. At the top, four javelins were placed in his hands.

"Arching throws," ordered Cephas. "Drop them in close but don't hit our men. On my command. Throw."

Eleven javelins disappeared against the night sky. When they reappeared, the shafts were embedded in the heads, shoulders, or chests of pirates.

"On my command," shouted Cephas. "Throw."

Again, eleven iron tipped javelins arched up and over before raining down on the second rank of pirates. Now, the first rank realized the pressure from behind had lifted. The Legionaries noticed the easing and the familiar shafts falling among the Illyrians. When a third flight struck down another eleven pirates, the squads shoved their shields forward and followed with their gladii.

As the squads folded in their flanks, trumpets sounded from the beach. Before Fifth and Fourth Squads mounted the stairs, the Illyrians broke off and ran for the steps leading down to the first level. With the Legionaries withdrawing and the pirates running, the second level plaza was soon empty.

***

"Good work. Clean your gear. Get some rest," Cephas said to one Legionary as he climbed to the third level plaza and filed by. Each man was greeted by the Garrison Commander as he reached the plaza. "Good work. Clean your gear. Get some rest."

Third Squad's temporary squad leader was the last to climb the stairs. He had an injured Legionary slung over his shoulder.

He stopped in front of the Commander. After the medics took the wounded man, Procopius asked, "Did we give the weapon's instructor enough time?"

"I don't know. But I do know this. Third Squad gave him all they had," Cephas offered. "Go clean your gear. And, get some rest."

Chapter 56 – Underestimate at Your Peril

Alerio crept around the side of the pavilion. He knew the Legion archers were on the hill watching, but he was cautious anyway. Peering around the corner, he saw the arrow ridden bodies around several of the closest campsites. Someone had fallen into one of the fires.

Flames around the naked man's head flared and burned with an intensity beyond simple burning cloth.

"Swift and overwhelming violence," Helicaon whispered from behind him. "Never give your foe a chance to organize or to bring in reinforcements."

Alerio didn't reply. His hands rose above his shoulders and he took a firm grip on both hilts. As he stepped around to the front of the pavilion, both gladii came free. He held them crossed at chest height as he approached the pavilion's entrance.

Without breaking stride, Alerio extended the crossed gladii and inserted the tips in the tent flaps. By jerking the blades to the sides, he threw the cloth entrance wide open.

Then, he squatted, tucked his head, and shoulder rolled through the opening.

A dagger and an arrow clipped the edges of the material as the flaps closed. By then, Alerio was through the opening and coming up on his feet.

Two men stood in the back of the pavilion. One held a Greek sword while the other fumbled to fit an arrow on a crossbow.

"You are too close for the bow, Navarch Martinus Cetea," Alerio sneered. "Sergeant Pholus has the right idea. This is sword work distance. And, I brought both of mine."

"Do I know you?" Martinus Cetea asked as he tossed the bow to the ground. He replaced it with two curved sicas pulled from his belt. "I don't recall us meeting."

Before Alerio could reply, the tent flaps opened and Helicaon shuffled through the opening. He seemed harmless with the gladius tucked into his belt and a comb in his hand.

"Are they dead yet?" the old Spartan asked. Then he looked around and added. "No? That could be a mistake."

The three combatants watched as Helicaon navigated the carpeted floor. As if his old legs could barely support his weight, the Spartan inched across the floor to a stool. He started to sit, but the gladius caught in the stool's legs. After fumbling with the hilt, he managed to pull the blade free of his belt. Holding it in his left hand, he eased down on the seat. As if to accentuate to his age, he grunted as he sat. The gladius ended up resting on his knees with the hilt hanging over his left leg.

He began to comb his beard.

"Alerio. You should just kill them," the old man suggested. "Too much talking."

"You side with a Legionary against a fellow Greek?" Pholus shouted at the old man. "So, you will die as well."

"You, a Greek? Your city state hired mercenaries from the Republic," the old Spartan replied. "When your King died, you sent the Sons of Mars away. They march on Messina. Where was your Greek pride when those thugs murdered all the men in the city? Leaving the Greek women widows and at the mercies of the Sons of Mars? You're not a Greek. You are a stupid, weak, cowardly piece of Syracuse merda."

Sergeant Pholus was a cunning leader and a brave warrior. He was also a vain, and prideful man. The tip of his blade came up and he ran across the pavilion screaming a war cry. The roar filled the tent and the hairs on Alerio's neck stood up. Most men would freeze from the beastly sound; others might, at least, rise to meet the threat. Helicaon sat combing his beard with his right hand while his left hand rested on the hilt of the gladius.

Pholus let his wounded ego take control. Wanting to make an example of the rude old man, he drew his blade to the side. It swung back with the intention of separating the weathered face and groomed head from the wrinkled old neck.

As the blade chopped, Helicaon's bones seemed to turn to liquid. At least that's how it appeared to Alerio. From sitting stiffly on the stool, the Spartan's entire body collapsed like a silk scarf. While sliding off the stool, his left hand slapped the hilt of the gladius. The weapon arched up and when Helicaon grabbed it with his right hand, the gladius' tip was pointed upward.

The blade rose and twisted as it penetrated Pholus' sword arm. Yelling in pain, the Syracuse Sergeant stepped back to inspect the wound. It shouldn't have been too bad. The gladius tip had barely touched him before he pulled away. Yet, there was so much blood. It bubbled around the wound and pumper from the jagged center.

Holding the injured arm, the Sergeant turned and ran for the tent flaps. Four steps from the exit, the blade of a gladius was thrust between his legs and he toppled to the floor.

"Going somewhere, Sergeant Pholus?" Alerio asked.

Pholus looked over his shoulder ignoring the Legionary. The old man had resumed his seat on the stool and sat combing his hair.

"Who are you?" Pholus asked weakly.

Blood continued to pump from the wound, but it no longer came out in spurts.

"Helicaon, the Spartan," the old man stated with no inflection or emotion. "Goodbye, Sergeant."

Chapter 57 – Make Sport Of

"So, it's you two against me," Martinus Cetea bragged. "I've faced worst odds and still came out alive. I can't say the same for my attackers."

"Don't look at me," the Spartan said. "I've talked too much. I'm becoming a regular orator."

"It's just you and me, Cetea," Alerio assured the Illyrian.

"At least you're honorable, Spartan," Martinus Cetea said. Then to the Legionary, asked. "What is your name?"

"Lance Corporal Alerio Sisera of the Third Century, Southern Legion," Alerio stated.

"Lance Corporal…Ah, the farmers at the inlet. Now I remember you," Cetea accused. "You killed members of my crew. Butchered them really. While they were defenseless. Wouldn't you agree?"

Alerio realized the Navarch was stalling for time. Despite the knowledge that reinforcements could arrive at any moment, Alerio couldn't resist.

"You murdered old men, old women, and children," Alerio stated. "They were mothers, fathers, and people's children. You killed them and threw their bodies in with their families. For that, I can't allow you to live."

"Wait. All this, the arrows and snakes while my crews were sleeping," Cetea ventured. "The night attack by the Legionaries and you charging into my tent. All this for a few farmers."

"Revenge is a better motivation then chasing a chest full of coins," responded Alerio.

Martinus Cetea laughed so hard the tent sides flexed.

"You believe I'd bring four warships, their crews, and soldiers for a box of coins?" Cetea asked between chuckles. "Lad, you have no idea. The Egyptian coin is for my crews. Me, I'm working on a bigger contract. Syracuse wants to expand on Sicilia. But, so does the Empire. They made an agreement. Syracuse gets Bovesia and the port and the farmland. That leaves Sicilia for the Qart Hadasht Empire to settle. Whether the Empire helps Syracuse defend against the Republic, when you come to take it back, I don't care. Illyrians have our homeland and the sea. As long as shipping continues, we'll continue to take what we want."

Alerio realized the value of the information for Tribune Velius. It caused him to hesitate. Suddenly, one side of the tent snapped as three arrows pierced the fabric. The arrows meant the Legion archers were leaving. Leaving because pirates were returning from the steps at Bovesia.

"My father is a farmer," Alerio said as he walked toward Martinus Cetea. "I have a mother."

"Well, good for you," Cetea congratulated the Legionary as he dropped into a fighter's stance. "Most of us do."

"And two sisters," Alerio added as he approached the Illyrian Navarch. "Do you know who doesn't?"

"Oh pray, tell me, Legionary of the Republic," Cetea said as he shuffled to his left.

Alerio jumped to his right blocking the Illyrian's path to the exit.

"The farmers at Occhio," Alerio stated as he brought his right gladius up in a high guard.

Cetea stepped back to get out from under the blade. As he moved, Alerio's left gladius swung upward while the Legionary took a giant step forward. The Illyrian slapped the blade away and leading with his sicas, stepped in.

He was an experienced enough fighter not to go for the torso. Rather, his target was Alerio's left wrist. Wound a wrist and the arm was useless. So, he sliced the air as his curved blades went for the first cuts of the duel.

Alerio, to Cetea's surprise, didn't pull the arm back. With the limb so close, he aimed to slice the arm with both blades. Cetea leaned forward so they would bite deeper; sufficiently deep to end the fight. Or at least, stop the Legionary, and allow Cetea to make it to the exit.

The curved blades closed with the Legionary's flesh. Then, the gladius fell from Alerio's hand. A puzzled thought ran through the Illyrian's mind at the action.

Both of Cetea's arms jerked to a stop. The Legionary stood with one leg far to the front in a split legged stance. His left forearm was bent at the elbow and in contact with the inside of the Illyrian's wrists.

Although it stopped the blades, it was a poor defense. All Cetea needed to do was…

The right gladius tapped the pirate leader on the crown of his head and he crumpled to the carpeted floor.

"Just kill him," the Spartan urged.

Alerio ignored Helicaon as he tied strips of cloth high on Cetea's ankles and around his wrists.

"Navarch Martinus Cetea. Wake up," Alerio said as he tapped the Illyrian's cheek. "I want you alert for this."

"For what?" asked an obviously groggy Cetea.

"Making sport," Alerio said as he hacked at Cetea's ankles.

Cetea screamed as the bones crumbled, the tendons separated, and the nerves reported the pain to his brain.

"That was for the old men and old women," Alerio said as he jerked the blade out of the crippling ankle wounds. "And this is for the farmer's children."

Cetea felt new pain in his wrists but the agony in his lower legs overrode the new injuries.

"And for throwing the babies' bodies in with the women and children," Alerio announced.

He ran a gladius across the bridge of Cetea's nose.

Oddly, the injury to his nose didn't hurt much, Martinus Cetea thought. Although he had trouble seeing. It was so dark in the pavilion; the Legionary must have blown out the lanterns.

Chapter 58 – Fleeing in the Dark

A ripping sound from the back of the pavilion drew Alerio's attention.

"Follow and try to keep up," Helicaon called as he stepped through the slit he made in the fabric.

Alerio swung the gladii over his shoulders and seated both blades in their sheaths. Then, he ran to the opening, squeezed through, and sprinted after the Spartan.

***

Alerio pulled alongside Helicaon further down the beach than he would have thought.

"You should have killed him," offered the Spartan.

"Strategy Helicaon," Alerio replied as they arrived at the boat.

The beach was deserted. Alerio looked around for the archers and Lupus. A figure separated from the shadows on the top of the bank and walked over.

"I sent the others on ahead," the Legion bowman explained. "We'll take to the hills and work our way back to the garrison. And, Lance Corporal Sisera, Private Lupus didn't make it. He did a good job creating the panic. So good in fact, not a blade touched him."

"How did he die?" asked Alerio.

"It had to be the snakes," the archer explained. "I was busy killing pirates, but one of the other archers saw him staggering around in his cloth cobra hood. He was holding two really big snakes in his hands."

"I guess the gift failed him," Alerio mumbled.

"Excuse me, Lance Corporal?" the archer asked.

"Nothing. I don't think the pirates will follow you far," commented Alerio. "But don't engage unless it's necessary. Now go."

A line of swaying torches appeared far down the dark beach. The archer pointed at the lights before jogging off. Alerio followed the arm and nodded. Then, he reached down to help the Spartan place the boat in the water.

"The water's cold," Helicaon warned as he stepped into the boat.

"This isn't cold," Alerio replied as he walked the boat through the surf and into deeper water. When the water reached his chest, he shivered while climbing into the boat. "Now it's cold."

"Grab a paddle and stroke," ordered the Spartan. "That'll warm you up."

The torches and a herd of angry Illyrian pirates moved across the beach. While they searched for the archers and the butcher of their Navarch, the small boat moved silently away from the shoreline.

***

The boat moved easily over the swells of the Ionian Sea in response to Alerio and Helicaon's steady paddling. They settled into a rhythm, which propelled the boat away from shore, around the biremes, and towards the fresh water. When they entered the mouth of the Kaikinos River their matched strokes fell apart. The choppy water and swiftly moving river threatened to overturn and swamp Helicaon's small boat.

Relentless driving strokes pushed them upriver and by the time the boat touched the pier, both of them were exhausted; the old Spartan from the exertion of paddling out and back. Alerio from the freezing swim and recovery, and the return trip. They climbed out and pulled the boat onto the wooden dock. Then, they staggered up the ramps to the garrison area.

***

The Legion garrison lay in darkness Where lanterns should glow from tents, the buildings, and manned guard posts, there was no light. Also, no sounds of marching sentries, snoring men, or Legionaries talking greeted them. For the limited distance Alerio could see in the dark, they could have landed at the wrong pier and climbed to a barren plateau.

Alerio started towards the path to Bovesia when the Spartan's fingers wrapped around his arm. Gentle pressure pulled him to his knees. Helicaon gripped his hand and pointed in the direction of the headquarters building. Then, the supply building, and finally, the hand indicated the first of the Legionary's tents. In his fatigued state, Alerio had forgotten about the Syracuse Raiders.

While waiting for a morning assault, a well-trained unit would have listening posts. Pairs of men located in front of where the assault squads were cloistered to warn of anyone approaching. Alerio had no reason to doubt the quality of the Raiders' training.

Even if he and Helicaon made it up the path to the town's entrance, they'd be stopped at the barricade. While negotiating with the Legionary guards for entry, their silhouettes would make perfect targets for the archers at the listening posts.

Alerio reached out. This time it was him taking the Spartan's hand. He placed it on his shoulder allowing Helicaon to follow in the dark. They soft-footed it to the base of the hill near the edge of the drop off. On one side was the silent Bovesia garrison, and far below, on the other side, the swift flowing Kaikinos River.

Helicaon dropped his arm from Alerio's shoulder when the Legionary bent forward. Cautiously, they climbed the steep hill using their hands to navigate the steep grade.

***

"Terrible place for a defense," whispered Helicaon.

They were perched at the top of the hill and leaning against the rear wall of a building. If it had been daylight, the two would look ridiculous, like two hikers stranded on a mountain ledge.

"Climb on my shoulders," ordered Alerio while turning sideways and squatting down.

Helicaon placed one, then the other foot on the Legionary's shoulders. Both used the wall to stand. Alerio reached up and worked his hands under the Spartan's feet. Once the older man's weight was resting on his palms, Alerio pressed him up and overhead.

At first, he didn't know if the combined height would allow Helicaon to reach the roof. When the weight lifted, Alerio dropped his arms and slumped against the wall. Despite the location and situation, he yawned. Wearily, he began creeping along the top of the hill in the direction of the alleyway and barricade.

Chapter 59 – The Barricade to Bovesia

Just Helicaon's fingertips reached the edge of the clay shingles. He pulled up until his chin came level with the rooftop. Using his chin as an anchor point, he walked his fingers forward to get a better purchase. As if he were a young boy in the Agoge, he nimbly scrambled onto the roof. Memories of Spartan training flashed through his mind. Some happy, some sad, but most bitter and better forgotten.

He heard whispering, but could only make out two of the Legionaries on guard duty. They were dark forms against the starry night sky. Staying near the edge, he crawled to the front of the building. Below him, lanterns lit the plaza and after a short scurry along the roof's edge, he located a ladder.

***

Commander Cephas lay wrapped in a blanket. No dreams came to the exhausted Legion Corporal. If they had, they would come as nightmares of howling Illyrian pirates and dead Legionaries. Luckily, he slept dreamlessly, although restlessly.

"Commander?" asked a voice with a Greek accent.

Cephas didn't think the speaker addressed him. He was an NCO; not a Commander.

"Commander Cephas. Lance Corporal Sisera is outside the barricade," Helicaon stated. "And there are Syracuse soldiers at your backdoor."

Realization came to Cephas and he tossed back the blanket and stiffly climbed to his feet. The weeks of holding down two senior NCO positions had beaten him down. Now, under the weight of Command, he was dipping into reserves he didn't know existed.

"Report," he ordered the Spartan.

"I'm not one of your Legionaries," Helicaon reminded Cephas. "Besides, it was Sisera's mission."

"Then, we had better get the Lance Corporal in so I can get my report," Cephas said as he crossed the plaza to where Third Squad slept. "Private Procopius. Get them up. You've got a mission."

***

Alerio squatted five feet from the barricaded alleyway. With a hint of pink in the eastern sky, he worried about the Syracuse archers. It would only take the weak predawn to highlight him and allow the bowmen to acquire a target.

A scraping noise, soft as if someone were lifting furniture, came from the barricade. Someone voiced a curse and suddenly the noise of lumber and boxes being tossed to the ground replaced the cautious scraping.

A torch lit and the shadows of five shields led by pointed javelins rushed from the alley.

"Password?" demanded Private Procopius.

Alerio racked his brain. Cephas had mentioned it before he left on the mission. Now, it was lost somewhere in the back of his weary mind. Four arrows slammed into the shields and the Legionaries holding the shields rocked from the impact. The archers were close.

"Password?" demanded Private Procopius.

Alerio recognized the voice and uttered the only thing he could think of, he howled.

The Legionaries standing in the alleyway howled back.

"Get in here, weapon's instructor," Procopius ordered as two shields parted.

The movement drew four more arrows. As soon as they slammed into the shields, Alerio dove between the Legionaries. He ended up sprawled on the pavers. Procopius reached down, and without letting him stand, dragged him back while shouting, "Third Squad, step back, step back."

Other Legionaries rushed forward pushing an upended supply cart. Boxes were stacked on either side of the cart bed and the alleyway was again barricaded.

"Lance Corporal Sisera," Cephas exclaimed looking down at the half laying Alerio. "Do you need a nap before reporting in?"

"No, Commander," Alerio replied as he climbed slowly to his feet. "But it's not a bad idea."

"We're rationing water. But after your report," advised Cephas after sniffing the air. "I'm authorizing a bath for you."

"Private Lupus didn't make it," Alerio said as they walked away. "Snake bites from what I know."

"It was bound to happen despite his squad leader's warnings," Cephas replied. "What about my archers? And the Illyrian Navarch?"

"As planned, the Legionaries have taken to the hills," Alerio said. "They did a great job of punishing the pirates during the panic. As for the Navarch? He's alive. But, the Syracuse Sergeant isn't."

***

They arrived at the command camp and a Legionary handed Alerio a clay mug. He took a gulp and chewed on a piece of meat he found in the stew.

"Do you mind if I sit?" Alerio asked as he swayed.

"Please, before you fall over," agreed Cephas. "I thought the purpose of the raid was to remove the leader of the pirates. What happened?"

Helicaon walked into the torchlight and squatted down. He too had a mug of stew.

"I'd like to hear the answer to that as well," he stated.

Both the Garrison Commander and the Spartan watched as Alerio chewed and thought of how to phrase his response.

"After the harvest, my father likes to go hunting. Have you ever seen a herd of Aurochs during rutting season? The young bulls fight among themselves for the chance to challenge the dominant male," Alerio explained. "The Illyrian Captains remind me of them. If Navarch Cetea was dead, the winner would become the undisputed leader. With Cetea alive but not able to command, the successful Captain will be weakened."

"How do you figure weakened?" demanded Cephas.

"Because the Captain is unable to challenge the leader," the Spartan offered. "Although Cetea can't fight, he still has the title of Navarch."

"Hopefully, they'll have to return to Illyria to settle the issue," Alerio added.

"So, you've based a strategy on the mating habits of wild cattle?" complained Cephas. "What about the human desire for revenge? Suppose the new top Captain decides to attack?"

"The pirates want the treasure from the Egyptian merchant ship," Alerio replied. "Bleed them enough and the cost will exceed the coin."

"That's what we plan to do. Get some rest. It'll get busy when the sun comes up," Cephas said as he walked away. Under his breath, he mumbled. "Rutting season and angry Aurochs, may the Gods help us."

Alerio unlaced his dual gladius rig and placed it beside his leg. After snuggling against a column on the merchant's porch, he promptly fell asleep.

Chapter 60 – Dawn Assaults

Legionaries marching by woke the slumbering Lance Corporal.

Alerio opened his eyes and looked from the porch to the plaza in the soft light of predawn. Barely perceivable were the First Squad on the left rooftop, Second on the stairs, and Third Squad lined up on the right rooftop. Another squad, the Fourth, stood guarding the rear alleyway.

Commander Cephas stood in the center of the plaza and divided his attention between the stairs and the alleyway behind him. To either side of him stood his acting Sergeant and Corporal. These Lance Corporals waited to pass on any orders from the acting Garrison Commander.

'There are no reserve infantrymen,' Alerio thought as he reached for his dual rig. Someone had left him a helmet and armor. He pulled them on before slinging the dual rig onto his back. 'When this started there were seventy heavy infantrymen. Now, the garrison is down to forty-eight fit to fight.'

He slid the helmet on as he approached the commander.

"Sir. Where do you want me?" Alerio asked.

"When it starts, report to Fourth at the alleyway," Cephas replied. "Right now, follow me."

They jumped the short distance to the roof of a second plaza's building and pushed between the shields of Third Squad. Cephas pointed down towards the beach.

"There are your young bulls," Cephas announced with a hint of sarcasm.

The three Illyrian Captains and a fourth man, possible second in command of Cetea's warship, stood around a raised platform. On the platform lay a large man with thick bandages on his ankles, his wrists, and a fifth wrapped around his head covering his eyes. He didn't move much, although, from time to time the four Captains stopped arguing, leaned in, and listened.

"Navarch Cetea has looked better. I'll grant you that," Cephas commented. "They've been arguing since I could see them. So far, they've stacked the Illyrian solders on the stairs and grouped the crews behind them on the first plaza. Then, they went back to their lively discussion."

"If it was you in that condition, I'd like at least one run at the enemy," confessed Alerio. "But, I'm not sure I'd risk losing too many men to revenge your honor, Commander. My apologies."

"None needed. And, we have the Syracuse soldiers around back still hidden," Cephas added. "I can't see how they're coordinating with the Illyrians."

Alerio glanced back towards the barricaded alleyway then back at the beach. After the third twist of his head, he inhaled deeply and locked eyes with the Commander.

"They can't be in communications. The only way the Syracusan Raiders will know when to attack is from the sounds of battle," Alerio stated. "It's why they haven't attacked yet."

"I agree with the idea," Cephas said. "They'll commit when we're busy with the Illyrians."

"How long will it take the Illyrian soldiers to march up two flights of stairs?" questioned Alerio.

"What are you thinking, weapon's instructor?" Cephas asked.

"That I lead three squads out the alleyway, hit the first group of Raiders, and race back," Alerio offered.

"And what do I do with eighteen Legionaries and two NCOs while you are leading a dismounted cavalry charge?" demanded Cephas.

"Defending the stairs and roofs until we return," Alerio remarked. "If we surprise the Syracuse Raiders, we can reduce their numbers before their assault."

Cephas squeezed his eyes together tightly. He opened them and locked eyes with Alerio.

"This is one of those suggestion where if I'm wrong people die," he said softly. "But we are outnumbered. If we don't take bold action, more of my Legionaries will die. Pick your squads and Lance Corporal Sisera."

"Yes, Commander," Alerio said.

"Bring them all back to me," Cephas requested.

Alerio turned around and shouted, "Third and First, form up on Fourth Squad."

As he walked towards the alleyway, Legionaries rushed by and converged on the plaza. Alerio pulled his helmet off and tucked it under his arm.

"Fourth Squad, half of you, grab as many javelins as you can find," Alerio instructed. "You are my doorway. The rest of the squad, bows, and arrows. You are my sweepers. Third and First, we're going to pay the Syracuse soldiers a quick and painful visit. Standby."

Thirty boots stomped and the Legionaries replied, "Yes, weapon's instructor."

Moments later, the boxes and cart were pulled back and Alerio, followed by thirty Legionaries, jogged from Bovesia.

***

As they raced down the path, four men with shields and javelins and four men with bows spread out to either side of the Legion column. Before Alerio reached the bottom of the hill, the Raiders at the listening posts were screaming and dying. The sweepers had cleared the line of retreat.

Rather than angling to the right and the garrison's gate, Alerio made a sharp left turn and ran along the thorn bush wall. When he was opposite the first Legion tent, he motioned for two Legionaries to pass him.

"Now," he shouted.

The two infantrymen pivoted right and threw their javelins high into the air. Before the tips hit the ground, they pushed their shields to the front and threw their bodies on the throne wall. The shields and the weight of the men crushed the bushes. Leaving the shields, the men rolled off them, grabbed their javelins, and spread to either side of the opening. Alerio stomped across the shield bridge and raced towards the tent. Behind him came twenty, silent heavy infantrymen.

***

In the tent, the ten-man Raider squad relaxed while awaiting the order to attack. They weren't ready when twenty-one gladii split the goatskin wall of the tent and Legionaries jumped through the rips.

Alerio stomped one Raider before engaging another. Behind him, he heard the soldier grunt as an infantryman ran his gladius through the man's chest. Lance Corporal Sisera's target parried the left gladius but was out of position to deal with the one swinging in from the right. He died with his neck almost severed.

"The tent is clear," a squad leader announced. "Orders, Sisera?"

The assault had gone so well, Alerio pondered the question for a moment. The supply building was close and if he could kill those Raiders?

He shook off the urge to press his advantage and turned to the squad leader.

"Withdraw," he ordered. "Everyone back to Bovesia."

They pushed through the slits and ran for the bridge over the thorn bushes. As they retreated, Raiders flowed from the supply building. Arrows arched through the air and began falling around the Legionaries.

"Put a roof on it," a Decanus shouted and half the men raised their shields overhead.

Six men stopped to let the two-man bridge team retrieved their shields. The thorn bushes bounced back to at least half their pre-crushed height.

"Give me a roof and a wall," the other squad leader ordered and four shields where held behind as four were held overhead.

All of the Raiders' arrows impacted solid shields as the Legionaries backed up the hill and the path to Bovesia.

"They're using our own arrows against us," a Legionary said as his shield rocked from an impact.

"So, next time, carry more," advised another infantryman. "Don't leave so many behind."

"I wasn't on arrow duty," the first Legionary protested. "I had water detail."

"Shut up. Step back, get it together First Squad," the squad leader ordered. "Less jawing, more stepping."

***

While the First moved steadily to the path, Third Squad rushed ahead. They passed the start of the path and formed an eight-man shield wall.

From the administration building, Raiders emerged and jogged through the garrison's gate.

Alerio stepped in behind the shields.

"Wait for them to be a step out, Private Procopius," he advised. "Then slam and stab them. Afterward step back so First can flow through and make contact."

The charging Raiders screamed as they reached the Legion line. They hadn't braced as their plan was to run the Legionaries down. Except, the line of stationary shields suddenly shot forward and staggered the running men. When the gladii tore between the Raiders' shields, they realized it wasn't going to be a pleasant day.

The Legion line stepped back and the Legionaries spread apart. Momentarily, the Syracuse soldiers had breathing space. Seeing light between the shields, the remaining Raiders on the start of the path stepped forward.

The lights winked out as First Squad's shields filled in the spaces and hit the Raiders with their shields and gladii.

Alerio was tempted to wrap his line of twenty Legionaries around the ten-man Raider line. But, the other squad of Syracuse soldiers had reached the garrison gate and Cephas needed his Legionaries back to defend the town.

"Smash them, and run," Alerio shouted as he turned and jogged up the hill.

Behind him, twenty shields hammered the Raiders back. Then the Legionaries turned and sprinted up the slope heading for First Squad's shields and bowmen.

Alerio raced around the shields of his doorway squad and slid to a stop. Below him, two lines of Legionaries were chugging up the hill. Slowed by the armor and shields, and the exertion of the attack, some were slowing.

"Come on Legionaries," he shouted as the lines began to accordion. Those lower down were falling further behind the faster men. "Come on, run. Run hard."

The distance between the leading Raiders and the last of the Legionaries was growing closer. In another five steps, the gap would close and Alerio would lose two of the Commander's Legionaries. He yelled in frustration, grabbed two javelins, and raced back down the hill.

***

The Raider was targeting the back of a Legionary. Another step and a slash to his leg and the man would fall. Then the Syracuse soldier would kill him. For a fleeting moment, he noticed a Legionary hopping down the hill. He discounted the man as he was too far away to be a threat.

Alerio skipped so every other move downward allowed him to set his feet. On the fifth, he drew back his left arm. When his feet landed solidly, he threw the javelin. Almost as if it were headed for the slow Legionary, the shaft slid by the man's helmet. Behind him, the iron tip entered the Raider's cheek and pierced his brain.

The next closest Raider watched his squad mate tumble back down the hill. He raised his shield to defend himself from the Legionary hopping down the hill with the javelin.

The move slowed his pace and the slow Legionaries were able to put distance between themselves and their pursuers.

As the two Legionaries reached Alerio, he yelled, "Extra duty for you both. Now run. If I beat you to the top, I'll kill you myself."

Arrows shot by the Legion archers rained down on the Raiders. Wisely, they fell back. When the last three Legionaries passed the four shields, the doorway fell back to the mouth of the alleyway. Soon, the cart bed and boxes were up and the barricade sealed.

Alerio didn't stop running until he was standing in front of Cephas.

"Fifteen Syracusan Raiders dead or wounded," Alerio blurted out as he huffed and puffed while trying to catch his breath.

"We cut their force in half," Cephas confirmed. Then he glanced at the medical area. "Looks like two minor arrow wounds and one with deep thorn scratches. I'd say the mission was a success."

"Yes, sir. I agree," Alerio answered. "What's happening on the beach?"

A trumpet blared from far down on the lower plaza.

"There's your answer," Cephas replied while spinning to the returning squads. They were milling around. "The day is not over yet, people. Squad leaders, get them into place."

Alerio looked up at the Legion bowmen on the rooftops facing the garrison. They seemed undisturbed. One looked back, smiled, and shook his head. Apparently, the Syracuse soldiers were taking some time to regroup.

***

Down on the stairs, Second Squad braced as the Illyrian soldiers jogged up the stairs, and came on line four abreast. With shields held high, they charged across the plaza at the Legionaries. The front rank of Second Squad was hunched over with the bottom of their shields hanging over the short wall. The front line of Illyrians must have thought the Republic was recruiting little people.

Just as they reached the Legion line, the Legionaries stood, lifting up their shields to reveal the short knee-high wall. Too late to alert those pushing from the rear, the front rank's lower legs slammed into the logs. Pressure bent them over and they died from gladii chops. The second rank Illyrians, expecting to power the first men through the Legion shields stumbled. They died from javelin thrusts. By the time the third rank figured out their charge had stalled, half of them fell from thrown javelins.

There was a jam up as the retreating Illyrian solders backed into a screaming hoard of pirates scrambling up the stairs.

Cephas pointed to his acting Sergeant, "First Squad, arrows."

As the NCO passed the order forward to the squad leader, Cephas spun to face his acting Corporal. "Third Squad, arrows."

By the time Third Squad received the order, First Squad was putting arrowheads into Illyrian pirates. When Third Squad added to the flurry of arrows, panic broke out on the second level plaza. Illyrians, both solders, and pirates began fighting for access to the stairs in an attempt to escape the slaughter.

Four trumpets sounded from the beach.

A smile creased Cephas' face and he slowly turned to his acting Sergeant. "First Squad stand down," he said before shifting his feet so he faced in the opposite direction. "Corporal. Third Squad, stand down."

The orders were passed from the NCOs to the squad leaders and then to the Pivot Privates. Soon, the arrows stopped falling but not until another ten more Illyrian pirates fell to the pavers on the second level plaza.

"Lance Corporal Sisera. A word?" Cephas called out. When Alerio approached, the Commander asked. "What do you suppose four trumpets mean?"

"It sounds like a recall from each warship," ventured Alerio.

"Do you suppose they have enough rowers to get away?" Cephas asked.

"Commander. You're not thinking about going down and engaging them, are you?" Alerio inquired. "There are still almost four hundred left."

"Not them. Once the Illyrians are away, I want those Syracuse cūlus out of my garrison," Cephas replied. "I'm putting Private Procopius and Third Squad in charge of the detail. What do you think?"

"It depends," Alerio stated.

"Depends on what?" demanded Cephas.

"On if you want prisoners," advised Alerio. "Because I don't think your wolves understand surrender."

"Then Third Squad should serve nicely. Now, go find a bath, Lance Corporal Sisera," ordered Cephas. "Because, Legionary, you smell."

Act 8

Chapter 61 – The Chain of Command

The next morning a Legion trireme beached at Bova. First Sergeant Gerontius was the first to jump from the warship. Following closely behind came Senior Centurion Patroclus.

They marched up the beach to where four Legionaries were laying in the sun. Behind them was a mound covered in goatskin.

"Where's Centurion Laurens?" demanded Gerontius.

"He's dead, First Sergeant," one of them replied.

"Then who is in charge?" demanded Gerontius.

"Garrison Commander Cephas, sir," another Legionary replied.

The Senior Centurion and the First Sergeant exchanged glances.

"And, what are you four doing?" Patroclus asked.

"We're on disposal detail, sir," a third answered.

"I don't see you doing anything," commented Gerontius.

"We're waiting, First Optio," a Private replied.

"You're disposing and waiting?" asked Patroclus. "Seems to me you're just laying around sunning yourselves."

"Commander Cephas said not to leave the beach until it's clean," the Private reported.

"Clean of what?" Patroclus demanded. He was losing patience with this game of question and answer.

The Private stood and walked over to the mound. Grabbing an edge of the goatskin cover, he tossed it back. Arms, heads, legs and other body parts stuck out from the pile of bodies. Once the cover was back, the smell of rotting flesh and merda rolled over the First Sergeant and the Senior Centurion.

"Who are they?" demanded Patroclus.

"Mostly Illyrians and I think this load has a few Syracusan solders, Centurion," replied the Private.

"This load?" inquired Gerontius. "How many loads were there?"

"Can't be sure," the Private replied, "But Commander Cephas said we had about one hundred and seventy-five on the beach. Although we brought thirty down from the garrison."

"What are you doing with them?" inquired Gerontius.

"Feeding them to the sharks," the Private explained while pointing to the horizon. "The patrol boats are dumping them way out. Commander Cephas said we didn't have time to bury them. We have to clean the beach and make our garrison combat ready."

"Where can we find Commander Cephas?" Patroclus asked.

"He's either at the tower build. Or, maybe at the grave site," the Private answered. "Or, at the Columnae Herculis questioning the Egyptians. Or, with the Spartan looking over our defenses. He moves around a lot. Or, he's…"

"I get it," Gerontius said interrupting the infantryman. "Cover that; the bodies stink."

"That's what we thought at first," the Private assured his First Optio. "But after a while, you kind of get used to it."

Patroclus and Gerontius marched through the sand and mounted the steps to the first level plaza.

"Pardon us, sir," a pair of sweating Legionaries said as they jogged down the steps.

By the time Patroclus and Gerontius crossed the first level plaza and started up to level two, the Legionaries passed them jogging up the stairs.

"What are you two doing?" Gerontius queried.

The infantrymen stopped and turned to face him.

"Running from Raiders, First Sergeant."

"I don't see any Raiders," declared Patroclus.

"No, sir. But if you do, we'll be able to out run them next time," the two said as they jogged away.

"First Sergeant. What is going on here?" the Senior Centurion asked.

"I believe, sir," Gerontius said. "That it's time Tesserarius Cephas was promoted to Optio."

"He's already a Commander according to everyone at Bovesia Garrison," the officer observed.

"If Garrison Commander was a Legion rank, I'd put him in the slot," offered Gerontius.

"Why is that, First Optio?" asked Patroclus.

"Because, our young Corporal took command after the death of his Centurion and fought a big battle here," Gerontius explained.

"And what do you base that on?" inquired the senior infantry officer.

Gerontius pointed at the buildings around the second level plaza. Four Legionaries were pulling arrows and javelins from the joints in the stonework and adding them to a huge pile in the center of the plaza.

"Legionaries. Why are you policing up the area?" Gerontius inquired.

"Because Commander Cephas said it's unsightly for citizens of the Republic to see the tools of war, First Sergeant," the Legionary replied. "This is a place of commerce, and we welcome foreign ships to do business here. I think that's what he said?"

"Well, Senior Centurion, does that answer your question?" asked Gerontius.

"It does. I look forward to reading Garrison Commander Cephas' report," the officer said as they continued across the plaza.

Chapter 62 - Columnae Herculis

"Steady there," a voice yelled from the roof top. "We've got one chance to get this up."

"What's the rush Lance Corporal?" a voice called out from the other end of the roof.

"Private. Commander Cephas said it has to be up before First Sergeant Gerontius comes for an inspection," the Lance Corporal replied.

"Why would the First Sergeant care if it goes up today or tomorrow?" the Private asked.

"Cephas explained that the First Sergeant likes to watch the sunset from the tower when he's composing his poetry," the Lance Corporal answered. "If the tower isn't up, it'll mess up his muse. Now, pull."

The Senior Centurion looked at the First Sergeant.

"Epic, or love poems?" teased Patroclus.

"I don't write poetry," growled Gerontius.

When they looked up, the top of a watch tower appeared. It had been laying on its side. Lines pulled from one end of the roof while poles pushed, and the tower rose into the air.

Gerontius glanced at Patroclus.

"Nice to know I can watch an unobstructed sunset," Gerontius uttered sarcastically.

"Good morning, Senior Centurion," a Lance Corporal said from the edge of the roof top. He was standing with his body squared to the tower, and his neck twisted so he could look down on Gerontius and Patroclus. "Don't worry First Sergeant, your muse is safe with Third Squad. We'll have the tower secured long before sunset. All right, people, we're wasting daylight. Let's get this tower leveled."

Patroclus started for the Columnae Herculis diner while motioning for the First Sergeant to follow.

"I don't write poetry. And, I don't watch sunsets," Gerontius grumbled.

"Don't tell them," Patroclus whispered as he pointed to the roof. "I think part of their pride and motivation is preparing the evening perch for their favorite poet."

***

The Southern Legion's infantry leaders walked across the porch and into a war zone. A clay mug flew across the dining room and shattered against the corner of a table.

"I want them out of my diner," Marija shouted. Her legs were set wide apart and slightly bent for balance. Her right hand rested threateningly on her short sword. "Get out. Three days of snooty, perfumed Egyptians is too much for anybody. Get out."

"Please love," pleaded Hyllus. "Where would the Ambassador and his staff..."

"Staff. He has four slaves and a scribe," Marija pointed out. "There's plenty of room on the porch or the plaza for them. My dining room is not an inn. If I wanted to hear men snore all night I could have stayed at my father's home in Macedonia."

When Marija mentioned Macedonia, the tall Egyptian in the richly embroidered robe stepped back as if he'd been struck in the chest. Patroclus noticed it but didn't say anything.

"We may be able to help," offered Gerontius.

Marija swung to face the door as if confronting a second challenge. Hyllus, on the other hand, smiled and held out both arms.

"First Sergeant, if you can help, I'd be ever so grateful," exclaimed the big Athenian.

"We sailed here for a day inspection," explained the First Sergeant. "We had planned to row back to Rhegium Garrison this afternoon. However, we didn't know Bovesia had lost its Centurion and was attacked. Senior Centurion, your thoughts?"

"I believe Tribune Velius would find it interesting to talk with the ambassador," replied Patroclus as he crossed the room. "We'll take the Egyptian with us."

"I must go to Athens," insisted the Egyptian. "Any detour would further my transit time. This layover has already cost me three days."

"What's your rush?" asked Patroclus. "Why is it so important that you get to Athens?"

The ambassador's eyes shifted to Marija. Then, just as swiftly, they returned to the officer.

"I am an ambassador of the King of Egypt," the man stated. "My business is that of my ruler and of no concern to a common soldier. I demand transportation to Athens as soon as it can be arranged."

Patroclus inhaled deeply and slowly let it out through his nostrils. Gerontius had seen his officer mad and recognized the pattern. He waited for the rage.

"I am the Senior Centurion of the Southern Legion," Patroclus said forcefully. "I command Legionaries and not one of them is a common soldier. You, sir, are on Republic soil and under the protection of my garrison commander, Cephas. You will speak to me with respect. Or, instead of transportation, I'll have you and your staff drowned in the Ionian Sea. Do I make myself clear?"

The Egyptian dropped his eyes and he deflated in the face of the Centurion's fury.

"Senior Centurion, my apologies. I spoke rashly," the ambassador said. "It's just this trip has been difficult and unpleasant."

"Unpleasant? That's it!" Marija shouted. "Get your bloated, overdressed, arrogant, snide cūlus out of my cafe. You dare to call this unpleasant after eating half my winter stores and turning half my dining room into your personal bedroom? Get out!"

"Ma'am, we will have the ambassador moved," Patroclus promised. "Either to my ship or to the garrison. I beg for your patience until the First Sergeant and I finish our inspection."

"Fine Senior Centurion, I appreciate it," Marija replied. Then her eyes softened and she added. "The next time you must stay longer. Hyllus and I will fix you and the First Optio a feast. That camp stew your Legionaries eat can't be good for the stomach."

"Thank you, Marija. We'll be back for the Ambassador," Patroclus promised. Then he turned to Gerontius. "First Sergeant, let's go take a look at the garrison."

"Yes, sir," replied Gerontius as both men headed for the door.

Chapter 63 – Mars, God of War

They marched through the alleyway and stopped at the top of the hill. On either side of the path, Legionaries were digging out the bottom of the slope. Other men hauled stone. An old man stood on a course of rock laid at the foot of the dig.

"Looks like Commander Cephas has ordered a construction project," Patroclus exclaimed.

They walked down the path and up to the old man.

"What are you building?" asked Gerontius.

"A wall. When the Syracusan Raiders set their listening post on the hills, they had us pinned," the old man replied.

"So, we're cutting the hill and shoring it up with a stone wall. It'll be too hard to scale once we're done."

Patroclus tapped the First Sergeant on the shoulder. When Gerontius turned, the officer pointed out a hospital tent. Poles allowing air to flow held up the sides of two joined ten-man tents. Within the tents, wounded Legionaries were resting in neat rows. Two medics moved between the injured.

It wasn't the tent or the busy medics. It was the number of wounded men that struck them.

***

"Good morning, Senior Centurion, First Sergeant," the Senior Medic said as they approached. He finished tying a bandage around a Legionary's leg before standing and walking over to them. "It's been a busy three days. But everyone is treated. None critical. Most of these men will return to full duty in a few weeks."

"Do you need anything? Supplies? An extra medic?" inquired Gerontius.

"No. Commander Cephas traded with the town's merchants for supplies," the medic reported. "The attacks could have been worse; a lot worse. But, between the Spartan and Lance Corporal Sisera's actions, and Commander Cephas' calm and steady control, we only lost twenty Legionaries."

"What did he trade?" Gerontius asked.

"Armor and weapons from the Illyrians and the Syracuse soldiers," the medic stated.

"What Spartan?" asked Patroclus.

"That's him," the medic said pointing to the old man standing and directing the placement of another load of stone. "Helicaon and the Commander were walking the area before first light. By daybreak, the word went out that Senior Centurion Patroclus trained as a stone mason before joining the Legion. It seems sir, that you have great affection for stone elements. The men didn't want to disappoint you, so they started right away on your wall."

After a few more words of conversation with the medic, they crossed the garrison compound.

"I never studied the stone mason's trade," declared Patroclus.

"I didn't think you had, sir," replied Gerontius. "But, I'm sure you will appreciate having a stone wall named after you."

***

They didn't locate Cephas until they were beyond the thorn bush wall of the garrison. At the far slope overlooking the goat trail down to the flatland, they spied Corporal Cephas.

Twenty sheep on twenty spits were being turned over twenty fires. In front of each fire was a fresh grave site. Cephas, naked and covered in sheep's blood, stood at the end of the rows of graves.

With his arms raised, he yelled, "Mars. God of War. These Legionaries, brave and fearless in battle, have passed from this realm. Each sheep, one for each warrior, I sacrificed in your name. We asked that you entreat Mercury to swiftly take these fine men to the Fields of Elysian."

Cephas walked to a grave, squatted down, and bowed his head. After a short time, he looked up at the Legionary turning the spit and said something. The spit turner laughed, and Cephas stood and moved to the next grave.

"What is Cephas saying to the Legionaries turning the roasting sheep?" asked Patroclus.

A smile drifted across the First Sergeant's face, and he nodded his head in approval.

"Words of encouragement for the living," Gerontius replied. "And a threat that if the Legionary falters in his duty of roasting the sheep evenly, the next animal to be sacrificed will be the Legionary."

"Then why do they laugh?" Patroclus asked. "It sounds pretty harsh to me."

"Because each man on a spit is a squad mate of a dead Legionary," Gerontius explained. "They wouldn't stop turning the sheep if Jupiter started throwing down thunderbolts. So, the threat is a way for the men to know someone is in charge. And everything will return to normal despite the squad's loss."

"It appears our Tesserarius Cephas has leadership abilities," offered Patroclus. Then he was silent for a while before adding. "Tribune Velius really needs to speak with that Egyptian. But, in light of the recent attacks, I'm not comfortable leaving a Corporal in charge of a garrison."

"What are you thinking, sir?" inquired Gerontius.

"Second Century will rotate out in two weeks," explained Patroclus. "So, we'll leave Optio Cephas in charge for that period. Now, let's get him promoted, collect the Egyptian, and row back to Rhegium. "

"What about Lance Corporal Sisera?" the First Sergeant asked. He was pointing down the steep slope at Alerio.

The Lance Corporal was standing over a grave and seemed to be having a long conversation with the dead Legionary.

"I suppose Velius will want his spy back," Patroclus remarked.

Cephas noticed the two men standing on the hill top. After throwing a cloak over his shoulders, he jogged up the hill. Half way up, he turned and slammed his fist into his chest. Twenty times he saluted the dead. Then he turned and continued to climb the hill.

"Senior Centurion. First Optio," Cephas said as he saluted. "I didn't expect you for another day or two."

"I understand you've assumed the mantle of Garrison Commander," stated Patroclus.

"Yes, sir. It seemed the best way to enforce discipline on Bovesia and the Garrison," explained Cephas.

"Perfectly good reasoning," Patroclus offered. "The First Sergeant and I agree that you did an excellent job holding the men together and fending off the attackers."

"We're taking the ambassador back to Rhegium. And, Lance Corporal Sisera," said Gerontius. "Do you need anything?"

"A Centurion and an Optio, First Sergeant," replied Cephas.

"Your Century will be relieved in a couple of weeks, so you'll not get an officer," Patroclus explained. "And you've been promoted to Sergeant. Now, go get cleaned up, put on a uniform, and walk us through the battle."

"Yes, sir," Optio Cephas said with a salute.

As the newly promoted Sergeant marched away, Gerontius turned and faced down the slope.

"Lance Corporal Sisera. Pack your gear," the First Sergeant yelled. "You're going back to Rhegium."

Chapter 64 – Office of Planning and Strategies

Alerio sat in the Legion offices. He had cleaned up before going to bed last night and made use of the baths again this morning. And for all his preparations, his reward was to sit for half the day waiting on Tribune Velius.

The Senior Centurion and the First Sergeant had disappeared and returned several times from the Planning and Strategies section. Each time one of them came down the long hallway, Alerio prepared to stand. Every time, he was waved down.

A Legion detail arrived earlier. They escorted the Egyptian and his staff out of headquarters. Other than a clerk, Alerio seemed to be the only person on this side of the building.

Finally, Senior Centurion Patroclus marched down the hall and made a come with me sign with his hand.

"Lance Corporal Sisera. We interviewed the Egyptian ambassador and his scribe. And we reviewed and went over Optio Cephas' report," the officer stated. "The Legion is satisfied, but Tribune Velius believes you can fill in some details. He's waiting for you."

"Thank you, sir," Alerio replied with a salute.

***

At the end of the hallway, Alerio pushed through the door. Despite all the talking, according to the Senior Centurion, and conversations with the Egyptian ambassador, the map table was still covered. The Tribune caught his puzzled look.

"That's right, we don't let foreigners see all of our intelligence," Velius said as he shuffled to a corner of the table. "Here, give me a hand."

Together, they peeled back the cover and exposed the map. Velius pulled his box of colored triangles off the shelf and placed them around the map.

"What am I missing?" he demanded once all the triangles were positioned.

Alerio walked to the area representing Bovesia and dropped one of the new black Illyrian triangles beside the hill. The Tribune leaned over to study it. But, Alerio held up his hand while he selected a blue Syracuse and a yellow Qart Hadasht marker. Both were laid beside the red Legion marker and the Illyrian's.

"Navarch Martinus Cetea was being paid by the Qart Hadasht Empire to capture Bovesia for Syracuse," he explained. "Because the Empire wants..."

He stopped talking and selected a yellow triangle. On another area of the map, he dropped the marker beside the city of Messina.

"They want all of northern Sicilia," Alerio concluded by pointing at the newly placed triangle.

Tribune Velius scrunched up his wrinkled face and stared at the map. He circled the table, studying the markers from different angles. Finally, he looked up at the young man.

"Bovesia was a diversion," Velius whispered. "The Empire wants to tie-up our Legions with small battles. While the Republic is occupied taking back our territory, the Qart Hadasht will stage an attack on Messina. We're strong on the west coast with the Capital anchoring that region. But on the east coast, our Legions are spread thin. And, it's only been twenty years since we made peace with the eastern Greeks, and the mountain tribes. If the Empire can create distractions and uprisings, the Republic will be too busy to protest their movement on Sicilia."

"What are you going to do?" Alerio asked.

"We, Lance Corporal. What are we going to do? I'm going to write reports to the Senate," Velius said. "And for you, there will be a new mission."

"One question, Tribune," inquired Alerio. "The Egyptian coin chests. I couldn't uncover what they were paying to have shipped?"

"The King of Macedonia is demanding the King of Egypt recognize him as King of both Macedonia and Egypt. If Egypt doesn't, Macedonia has threatened to attack," Velius explained. "So, Egypt is secretly sending coins to Athens so the Athenians can rent transport ships to carry grain from Egypt."

"Why don't they pay for the transportation when the Athenians buy the grain?" asked Alerio.

"Because they aren't paying coin for the grain," said Velius. "The Egyptians are giving the grain to Athens. To pay for the grain, the Athenians will attack Macedonia. With the King of Macedonia at war with Athens, he'll be too busy to attack Egypt."

Alerio placed his fingers on the table and moved them until they were off the map. He pointed to a space where Egypt would be located and back to the location of Macedonia.

"What's my mission?" asked Alerio. "When do I leave?"

"I need a response from the Senate before sending you out," Velius explained. "Until then, you have something to complete."

Chapter 65 – Attack Rowing

Lance Corporal Alerio Sisera stood in the cool predawn with nine other Legionaries. Over the last few days, new graduates from Legion training had reported to headquarters Southern Legion. Once assembled in groups of ten men, the Legion's First Sergeant sent them for training. Ordered to report for the first day of rowing instructions, the new squad waited in the dark for the instructor.

"Good morning, Legionaries," a deep, raspy voice greeted them from beyond the light of a lantern. "My name is Sergeant Martius. Some in the Southern Legion call me Chief of Boats. Some have less savory terms to describe me. For you, right now, I am your rowing instructor."

A few Legionaries moaned.

"I take it from your enthusiastic responses that some of you have boating experience," Martius continued from the shadows. He was still an invisible, disembodied specter from the dark while the training unit stood between four bright lanterns. "But I'm not asking about fishing boats, merchant ships, nor rowing your lass around on a pond; I'm asking for attack rowing experience. Those of you trained in warship rowing raise your right hand."

While the Chief of Boats talked, Alerio's mind drifted, and he gazed across the dark waters of the strait. On the far shore, a few night lights of Messina glowed. The Sons of Mars occupied the city and the harbor, only a bowshot from Republic soil.

In the near future, Messina could fall under the control of the Qart Hadasht Empire. Tribune Velius and the leadership of the Southern Legion weren't pleased with the prospect. What the Republic's response would be, only the Senate could decide. Alerio would let the Tribune worry about the politics.

He returned to the present and prepared to run onto the dark beach with the training squad. There, they would launch an oar less patrol boat and swim it back to the Chief of Boats. Legion training was simpler than the intrigue of international politics; colder too but, more straightforward. Something weapon's instructor, Lance Corporal Alerio Sisera, preferred.

The End

Bloody Water

A note from J. Clifton Slater

Thank you for reading Bloody Water. The use of proxies by large governments to fight small battles to advance their position isn't new. In 265 B.C., the Athenians were paid to fight and prevent Macedonia from attacking Egypt.

History shows that few human quirks are new. As it gives illustrations of commitment and courage. At the start of the siege of Sparta, the women and seniors of the unwalled city, dug a deep and wide trench. The obstruction delayed the attacks by King Pyrrhus. The siege ended when the Spartan army arrived after rowing all night. They landed and, being Spartans, they marched directly into battle.

One of my favorite characters in these stories is the Messina Strait. Like any good foil, the strait effects anyone who comes into contact with it. The central channel and both shorelines flow in opposite directions. And the entire strait reverses direction several times a day. The strait is just as dangerous today for sailing vessels as it was in 265 B.C.

Lance Corporal Sisera's adventures continue in book #4 Reluctant Siege. With the Empire encroaching on the Republic and the Senate in turmoil, Alerio is forced into dangerous roles and situations. And in the end, he'll battle for his life in a reluctant siege.

If you have comments, I want to hear from you.

E-Mail: GalacticCouncilRealm@gmail.com

To join my newsletter and to read blogs about ancient Rome, go to my website:

I write military adventure both future and ancient.

Books by J. Clifton Slater

Historical Adventure – 'Clay Warrior Stories' series

#1 Clay Legionary   #2 Spilled Blood

#3 Bloody Water   #4 Reluctant Siege

#5 Brutal Diplomacy   #6 Fortune Reigns

#7 Fatal Obligation   #8 Infinite Courage

#9 Deceptive Valor   #10 Neptune's Fury

#11 Unjust Sacrifice   #12 Muted Implications

#13 Death Caller   #14 Rome's Tribune

Terror & Talons

#1 Hawks of the Sorcerer Queen

#2 Magic and the Rage of Intent

Call Sign Warlock

#1 Op File Revenge   #2 Op File Revenge

#3 Op File Sanction

Galactic Council Realm

#1 On Station   #2 On Duty

#3 On Guard   #4 On Point

Made in the USA
Las Vegas, NV
12 December 2021

37135892R00174